P9-DEI-449

PRAISE FOR
Girls Like Us

A *Library Journal* Best Book of the Year

"Riveting . . . I'm a fan of Cristina Alger, who now proves that she can write about anything, anywhere."
—Lisa Scottoline

"A smashing read. Instantly gripping and compulsively readable, with a heroine as vulnerable as she is tenacious." —Riley Sager, author of *The Last Time I Lied*

"*Girls Like Us* is something special: A beautiful, deeply textured novel and a poignant, surprising mystery. I loved it, every chapter and every word. I'm going to be thinking about it as a reader, a father, and a storyteller for a long, long time."
—Chris Bohjalian, author of *The Flight Attendant*

"The type of thriller that will keep you guessing until the last page." —PopSugar

"What better way to start the summer than this? . . . I read it in six hours. On a Saturday. I loved it, could not put it down. . . . So well-written . . . Highly recommend." —Dana Perino, host of *The Five*

"A truly timely, ripped-from-the-headlines tale of exploitation, abuse, and corruption. Tautly wound police-procedural-thriller aside, Alger's novel is a smart, searing indictment of just one of the many contemporary examples of the haves vs. the have-nots."
—*Seattle Review of Books*

"Alger's novel is highly political, deeply felt and fast-paced." —*The Sunday Times* (UK)

"Gripping . . . Nell's work on the case is smart and efficient, which gives the book a crisp tone and pace. . . . Readers will hope to savor more of her gimlet-eyed takes." —*Newsday*

"If you like mysteries with thriller endings . . . and a main character you root for, don't miss this one." —BookRiot

"[*Girls Like Us* meets] the hype and then some. With fascinating, deep characters and excellent plots with good twists, I was enthralled." —MysteryPeople

"Cristina Alger has perfected the character of the smart, spunky heroine. . . . [I] couldn't put down *Girls Like Us*." —*Shelter Island Reporter*

"This thriller will keep you on the edge of your seat until the last page." —The Everygirl

"[An] excellent crime novel . . . [Alger] captures the social dynamics of Suffolk's eastern extremes perfectly. The first-person narrative is appropriately terse—Nell delivers a thorough report—but it occasionally surprises with a gripping depth. . . . Highly recommended." —*Booklist* (starred review)

"[A] propulsive thriller . . . Alger expertly ratchets up the suspense all the way to the explosive finale. Readers will hope to see more of tough, smart Nell." —*Publishers Weekly*

"The tension becomes nearly unbearable as Nell realizes she truly can't trust anyone. . . . Readers can expect a few genuine surprises, and the light Alger shines on society's most vulnerable members is an important one. Melancholy and addictive."   —*Kirkus Reviews*

"This fast-paced psychological thriller . . . will intrigue mystery readers as they shadow Nell's precarious quest for the truth at all costs, despite the consequences."
                                              —*Library Journal*

PRAISE FOR
The Banker's Wife

"First-rate . . . Slick, heart-hammering entertainment."
                    —*The New York Times Book Review*

"[A] smart, incisive page turner . . . The thriller moves swiftly as the desperation and violence escalate, gliding by on clear, competent prose that never gets in the way. . . . Alger delivers an addictive dose of suspense and intrigue with a surprisingly believable plot. And all power to the bad girls, the gone girls, the difficult characters— but it's nice to remember that women don't have to be unlikable to be nuanced, or to take down villainous men."   —*USA Today*

"*The Banker's Wife* is a page-turning, plot-twisting international thriller of the first order. Cristina Alger's writing is as sophisticated and self-assured as the characters she's created. A remarkable and intriguing journey into the rarefied world of power and money. A perfect blend of mystery, suspense, and betrayal."   —Nelson DeMille

"Immersive, satisfying, tense—and timely: This is probably happening for real right now." —Lee Child

"With a global conspiracy about the 'world of dirty money, hidden away in shadow accounts' fueling a plot that soars from Geneva to London to Paris to New York, led by two intriguing women, this is a thriller to bank on." —Minneapolis *Star Tribune*

"[The] intriguing, fresh tale is that of the three women. Invited into the world of wealth, they flirt with all its trappings, even as they are aware of the sacrifices they make to be part of it. (Will they leave their jobs to support their husbands' careers? Let someone they know get away with murder?) Their choices about accepting or rejecting the easy life are the real thriller here."
—*Bloomberg*

"Gripping financial thrillers are rare. . . . Cristina Alger passes all the tests. . . . An exciting journey into the dark underbelly of the ultra-rich world of banking."
—*The Times* (UK)

"Buckle up—*The Banker's Wife* is an international thriller that moves at a breakneck pace, keeping you on the edge of your seat." —PopSugar

"One of the best thrillers you'll read all summer."
—Hello Giggles

"Warning: You'll want to clear your schedule for this thriller." —PureWow

"Fast-paced, smart, blessed with strong women characters and surprisingly believable." —*American Banker*

"A powerful page turner . . . A fast-paced, entertaining narrative."
                                                    —*Greenwich Time*

"There's plenty of suspenseful plotting and a quest for conclusive answers as the story swings convincingly between Geneva, Paris, London, New York, the South of France, and ultimately, the Caribbean."
                                              —*The East Hampton Star*

"Readers riding this international financial roller coaster will be kept on edge through its many twists and turns. Highly recommended for fans of fast-paced thrillers in the tradition of John Grisham."
                                   —*Library Journal* (starred review)

"Alger perfectly nails her twisty plot, wrapping everything up in a completely satisfying ending. Readers will be eagerly turning the pages of this fast-paced financial thriller."
                                                           —*Booklist*

"An engrossing financial thriller . . . Alger presents the world of wealth management in a way that a novice can understand the intricacies but also appeals to the sophisticated reader. This complex tale of how greed can upend innocent lives will resonate with many."
                                                   —*Publishers Weekly*

"A sharp, compelling thriller . . . This brisk, tense page-turner will mesmerize fans of international mysteries."
                                                     —*Kirkus Reviews*

"A more intellectually stirring, sophisticated mystery . . . With global settings, covert government agencies and intricate plotting, *The Banker's Wife* reads like an old-fashioned international thriller."
                                                           —*BookPage*

"A knockout of an international thriller, with glamorous lives on collision courses with high-stakes crime and high-level politics through the corridors of power in Europe and America."   —Chris Pavone, author of *The Expats*

"In Cristina Alger's expert hands, the world of complex international finance is the perfect setting for a gripping, twisty thriller that asks how well we really know the people closest to us. *The Banker's Wife* is smart, savvy, and beautifully written. It grabs the reader by the gut and doesn't let go until the last page."

—Alafair Burke, author of *The Wife*

"Behind every great fortune, there's a crime . . . and a bank. From Geneva to London to New York, Cristina Alger takes us inside the secretive and corrupt world of the super-rich—and three women who struggle to survive its deadly undertow."

—Alex Berenson, author of *The Prisoner*

"Cristina Alger takes an inside look at the lucrative, high-stakes—and sometimes murderous—world of private banking in this stunning masterpiece. Whip smart and fraught with tension, *The Banker's Wife* packs a punch that doesn't let up. Brilliant."

—Mary Kubica, author of *The Good Girl* and *Every Last Lie*

"Cristina Alger's ripped-from-the-headlines thriller is a fascinating glimpse into the mysterious world of billionaire banking, and kept me guessing until the very last page. I couldn't tear myself away."

—Janelle Brown, author of *Watch Me Disappear*

"If you enjoyed *The Darlings* like I did, you'll LOVE *The Banker's Wife*. International intrigue, glitz, and glamour all tangled in an intricately crafted plot. Both Annabel and Marina are smart, strong female leads who make bold choices—my favorite kind of characters. This is Alger's best book yet!"

—Kate Moretti, author of *The Blackbird Season* and *The Vanishing Year*

"*The Banker's Wife* is a glamorous and twisting novel of international intrigue, the secrets and lies that stitch a marriage together, and a wife's desperate search to understand the husband she thought she knew. The rocket-paced plot and transporting sense of place will sweep you away, but it's the smart, determined women at the heart of the story that keep you riveted through the breathless ending. Cristina Alger delivers on every level."

—Lisa Unger, author of *The Red Hunter*

"*The Banker's Wife* is the best kind of thriller: break-neck pace, gutsy women characters who are their own heroes—and if the action and dazzling locales don't take your breath away, the twisty surprises will."

—Kate White, author of *Even If It Kills Her*

"A mysterious plane crash and a suspicious home invasion unknowingly intersect two women, sending them on parallel paths to discover the truth about the people they love. *The Banker's Wife* will leave you breathless as you turn the pages, gasping as you uncover each delicious layer of this perfectly plotted thriller. We promise you'll be guessing until the very end."

—Liz Fenton and Lisa Steinke, authors of *The Good Widow*

ALSO BY CRISTINA ALGER

The Darlings

This Was Not the Plan

The Banker's Wife

Girls Like Us

CRISTINA ALGER

G. P. Putnam's Sons
New York

PUTNAM
— EST. 1838 —
G. P. PUTNAM'S SONS
Publishers Since 1838
An imprint of Penguin Random House LLC
penguinrandomhouse.com

Copyright © 2019 by Bear One Holdings LLC
Penguin supports copyright. Copyright fuels creativity, encourages diverse voices, promotes free speech, and creates a vibrant culture. Thank you for buying an authorized edition of this book and for complying with copyright laws by not reproducing, scanning, or distributing any part of it in any form without permission. You are supporting writers and allowing Penguin to continue to publish books for every reader.

The Library of Congress has catalogued the G. P. Putnam's Sons
hardcover edition as follows:

Names: Alger, Cristina, author.
Title: Girls like us / Cristina Alger.
Description: New York : G. P. Putnam's Sons, 2019.
Identifiers: LCCN 2019018651 | ISBN 9780525535805 (hardcover) |
ISBN 9780525535812 (epub)
Subjects: | BISAC: FICTION / Thrillers. | FICTION / Contemporary Women. |
GSAFD: Mystery fiction. | Suspense fiction.
Classification: LCC PS3601.L364 G57 2019 | DDC 813/.6—dc23
LC record available at https://lccn.loc.gov/2019018651
p.   cm.

First G. P. Putnam's Sons hardcover edition / July 2019
First G. P. Putnam's Sons international edition / July 2019
First G. P. Putnam's Sons international trade edition / January 2020
First G. P. Putnam's Sons trade paperback edition / April 2020
First G. P. Putnam's Sons premium edition / July 2021
G. P. Putnam's Sons premium edition ISBN: 9780593331491

Printed in the United States of America
1 3 5 7 9 10 8 6 4 2

This is a work of fiction. Names, characters, places, and incidents either are the product of the author's imagination or are used fictitiously, and any resemblance to actual persons, living or dead, businesses, companies, events, or locales is entirely coincidental.

If you purchased this book without a cover, you should be aware that this book is stolen property. It was reported as "unsold and destroyed" to the publisher, and neither the author nor the publisher has received any payment for this "stripped book."

For my girl. For every girl.

His desire to set a new beginning to the chain of events to which he belonged encountered the same difficulty that it always does: the fact that everybody has a father, that nothing comes first and of itself, its own cause, but that everybody is begotten and points backward, deeper into the depths of beginnings, the bottoms and abysses of the well of the past.

—THOMAS MANN

Girls Like Us

1.

On the last Tuesday in September, we scatter my father's ashes off the coast of Long Island. Four of us board Glenn Dorsey's fishing boat with a cooler of Guinness and an urn. We head east, toward Orient Point, where Dad and Dorsey spent their Saturdays fishing for albacore and sea bass. When we reach a quiet spot in Orient Shoal, we drop anchor. Dorsey says a few words about Dad's loyalty: to his country, his community, his friends, his family. He asks me if I want to say anything. I shake my head no. I can tell the guys think I'm about to cry. The truth is, I don't have anything to say. I hadn't seen my father in years. I'm not sad. I'm just numb.

After Dorsey finishes his speech, we bow our heads for a minute of respectful silence. Ron Anastas, a homicide detective with the Suffolk County Police Department, fights back tears. Vince DaSilva, Dad's first partner, crosses himself, muttering something about the Holy Spirit under his breath. All three men go to Mass every Sunday at St. Agnes in Yaphank. At least, they used to. We did, too. Except for a small handful of weddings, I haven't stepped inside a church since I left the island ten years ago. I'm grateful to be outside today. The air inside St. Agnes was always stagnant and suffocating, even after the summer heat subsided. I can still hear the whir of the ancient fan in the back. I can feel the edge of the scrunched-up dollar bill pressed against my sweaty palm, bound for the collection plate. The thought of it makes me squirm.

It's a calm day. They say a storm is coming, but for now, the sky is cloudless. Dorsey holds the silence longer than necessary. He clasps his hands in front of him and his lips move as if in prayer. The guys start to get antsy. Vince clears his throat. Ron shifts from one foot to the other. It's time to get on with it. Dorsey glances up, hands me the urn. I open it. The men look on as my father's ashes blow away on the wind.

The burial is, I believe, what my father would have wanted. Short and sweet. No standing on ceremony. He is out on the water, the only place he ever seemed at peace. Dad always fidgeted like a schoolboy during Mass. We sat in the back so we could duck out before Communion. Dad claimed to hate the taste of the stale wafers and bad wine. Even then, I knew he was lying. He just didn't want to confess.

After it's over, Dorsey hands us each a Guinness and we toast. *To the too-short life of Martin Daniel Flynn.* Dad had just turned fifty-two when his motorcycle skidded off the Montauk Highway. It was two in the morning. I imagine he'd been drinking heavily, though no one dared say as much. No sense in pointing fingers now. According to Dorsey, Dad's tires were worn, the road was wet, the fog clouded his visibility. End of story.

With these guys, what Dorsey says goes. Of the four, Dorsey went up the ranks the fastest. He got his gold shield first, then quickly pulled Dad and Ron Anastas out of plainclothes and put them into homicide. When he became chief of detectives, Dorsey made sure that Vince DaSilva got elevated to inspector of the Third. The Third Precinct of Suffolk County covers some of the island's rougher parts: Bay Shore, Brentwood, Brightwaters, Islip. It's where the four men spent their early years together as patrolmen. It's also where my father met my mother, Marisol Reyes Flynn. Dad always called the Third a war zone. For him especially, it was.

Dorsey and Dad went way back. Our families have been in Suffolk County for three generations. Before that, we hailed from Schull, a small village on Ireland's rugged southwest coast. They used to joke that we were all probably related somewhere down the line. The men certainly looked it. Both were tall and dark-haired, with green eyes and sharp, inquisitive faces. My father wore his hair in a military crop his whole life. Dorsey, over the years, has had a mustache, sideburns, a shag. But when Dorsey's hair is short, as it is now, you might mistake him for my father from a distance.

We put out some lines and the guys tell stories about

their early days in the Third Precinct. As plainclothes officers, they would show up to work wearing Vans and Led Zeppelin T-shirts. Glory days stuff. They didn't shave. If they had too much to drink the night before, they didn't shower. Just rolled out of bed and cruised around in unmarked beater cars, looking for trouble. They never had to look far. In the Third, gangs were—and are still—prevalent. Violent crime is high; drugs are everywhere. For all the wealth in Suffolk County, nearly half of the Third Precinct lives at or just above the poverty line. Dad used to say that there was no better training ground for a cop than the Third Precinct. Most of the top brass of the Suffolk County PD came up from the Third.

Dorsey remarks that Dad was the toughest cop in the Third, and the best teacher a young patrolman could ask for. The guys nod in assent. Maybe that's true. Dad had an unshakable, almost evangelical sense of right and wrong. But there were contradictions. He loathed drugs but felt comfortable pickling his liver in scotch. He routinely busted gamblers but hosted a monthly poker game that drew district attorneys and a few well-known judges from around the island. The criminals he most despised were abusers of women and children, but I once saw him strike my mother so hard across the face that a red outline of his hand was imprinted on her skin. Dad had his own code. I learned early not to second-guess it. At least, not out loud.

Dad's was a rough sort of justice. He taught lessons you wouldn't soon forget. Dorsey's favorite story about

Dad was the time he made Anastas lie down on a gurney under a sheet at the medical examiner's office. There was a rookie fresh out of the academy named Rossi. His dad was a judge and Rossi thought that made him a big shot. He liked to wear designer clothes to work—Armani and Hugo Boss—and that rubbed Dad the wrong way. Dad took Rossi down to the ME's and had him pull back the sheet. Anastas sat up screaming and Rossi pissed himself, all over his six-hundred-dollar pants. After that, he shopped at JCPenney like everybody else.

Dorsey's told that story a hundred times, but he tells it again, and we all laugh like we've never heard it before. It feels good to remember my father as funny because he was, he really could be. He'd be quiet all night and then pipe up with one perfect, cutting remark. Dorsey and I exchange smiles. I nod, grateful. This is the way I want to remember Dad today. Not for his temper. Not for his sadness. And not for the alcohol, which had finally taken him out on a quiet stretch of wet highway in the early hours of the morning.

Eventually, the sun dips low on the horizon. The sky turns an electric plum-toned blue. Dorsey decides it is time to head home. We're carrying well more than our quota of sea bass, but with three cops on board—especially these three cops, who, like my father, were all born and raised and will probably die inside county lines—no one's going to say squat about fishing limits. These men, Dorsey especially, are the closest thing Hampton Bays has to hometown heroes.

The guys are good and sauced. They talk loudly and

repeat themselves; they hug me hard in the parking lot, not once but twice, three times. Anastas invites me home for dinner. I beg off, saying I'm tired, I need some time alone to decompress. He seems relieved. Ron has a wife, Shelley, and three kids. He doesn't need a dour-faced twenty-eight-year-old hanging around his house. DaSilva is in the middle of a divorce. My guess is he'll head to a bar once we're done here.

After another round of jokes, Anastas and DaSilva stumble off in separate directions. They both drive away in minivans, cars built for booster seats and lacrosse sticks and car pools. Dorsey points to the silver Harley-Davidson Sportster that I rode over here. It was Dad's favorite. He bought it cheap years ago; restored it himself over time. Dad had four motorcycles, or he did, before the accident. Now, I guess, there are three. His babies, he called them. Each one meticulously restored and cared for, swallowing up his off-duty hours like hungry fledgling birds.

"Nice ride." Dorsey drops his arm around my shoulders and gives me a paternal squeeze. Dorsey married his high school sweetheart. He lost her in a car crash just a few years later. He never remarried or had kids. Dad made him my godfather, a job he took seriously. All four of my grandparents have passed. Both my parents were, like me, only children. It occurs to me now that Dorsey is the closest thing I've got left to family. I feel a pang of sadness. I wish we'd kept in better touch.

"Yeah," I say, tilting my head against his arm. "It's a good-looking bike. I miss riding."

"You don't have one in DC?"

"I'm not there enough to take care of it."

"You move around with every new case, huh."

"I'm a great packer. Been living out of a suitcase since the academy."

"Your dad was like that. I think that's why he liked camping so much."

"He taught me well." I take a step toward the bike.

"You sure you're okay to operate heavy machinery? I can give you a lift home if not."

I wave him off. "Don't worry about me."

"The road might be wet."

"I'm okay. Really." I know what he's thinking. He's drunk, and I've had enough to put me over the limit. I have a wooden leg, though, and unlike my father, I know when it's time to stop. I never drink the way Dad used to, well past the point of sloppiness. At least, not in public. Like a lot of agents, I save my drinking for the privacy of home.

"You know, I always wanted to ride this bike." I smile, trying to lighten the mood. "Dad used to make me work on it on the weekends, but I was too afraid to ask to try it out." We both laugh.

"Marty loved those bikes of his."

"He sure did. If there was a fire, I'm pretty sure he would've saved them first and come back for me afterward."

"Don't say that." Dorsey shakes his head, a reprimand. "Your dad loved you more than you know."

"Do you know what happened to his bike? The one he

was riding, I mean." It's something I've wanted to ask but haven't quite found the right moment. It seems like a relatively shallow thing to consider, having just lost my father and all. But it's one of the many small loose ends I know I need to tie up before I leave Suffolk County for good.

Dorsey frowns, thinking. "It went to impound. I guess it's still there. I can check."

"Not the crime lab?"

"Nah. Pretty clear it was an accident. I signed the release form for it. I didn't think about getting it to you. It's basically junk metal now." He winces, realizing how that sounds. "Sorry. I just meant—"

"I know what you meant. It's okay. Should I pick it up from impound, then?"

"I can have them take it to the scrap yard for you if you want. Save you the time."

"No, it's fine. I'd like to do it myself."

"It's pretty badly mangled. I don't know if you want to see something like that."

"I'm a big girl, Glenn. I've seen what happens in a fatal crash."

"I know you have. It's just different when it's family." Dorsey looks away. His eyes are glassy with tears.

I nod, considering. "You're right. I'll call impound tomorrow. Cole Haines still running it?"

"Yep. He'll take care of it. I'll check in on you in the morning." He watches me straddle the bike. "Listen, did you get in touch with Howie Kidd?"

"Dad's lawyer? Yeah. He's dropping by tomorrow to

go through some estate stuff. Glad you reminded me. I'd forgotten about it."

"You want me there? I can sit with you. Help you go through paperwork."

"No, no. Thanks. I'm sure it's all straightforward."

"Okay. Well, you call if you need anything. That stuff can get overwhelming."

"Thanks, Glenn. For everything." He gives me a two-finger salute and starts to walk away. I rev the engine and he turns back, giving me one final, sad smile.

"Hey, hon?"

"Yeah?"

"I love you."

"I love you, too," I say, my voice husky. It's been a long time since I said those words to anyone.

I pull out of the lot before Dorsey does. It feels good to get moving after so many hours on the boat. The cold air puts life back into me. I putter down the Sunrise Highway, across the Ponquogue Bridge, to the house at the end of Dune Road.

It's my house now, though it's hard for me to see it that way. It won't be for long. I need to sell it. I can't afford to keep it. Even if I could, it doesn't make sense for me to hold on to it. I haven't taken a vacation in six years. I have no use for an old house on the South Fork of Long Island, in a county that holds as many bad memories as good ones.

My grandfather Darragh Flynn, who I called Pop, built this place back in the 1950s, when you could still buy a sliver of land with a bay view on a policeman's salary. Views like this cost a half-million dollars now, maybe more. The house has about as much charm and space as an RV. I know that anyone who buys it is likely only interested in the land beneath. It is a squat, weather-beaten box with faded gray shingles and cheap sliding doors. Still, it's not without a certain charm. It has a wraparound deck with views of Shinnecock Bay to the north and acres of rolling dune grass on either side. I hate thinking about someone bulldozing this patch of marshland just to throw up a McMansion with a pool and a tennis court. I know my father would hate that, too.

I came here a little over a week ago, after Dorsey called me with the news about Dad. I have no return date in mind. As of now, I have no job to go back to. I live in a small walk-up apartment in Georgetown that I don't miss, with an unreliable AC unit that leaks puddles on the kitchen floor, and the scent of curry wafting up from the Indian place on the ground level. My neighbors are graduate students, prone to smoking weed and listening to EDM after midnight. Sometimes I can hear them fighting or making love, and when they play music, my walls vibrate from the bass. I think about complaining, but I never do. It's not like I sleep much, anyway. When we see each other in the hall, they nod politely and go on their way. I'm certain they know nothing about me. I have to assume that if they knew I was in law enforcement, they might be more discreet about the weed. It's not their fault. I'm gone for weeks at a time. When I'm home, I come and go at odd hours, leaving for work early in the morning, often returning well past midnight. I have no pets, no plants, no significant other. I can fit most of what I own in a single large duffel bag. I wonder how long it will take for them to notice I'm gone. Maybe they never will.

The only person who has called me while I'm here in Suffolk County is Sam Lightman, the head of the Behavioral Analysis Unit and my boss at the FBI. Last month, I shot and killed someone in the line of duty. His name was Anton Reznik. He was an associate of Dmitry Novak, one of the Russian Mafia's most profitable traffickers of drugs and women within the United States. Reznik was known to his friends as the Butcher, for obvious reasons. Not someone I will miss. Still, killing a man is never pleasant and this time has been particularly hard on me. For one thing, a bullet nicked my shoulder in the exchange. I was lucky, technically speaking. An inch to the right and it could have opened my brachial artery, almost certainly killing me on the spot. Instead, I traded my badge and my firearm for a couple of stiches, a paid medical leave, and the business card of a Bureau-endorsed therapist who specializes in PTSD. By now, the doctors say my shoulder should've healed, and it mostly has. It still feels sore now and then, particularly in the evenings, but that's probably because I haven't found the time to do physical therapy to rehabilitate the muscles beneath the wound. The Bureau thinks my head should be on straight, too. It isn't yet. Maybe it never was to begin with.

My father's death has earned me a reprieve of sorts. "Take the time you need," Lightman said when I told him, which we both knew meant "as little time as possible." I can tell Lightman's patience with my recovery is wearing thin. I'm sure he's getting pressure from the higher-ups to either put me back in the field or cut me loose. These days, I've started to think that the latter is the right thing to do.

I pour myself a stiff glass of Dad's Macallan and retire to the porch with a wool blanket. I drink quietly and alone, as I imagine he did most nights, until the last streaks of sunset fade and stars light up the sky. I listen to the roar of the ocean and the faint shudder of music from one of the bars across the bay.

It's over. I will never feel a gravitational pull back here, back home. Not for holidays or for birthdays or for weddings of people I once considered friends but no longer think about. I won't feel obligated to call my father and I won't feel guilty when I don't. I can burn his things; sell this house; never return to Suffolk County again. For the first time in years, I don't need to medicate myself to sleep. I lie back on the deck couch, put my feet up on the driftwood coffee table. I close my eyes and let the darkness take me.

2.

The cry of a seagull rouses me. My eyes open. It's light. For a few seconds, I'm disoriented. I sit up, startled, and take in my surroundings. The faded wood decking. The openness around me. I'd forgotten the singular pleasure of waking up to clouds overhead.

The air has an edge to it that it didn't a few days ago. I pick up the smell of salt and peat and, for the first time, something else: firewood. There is smoke coming from a chimney a few doors down. I get up and watch it rise in tufts and then dissipate into the slate-colored sky.

Fall has arrived. My favorite season on the island. The colors fade from vibrant greens and blues to gentler shades of brown and gray. Light dapples the marsh. Just beyond the deck, a snowy egret stands stock-still in a sea of sumac and switchgrass. In a flash, the bird dips its beak into the water and swallows a killifish whole. Then it morphs back into a statue, lying in wait for its next victim. I used to watch the egrets for hours when I was little. I admired their pure white feathers and long, graceful necks. I thought they looked like ballerinas. Pop told me that they almost died out years ago because women so admired their plumage that they killed them and turned them into hats. It broke my little heart to hear that.

Egrets are ruthless killers, too. They know how to extend their wings out while hiding their beaks, fooling small fish into seeking refuge from the sun beneath their shadow. Sometimes you can see them moving their reed-thin legs in the water in a rhythmic, hypnotic way. It looks as though they are dancing. But really, they are shaking up prey from sediment around their feet. When something moves, they pounce. Knowing this made me feel better. We kill them. They kill small fish in return.

Soon, the waters here will grow cold. The egrets, like the plover and the gulls, will be forced to move farther south in order to survive. The change will happen overnight. One day, I'll wake up and they'll be gone. As a child, I always mourned the day they left. The migration marked the end of the outdoor season, and the beginning of a long winter cooped up in the house with Dad. Winters on Long Island are cold and dark. Most of the folks who stay for it drink more during those hard months, and my father was no exception. I wonder if I'll still be here when the birds leave this year, or if I, too, will have headed south by then. It's probably time I start thinking about packing up and moving on. The bite in the air is a good reminder.

I open the sliding door and go back into the house. In

the bathroom, I turn on the tap and splash cold water on my face. I fill a glass to the brim and drink it down, trying to offset the effects of drinking too much scotch on an empty stomach the night before. I stare at my reflection in the mirror. I've lost weight. My cheekbones protrude. The hollows around my hazel eyes seem more pronounced. I've stopped preparing proper meals. I can't remember the last time I showered. It's hard to do it with my shoulder. I fatigue easily, even when washing my hair. The bandaging gets wet and needs to be changed, and that seems like a lot of effort for me these days. It isn't as though I'm expecting much in the way of company. Still, I am startled by my appearance. I'm not caring for myself. It shows.

I flick on the shower. I need to pull myself together before Howard Kidd stops by this afternoon. There are papers to sign, bank accounts to close. A house to sell and bills to pay. My clothes drop to the tile floor. The tap rumbles and then sputters out water the color of bourbon. Rust. The pipes need replacing. So does the roof, the deck, the dented screen doors. One of the windows blew out in the last hurricane and no one bothered to replace it. My father used to hammer boards over the windows when hurricane season came. Nail marks mar the wood frames. Any broker will tell me to paint over them when I'm ready to sell the house. But I love those marks. As a child, I used to run my hands over them, my fingers feeling out each bump and rivet. They are scars from battles this house has fought and won.

The whole house needs replacing, really. I know that.

Maybe there's no point in painting walls and putting in new screens when, more likely than not, a buyer will tear it down. Maybe all I need to do is tidy things up so that it looks presentable. Put away personal effects. Remove my father's hunting trophies: the stag's head with its glistening, dead eyes. The needle-nosed sailfish arched over the front door. I need to ensure that the air conditioner doesn't leak and that the fridge stops making that strange, rattling sound. I have to clear out my father's clothes from his bureau. His office door is locked. So is his gun closet. The guns need to go. So does his toothbrush, its frayed bristles hanging downward off the edge of his sink. My mother's ashes are probably still stashed in the back of the office closet, in the brass-necked urn that has long since dulled from neglect. I don't know for sure that the urn is still there, but I bet it is. I haven't had the heart to check.

I want to pick up Dad's bike from the impound lot. If it's at all restorable, I want to keep it. If not, I'll take it to the junkyard myself. It seems like a personal job, something I shouldn't farm out to Cole Haines. The bike, like my dad, deserves a decent goodbye.

So much administrative work remains. The thought of it all exhausts me. I've been ignoring it, hoping it will dissipate, like the fog that hangs over the house in the early morning. But it won't, of course. There is no one else to do these things but me. The stream of water begins to run clear. I step beneath it. It's cool, but that's good. The chill wakes me up, wipes the cobwebs from the drainpipes in my head. The water in this house has always been finicky. My father, a military man at his core, believed in cold showers. As a teenager, I resented him for making me bathe beneath an icy tap. His own showers were two minutes long, maybe three. They always seemed like punishment, as though he was repenting for his sins of the night before. Short, hard, cold showers. He didn't understand how long it took for a teenage girl to wash her hair, to condition it, to shave her legs. Or maybe he did, but he wanted to punish me, too. I cut off my hair when I was fifteen. Used my own scissors and everything. My father approved. He applauded practicality. He thought blow-dryers and curling irons were frivolities, especially for a girl who played sports and didn't much care what she looked like. He had a point. I've worn it short ever since.

I step out of the shower and dry myself off. I fish the last bandage out of the box below the sink and apply it to my shoulder. I slip on my jeans and a T-shirt, the kind with thumbholes at the cuff, so that the sleeves stay in place. I throw on a shoulder harness and, over that, an old FBI fleece vest that I borrowed from Lightman and never returned.

From the drawer in the bedside table, I withdraw my Smith & Wesson. It's my personal weapon, the one I've been carrying ever since my Bureau-assigned firearm was confiscated last month. I carry it in my harness, hidden beneath the long sides of the vest. I will continue to do so, at least until Dmitry Novak—the man we were hoping to arrest when I shot Anton Reznik—is in custody. I imagine Novak is unhappy with me for killing his favorite butcher. I won't be safe until he's behind bars, and perhaps not even then. With six years at the BAU under my belt, I've made plenty of enemies in addition to Novak. Enemies with long memories and violent tempers. I'll likely always carry a gun. Dad did. He kept an arsenal in the closet of his office, locked of course, and pristinely maintained. If he was awake, he was carrying, and if he wasn't, he was sleeping with a firearm in reach; usually in the drawer of the nightstand next to his bed. It never occurred to him not to. In his world, you were either predator or prey. Egret or killifish.

In the kitchen, I set coffee to brew. I look up the number for the Suffolk County Police Impound Lot in Westhampton and dial. I know Cole won't be there—it's too early—and I'm happy enough not to have to make conversation about Dad's passing. I leave a brief message with my name and cell phone number, saying that I'd like to swing by and pick up my dad's bike as soon as possible. I want to do it quickly, without too much fuss. The idea of seeing Dad's bike torn apart or reduced into scrap makes my stomach twist. In the sober light of morning, I realize Dorsey is right. I may have seen a lot of crime scenes, but everything's different when it involves family.

As soon as there is enough coffee in the pot, I pour myself a mug and step back out onto the deck. I take one sip before my phone rings. I set my coffee down, check the number. When I see that it's Sam Lightman, I grit my teeth. After a moment's pause, I pick up the call.

"Flynn here."

"How are you doing, Nell?"

"Fucking fantastic."

"How's the shoulder?"

"Barely a scratch."

"And your dad's service?"

"Over."

"Sounds like you're ready to come home."

"Are you ready to bring me home?"

Lightman clears his throat, something he does before he delivers bad news. "About that. I talked to Maloney."

Paul Maloney is the assistant director of the Office of Professional Responsibility, an arm of the FBI that I didn't know existed a month ago and very much hope to never encounter again. After the shooting, Maloney insisted that I undergo counseling with Dr. Ginnis, a psychiatrist kept on retainer by the FBI. Ginnis reports to Maloney, and Maloney has the ultimate say on whether or not I'm fit to work. I get the sense that he's not inclined to sign off on me unless I do what he tells me to do, and that includes a lot of therapy I've been avoiding.

"And?"

"Maloney's concerned. He said you don't keep your appointments."

"I don't need PT. I feel fine." I cup my hand over my shoulder, my fingers probing the wound to see if it's still tender. It is. I stop.

"Not just physical therapy. You need to see Dr. Ginnis, too."

"I've talked to Ginnis."

"Nell, come on. You can't go once and call it a day."

"It's not my fault I had to leave DC."

"Of course not. But you could do sessions over the phone. Ginnis needs to write up a full report about your mental fitness. You won't get a clean eval until then."

"I get it."

"We need you back, Nell. I need you back."

"Are you begging?"

"I would if I thought that would help."

"Can't you get Ginnis to sign a form or something? I don't want to lie on a couch and talk about my childhood." My voice has taken on a petulant tone that annoys even me.

"No one has asked you to do that."

"That's exactly what he wants me to do. He has an actual couch. I've seen it. I lay on it. Once. That was enough."

Lightman chuckles despite himself. "Well, he's a psychiatrist. They all want a little of that. You might feel better, you know."

"How about we find the guys who blew off a piece of my shoulder? I'd feel better then."

"We all would. We're working on it."

"Work harder. Or better yet, let me come back to work and I'll do it for you. I spent eight months hunting Novak. No one is closer to that case than I am."

Lightman sighs. "I'm worried about you, Nell. You've had a hell of a month. I can't in good conscience send you back into the field on such a dangerous assignment. You know that. You need to take care of yourself. I can get you other names if Ginnis isn't the right fit."

"Ginnis is fine."

"Then talk to him. That's what he's there for. You know, Ginnis lost his mom when he was young, too. He was raised on a military base. Just him and his father."

"So?"

Lightman sighs. "So I think you have some stuff in common."

"Fine. I'll talk to him. Don't expect a miracle."

"I don't. I'll give him your cell number. You can call me, too. I know what it feels like to take a life. It's brutal, Nell. It stays with you. It can really fuck you up if you aren't careful."

I hear the rumble of a car approaching on Dune Road and then the crackle of tires on the gravel outside the house.

"Thanks for the pep talk. Someone's here. I gotta go."

I hang up before Lightman can protest. My hand falls to my firearm. It's daylight. The driveway isn't too far from the parking lot for the local beach. Sometimes folks get the two mixed up. Still, I'm not expecting anyone, especially not this early. In my situation, unexpected visitors aren't exactly welcome.

I hear the gate at the back of the house creak open. I move across the deck and flatten my body against the corner of the house. The wooden shingles press into my shoulder blades. A fly, trapped between the screen door and the window, buzzes overhead. I steady myself, ready my weapon. A rustle of birds shoots up from the dune grass, startled by the visitor. They're as skittish as I am, and as unaccustomed to guests.

I count the footsteps. Five will take you to the top of the stairs. A tall male figure appears. For a brief second, I panic. From behind, he looks like Dmitry Novak.

My heart rate spikes. My finger grazes the trigger. I step out of the shadows.

I don't need to say anything; the man raises his hands slowly in surrender. "It's me, Nell. It's Lee." He turns slowly.

When I see his face, I lower my weapon.

"Lee Davis. Jesus Christ. You scared the living shit out of me."

"Hi, kid." Lee has always called me *kid*, even though we're the same age. I think it has something to do with the fact that he's a solid foot taller than I am. He moves in and hugs me so hard that I groan in pain.

"What's wrong?" He withdraws, his face pinched with worry.

"It's nothing. Just a flesh wound." I tap my shoulder, feeling the color slowly return to my face. "Lightly grazed by a bullet a month ago. Still a little sore."

"Lightly grazed. That sounds like something your dad would say. I'm glad you're okay."

"Never better."

He nods and looks me up and down; I do the same. He hasn't changed much since our days together at Hampton Bays High School. Tall and thin as a pencil. His shoulders hunch inward, like he can't quite hear people talking down below. His hair, once jet-black, has a few strands of silver in it now. He probably hates that, but I think it makes him look distinguished. His face, freckled and lineless, is still boyish enough to carry him. He's hand-some in a quiet sort of way that I find appealing. I glance at his ring finger. It's bare, which surprises me. He always seemed like the sort who'd be driving his kids to soccer games by the time we were in our thirties.

Lee dated nice girls in high school, field hockey play-ers and cheerleaders who smiled a lot and flipped their hair when they laughed. The kind of girls who pretended I didn't exist. I tried hard to convey that the feeling was mutual, but no one at Hampton Bays High School really cared one way or another what I thought about them. I was just the quiet, skinny girl who wore a black leather jacket to class and was taking college-level math by the time I was in ninth grade. The girl whose dad was a ho-micide detective, whose mom was a homicide victim. My mother's brutal murder was well publicized in our area. For years afterward, there were whispers about it, about her, about us. Suffice it to say, I was given a wide berth at school.

"Sorry about the greeting," I say, running a hand through my hair. "Occupational hazard."

Lee waves me off, like a gun in his face first thing in the morning is no big deal. "How was the service? Dorsey said it was nice."

"It was. What Dad would have wanted, I think."

Lee gives me a tight smile. I wonder if we should have invited him. A newly minted homicide detective, Lee was Dad's latest partner. We mostly lost track of each other after high school. I'd heard through the grapevine that he was also living in DC, attending law school at George

Washington. He was in his third year when he found out his mom had Parkinson's disease. Moved back to the island and became a cop. Not unlike my father. Dad was a marine who managed to knock up my mom while he was home on leave. He did what he thought was right: he married her and then, when his tour was over, returned home to Suffolk County. They bought a small house with a white fence and Dad joined the SCPD. I always wondered what might have happened to Dad if my mother hadn't gotten pregnant. My guess is he would have stayed in the military and never looked back.

Lee seems more like a lawyer than a cop. I'm surprised he made it into homicide. Homicide is a tight-knit group, clubby and exclusive. Lee seems too young and eager to command any respect with that crew. Dad rarely spoke about him, and frankly, I'd forgotten they were partners until Dorsey mentioned it last week. Anyway, it didn't occur to me to invite Lee along and it probably should've. Then again, maybe Lee was relieved not to have to spend the afternoon getting wasted with a bunch of weathered, heavy-drinking cops pushing retirement age. He probably does that plenty as it is.

"Can I join you for a few?"

"Sure."

We both sit at the wooden table on the deck. Lee locks his hands behind his head and rocks back in his chair, soaking in the view. A fishing boat glides beneath the Ponquogue Bridge and he watches it until it disappears. His knee bounces nervously beneath the table. It occurs to me that this isn't a friendly visit. It's too early in the morning for that, and too soon after Dad's service.

"How long you planning to stick around town?" he asks.

"I don't know. A few more days, anyway."

"Bureau gave you leave?"

"Something like that." I feel a ping of impatience. "So what's up, Lee? I'm guessing you're not just here to check in on me."

Lee's jaw tenses slightly. "Something happened early this morning, out in Shinnecock County Park. A woman walking her dog found a body. A girl, buried in the dunes."

"That's too bad."

"The body was hacked up and wrapped in burlap."

"Ah." Our eyes meet. He doesn't have to elaborate. The previous summer, the body of a seventeen-year-old girl was found in the Pine Barrens, a sprawling, densely wooded preserve in the center of Suffolk County. She'd been dismembered and covered in burlap. It was my father's case. As far as I knew, he was still working it when he died.

"Same guy, you think?"

"I have to assume so. Or a copycat."

"ID?"

"Not yet. The vic has a metal plate in her jaw, so that's something."

"Any recent missing persons?"

"There was a local girl who disappeared around Labor Day. Could be her, but we can't say for sure."

"Okay."

"There isn't much at the office on Pine Barrens. I know your dad kept working on it, though. I was wondering if maybe he kept his own records at home? Notebooks. Laptop. Anything."

"He had a home office. I haven't gone in there yet. You're welcome to poke around if you like."

"That'd be great. Maybe I can stop by later today or tomorrow." He checks his watch. "I should head back to the crime scene."

"So that's it?"

Lee hesitates. "I was hoping I could get you to come with me. Lend a hand with the investigation."

My shoulder begins to throb, as if to remind me what a shit state I'm in. I cover it with a hand and curl my feet up onto the chair. "Oh, I don't know. I've got stuff to do. Howard Kidd's coming by later with some paperwork."

"Howie's coming when?"

"After lunch, I think he said."

"Come on, Nell. That's in, like, five hours. I promise I'll have you back in time. We sure could use the help. If this is a serial thing . . ." He shakes his head, unwilling to finish the sentence.

"Why doesn't Dorsey call in the FBI? Officially, I mean."

"Between you and me? Because he's about to retire and the last thing he wants is mass hysteria over a serial killer in Suffolk County."

"Maybe a little hysteria is appropriate."

"Maybe it is. But not on Dorsey's watch. So no. No

FBI. Just you. I've already asked him if you could come on as a consultant. No commitment. Just as long as you're in town."

"And he was okay with it?"

"He said it was fine, just be quiet about it."

"How much do I get paid?"

It takes him a second to realize that I'm joking. He smiles, a lopsided, embarrassed grin. "Jesus, Flynn. You had me there for a sec."

I sigh. It's not like I have anything else going on. The thought of boxing up our house is unpleasant enough; I'd rather prowl around a crime scene instead. At least I'd have to turn my brain on again for a few hours. Make sure it still works. I drain the last of my coffee. "Shinnecock County Park East or West?"

"East. Come on. I'll give you a lift. I'll even buy you a bagel on the way. You look like you could use it."

3.

Lee drives and I stare out the window. We cross the Ponquogue Bridge and make our way through Hampton Bays. It hasn't changed much. The houses are small and nondescript. There isn't a real town center: just a few mom-and-pop shops lining the highway and a handful of cheap bars down by the waterfront. There aren't chain restaurants or tourist-type boutiques to browse in. Just fish markets and bait-and-tackle stores and gas stations and thrift shops that scatter their wares on patchy lawns out front.

There's a small strip mall now, with a Starbucks and a King Kullen and a stoplight in front of it, all of which I'm certain Dad hated. He wasn't a big fan of development in what he called "our part" of the island. Other than that, everything is the same. We pass a half-dozen signs for the annual pancake breakfast at the fire station. My heart lurches when I see the park where my mother used to whirl me around on a roundabout after school. It sat at an awkward angle, and it groaned while she sang to me. I sit up and catch a glimpse of it as the car rolls past. It's still there, rusted and tilted as always.

At the edge of town, we pass the marina where Dorsey keeps his boat. There's a joint next to it called Hank's, where Dad and the guys used to go for beers after work. After that, the Shinnecock Canal bisects the land in two. Locals call it the Cut. The highway narrows to a bridge, which spans the Cut like a tourniquet. When you see it on a map, you realize that this bridge is the only thing tethering the eastern tip of the South Fork to the main island itself. The Cut is as psychological as it is physical. It's the demarcation line between the summer people and everybody else.

Once we cross the bridge, we're in the Hamptons. The change is immediate and noticeable. To the east of the Cut, there are no pawnshops or bait-and-tackles. Main Street in Southampton is populated with designer clothing and jewelry boutiques. Restaurants serve over-priced seafood and French wine. The lawns here are manicured. Hundred-year-old elms line the streets like sentinels. The summer people like their towns perfect. God knows they pay enough for it. It's strange to think of this as Suffolk County, but it is just the same. The people who reside here don't know there's anything else. To them, our part of the island is just something they have to drive through on the way to the beach.

We pass a gardener on a ladder, shearing the top of a hedge with surgical precision. He wields a long, silver chain saw; the blade glints in the sun. The man looks at us, his eyes trailing our car with suspicion. I'd guess he's not documented; a lot of the landscapers around here aren't. My maternal grandfather was one of them. He and my grandmother crossed the border from Juarez just in time for my mother to be born here. They stayed awhile in Texas before moving north, eventually settling in Central Islip. My grandfather owned a small farm back in Mexico. He found work as a landscaper. My grandmother cleaned rooms in a retirement home. They lived in a trailer with my mother and one other family. As rough as the Third Precinct was for them, it was better than Juarez.

I roll down the window and catch the faint scent of ocean air. The chain saw falls silent. Cicadas buzz. On the other side of the street, sprinklers turn on and water the already wet, lush grass. Two girls in tennis dresses and matching windbreakers ride bicycles side by side. They head south, toward the beach. I always went back to school the week before Labor Day, but the private schools in Manhattan don't open until late September. The girls' slim legs pump in unison. Just as we're about to pass them, one lifts her arms over her head and raises her feet from the pedals. The wheels wobble, and for a moment, I think she might fall. She swerves toward us, regaining her balance just before she nearly collides with the passenger-side door. I suck in a breath; Lee slams on the brake. I hear the hush of her ponytail against the glass. She has a pink ribbon in her hair. It presses against my window like a kiss.

"*What the fuck*," Lee mutters.

The girls sail by, laughing. They both look back at us, their sun-streaked ponytails shaking in the breeze, their heads bobbing in disbelief at their near-miss. I expect Lee to speed up and pull alongside them. Give them a lecture about street safety. He doesn't. He just lets them go. Nothing bad ever happens to girls from Gin Lane, I guess.

We pass the turnoff for Coopers Beach and take a right onto Meadow Lane. Meadow Lane is known as Billionaire's Row. It's a thin strip of land with Shinnecock Bay on one side and the Atlantic Ocean on the other. The houses on Meadow Lane are enormous. They make the other houses in the area look like guest cottages, which is saying something. They have oceanfront pools and tennis courts. The lawns go on forever. One is studded with large, bizarre sculptures. A giant balloon dog made of shiny, magenta-colored metal. A naked, obese woman cast in bronze. It looks like a museum, and one I'm not particularly eager to visit. Toward the end of the lane, there's a rectangle carved out of the sand. It's marked with a large *H*. A helicopter lifts off from it as we approach, its sleek, silver form disappearing into an overcast sky.

The irony of Billionaire's Row is that it dead-ends into Shinnecock County Park East, a public preserve where, for thirty bucks, you can park a camper van overnight. The park is a favorite spot for locals to bass fish and take their off-road recreational vehicles. My father loved it there, especially in the off-season. It's where he taught me how to fish. In high school, my classmates would drive down to the park to drink beer and smoke in the dunes. I'd tag along now and then, not because I enjoyed parties but because anything was better than spending a night at home with Dad when he was drunk. We'd chuck bottles and butts as far as we could in the direction of Meadow Lane. It was just a little fuck-you to the summer people, who acted as though this part of the island belonged to them and them alone.

Today it's a festering crime scene. I can envision the headlines already. The tabloids will eat this up: a dead girl, dismembered and buried amid multimillion-dollar oceanfront mansions. It's hard to imagine a more glamorous burial ground. Once the press connects this case to the body found last summer in the Pine Barrens, the floodgates will open. A murder is one thing. Serial killings catch national news interest. Web forums light up with chatter. Conspiracy theorists and true-crime junkies take notice. The killer himself might even crawl out of the woodwork, unable to stay away from the media circus. It might inspire him—or someone else—to kill again.

It wouldn't be the first time. Long Island has always been a breeding ground for men who hunt women. Joel Rifkin killed at least nine women back in the nineties. Robert Shulman killed five. The Long Island Serial Killer—said to be responsible for anywhere from ten to sixteen murders over the past twenty years—still remains at large. And that's to say nothing of the scores of cold cases that remain in boxes on the shelves at SCPD headquarters and the bodies that never got found at all.

"How does it feel to be home?" Lee says.

I give him a look. "This isn't home."

"I mean the island. Did you miss it?"

"No."

"How long has it been?"

"Ten years."

Lee whistles. "You left for college and never came back?"

"Yep."

"Whatever happened to Tommy Street?"

I must look shocked because Lee turns crimson. "Sorry. Too personal?"

It *is* too personal, but Lee doesn't know that. He's just trying to make casual conversation. Tom was my high school boyfriend. The first and perhaps most important relationship of my life. We started dating at the beginning of sophomore year and broke up at the end of senior year, right after I got pregnant by accident. Tom wanted to get married. I considered giving up my scholarship to MIT and staying put in Suffolk County so that we could get married. Dad told me he'd disown me if I did. Lee doesn't know that, despite my father's outrage, I decided to keep the baby only to lose it a few weeks later. He doesn't know that all of this changed the course of my life irrevocably. I stopped speaking to Tom, though none of it was his fault. I stopped speaking to my father, too. I packed up my secondhand Civic and drove myself up to MIT without saying goodbye.

"I don't know about Tommy. We're not in touch," I say, though it's only half-true. I've kept tabs on Tom's life over the past decade. He still lives in Suffolk County. He's married to a woman named Beth, who looks like me except she's always smiling. They have twin girls, Hannah and Ellie, who wear matching outfits. He's an insurance broker, just like his father. He coaches Little League on weekends. They have a rescue dog named Hester. They look, on social media anyway, well-adjusted and happy. Occasionally, I wonder what would have happened if I'd stayed. Could I have been Mrs. Thomas Street? What if we had a little girl or boy, now ten years old? Would I have felt trapped, like my father had? Or is it possible that, like Beth, I would be smiling in every photo?

"I always thought you two would get married," Lee says. "Everyone back then did."

"It was high school. Puppy love."

Lee shrugs. "Looked real to me."

"It was ten years ago."

"You and your dad fell out of touch, I take it."

"Something like that."

"Did he ever talk about the Pine Barrens case?"

"He didn't talk much about anything. At least, not to me."

"He talked about you."

I turn, surprised. "He did?"

"Yeah. He was proud of you. Of the work you do. He'd bring you up every chance he got."

We're both quiet for a minute. "We didn't speak for years after I moved away," I say quietly. "I wanted nothing to do with him."

"And yet you ended up in law enforcement, just like him."

"True. It's in my blood, I guess. Dad came down to

DC a few years back. We patched things up a bit. We'd talk now and then. Not recently, though. We hadn't spoken in months."

Lee nods like that doesn't surprise him. "Last year was tough on your dad. Pine Barrens shook him up. It was a horrible case. The girl was young. Just turned seventeen. Your dad took it real personal. He told me once that he felt like he was the only one who seemed to care that she was dead."

"Did anyone care?"

Lee shrugs. "There wasn't exactly a media frenzy. She was a working girl from a bad neighborhood. You know. Same old story."

"Where was she from?"

"Brentwood."

"Latina?"

"Yeah."

"And killed the same way as this one?"

"Shot at point-blank range in the head. Cut up and wrapped in burlap like a goddamn Christmas tree and buried way out in the middle of nowhere. Ria Sandoval was her name."

"Sexually assaulted?"

"Hard to tell. Animals got to her pretty bad. She'd been dead for more than a month when some hikers found her."

"When did she go missing?"

"Over July Fourth weekend, last summer. Told a friend she was going to work a job out east. Never came back. No one bothered to file a missing persons."

"Well, right. Because then ICE would come knocking."

"No one really seemed to notice she was gone. Took them almost two months to ID her."

"What about her parents?"

"Dad was never in the picture. Mom's a mess. She'd go MIA for weeks at a time. The girl bounced around. Sometimes she'd stay with her neighbors. She was tight with one of them. Girl named Luz Molina. Both did some escorting. They used a driver sometimes to take them to motels or clients' houses. An ex-con named Giovanni Calabrese. He runs a limo company out of Wyandanch. Thinks he's a pimp. Drives a tricked-out white Escalade with custom rims." Lee rolls his eyes.

"How'd they find themselves a driver?"

"Not sure. Maybe online? Once Ria met Calabrese, she stopped advertising on Craigslist and Backpage. He connected her with clients directly. Rich ones, according to your dad. Calabrese runs a high-end operation."

"Was Calabrese driving Ria the night she went missing?"

"Yeah. He said he dropped her off in a motel parking lot. GPS backed that up, and the motel attendant remembered seeing his car pull into the lot, idle by the curb, and then leave. Ria was supposed to spend the night with a client and call Calabrese to pick her up in the morning. He never heard from her again."

"I assume he had an alibi?"

"He did. It checked out. He was out all night, partying with friends."

"And the client?"

"Never did figure out who it was."

"Did the motel have security cameras? Client records?"

"Cameras were broken. Had been for months. Most of the clients paid in cash. It's that kind of establishment."

"Were there any leads at all?"

Lee sighs. "There was a landscaper. Alfonso Morales. He lives in Brentwood, down the street from the Sandoval house. Ria's friend Luz said he used to stare at Ria when she passed by. Followed her a couple of times, too. Luz said that she once heard footsteps around the house late one night when Ria was staying over. She thought she saw a man staring in at them through the back window."

"And she thought it was Morales?"

"That was her guess, but she never called the police or anything."

"Does Morales still live in Brentwood?"

"Last I checked."

"And what about Luz?"

"Not sure. I assume so. She works at a bar down by the marina now. Hank O'Gorman's place. Remember him? I see her there sometimes. I hope what happened to Ria scared her straight, you know?"

"Scared her straight?"

"Got her to stop selling herself."

I take a beat. "You do understand that most girls don't choose that life, right?"

"Everyone makes choices."

I take a deep breath and decline to respond.

"Oh." Lee snaps his fingers. "There was a thing about a red truck. Morales drives a maroon pickup. The motel clerk said he thought he saw a red truck in the lot the night Ria was there, but he couldn't say for sure. And he couldn't positively ID Morales."

"Did you talk to Morales?"

"We picked him up a couple of times. I always thought there was something off about him myself. He looks all around when you talk to him, but never right in the eye. Got nervous when we started asking questions about Ria. At first, he tried to claim he'd never seen her before."

"Maybe he's scared of cops."

"Maybe. I got a bad feeling, though. He does some work for the South Fork Preservation Society. You heard of them?"

"The plover people?"

Lee snorts. "Yeah. They care a lot about the plover. They do projects all over the island. Run by a bunch of bored hedge-fund wives, mostly. Too much time on their hands and definitely too much money. They buy up land for preservation and do sand dune restoration and that kind of thing. Last summer, Morales was working at one of their sites in the Pine Barrens, not too far from where the body was buried. He was planting trees out there. And guess what the tree roots were wrapped in?"

I raise my eyebrows. "Burlap."

"You got it. He had yards of it in his truck. Same make, everything. That said, it's pretty common. You can find it in most of the nurseries on the North Fork."

"You find anything else? Hair, blood?"

"Nah. We searched the car, his house. Nothing."

"What about DNA?"

"Vic's body was too badly degraded to find anyone else's DNA. Morales had scratches on his hands and a big, nasty gash on his leg. Looked like it was healing up, so maybe a few weeks old. Matched up with our time-line."

"Did he have an explanation?"

"Claimed he got injured on the job."

"Plausible."

"I guess. In the end, we had to let him walk. Your dad didn't think we had enough to hold him."

"What did you think?"

Lee sighs. "I thought he might be good for it. At least, I thought we should have turned him over to ICE, let them get rid of him. Better safe than sorry, right? But what did I know? I was two weeks into homicide. And your dad wasn't really into friendly suggestions."

"You're telling me."

Lee pulls over on the sandy shoulder of the road and cuts the engine. "He was tough on you, huh?"

"You could say that. He had a well-developed sense of right and wrong."

"Couldn't have been easy, growing up with him. I mean, he was a good man and all. But he scared the crap out of me."

"Scared the crap out of most people." I push open the car door.

There is a news van up ahead, parked behind an SCPD cruiser.

"Fuck." Lee shakes his head. "These guys are like vultures. They smell blood and come running."

"What do you expect? You can see the crime scene from the Ponquogue Bridge. And hey, maybe it's a rich white girl this time."

Lee hands me an SCPD baseball cap from the back seat of his car. "Put this on. Last thing you need right now is a spot on the five-o'clock news."

4.

We hop out of the car. Sand slips into my sneakers, under my toes. I halt when I see a woman step out of a Jeep on the side of the road. Lee is talking, but I've stopped listening. I watch the woman as she closes her car door, her cherry-red lips parting into a smile as she greets a passing police officer.

Twenty-one years ago, Ann-Marie Marshall was a cub reporter at *Newsday*. I was seven years old. While my father and I were out camping in Sears Bellows County Park, my mother was murdered in our house in Hampton Bays. By the time we got back home, our block was swarming with cops and reporters, Ann-Marie Marshall among them. While I don't remember the details of the night she died, I have a visceral impression of the following morning. I knew something was wrong as we approached our house because of all the flashing lights. To this day, I seize up at the sight of police lights cutting through fog. Dad made me stay in the car while he got out to see what the fuss was about. I remember that the windshield wipers were on; I can hear them when I dream about that day. I can smell the faint scent of the cigarettes Dad smoked in the car when he was angry and the pine-scented air freshener he used to cover it up. I pressed my face against the window as techs wheeled my mother's body down the driveway. A sheet was draped over her, but I knew it was her. Dorsey was there. Dad ran to him; collapsed into his arms. It was one of the few times I ever saw either man cry.

Dorsey took us both down to the station. For an hour or so, he separated me from my father. He brought me a soda and asked me questions about the night before. Where had we camped? What did we eat for dinner? What time did we go to bed? Did I sleep through the night? Had Dad and I been together the whole time?

I answered most of the questions silently, just nodding yes or shaking my head no. I knew my answers were important, and my hands shook so hard that I sat on them to make them stop. Eventually, Dorsey patted me on the shoulder and told me I could go home. *She did good*, he whispered to my father in the hallway. Dad looked relieved. He put his hand on my shoulder and gave me an affectionate squeeze. Dorsey winked at me and smiled.

Not long after, a seventeen-year-old boy from down the block confessed. It wasn't Sean Gilroy's first brush with the law, but it would be his last. The previous year, a neighbor claimed he'd been watching her shower from

a tree outside her window. There were all kinds of rumors about him. People said he killed cats and rabbits,
skinned them and kept their pelts in his basement. I
never found out if that was true or just a suburban myth
about a quiet, strange boy who'd never really fit in. According to his initial confession—one that he would re-
count and then retell in a narrative that shape-shifted
over the course of his sentencing and incarceration—
Gilroy saw my mother washing dishes through the window. Her long black hair was down; she wore a low-cut
top and a skirt that skimmed her narrow hips. She was
tan from the summer, and Gilroy said she was smiling to
herself like she had a secret. He was overcome by his sexual desire for her. He knocked on the door and she let
him in willingly, even offering him a cold drink from our
fridge. He attacked her in the kitchen and they struggled.
She pulled a knife out of the butcher's block on the counter to defend herself. Gilroy overpowered her, seized the
knife, and stabbed her in the chest with it, not once, but
eight times, straight through the heart. Then he took a
shower in my parents' bathroom, changed into clean
clothes that belonged to my father, and returned to his
house as though nothing had happened. When the police
came to question him, he was sitting on the couch watching baseball. He was still wearing my father's T-shirt and
jeans. His sneakers were splattered with her blood.

Gilroy was sentenced to life in prison without parole.
On the morning Gilroy was sentenced, a small cluster of
reporters waited for my father and me outside our house.
My father instructed me to ignore them. I did, on what

felt like an eternal walk from our doorway to the SCPD cruiser that was waiting for us at the curb. I kept my eyes down and counted the cracks in the sidewalk cement. I had almost made it into the car when Ann-Marie Marshall called out, "Nell!" I looked up, and for a second, we locked eyes. Then my father stepped between us and hissed to her that if she approached us again, he'd have her arrested for harassment. At night, I dreamed not about my mother but about Marshall, those red lips of hers calling my name. Not long after, we moved to Pop's place on Dune Road. Our house was sold and razed to the ground. No one wanted to live in the house where a detective's wife had been murdered, especially not us.

Ann-Marie won't recognize me now. I was just a child then. But I recognize her. Even after Sean Gilroy was sent up to Shawangunk Correctional Facility and everyone lost interest, she kept writing about him, about the case. She argued that Gilroy was slow and unable to understand the questions the police had asked of him. She wrote about how he was kept for hours without an attorney present, without food and water, and how he eventually produced a statement that was riddled with contradictions and inaccuracies. She said he left the interrogation room with a freshly broken finger. She argued that he confessed because he wanted to go home. Even though he admitted to her, in an interview years after his sentencing, that he had, in fact, murdered my mother, Sean Gilroy became a touchstone for Marshall. She kept coming back to him in subsequent articles, as a reminder, a warning, a sign that Suffolk County was rotting. If they would treat a poor, slow young white boy like this, she seemed to say, think about what they would do to the rest of us.

I'm surprised by how much she looks like her byline picture. Silver hair, cropped short, with bangs. Sharp, serious face with brows that seemed knit together in constant contemplation. She looks up, and for a moment, I think she sees me. Her chin lifts, her eyes narrow in recognition. But then she waves at a car coming down the road. My shoulders drop from around my ears.

"You okay?" Lee asks. He puts his hand gently on my back. I flinch at his touch, and he takes the hint. He steps away from me, giving me space.

"Yeah. Sorry. Thought I saw someone I knew."

We take the long way around the barricades that have been set up at the entrance to the park. A camera flashes as we pass. I turn my face down, angling my body behind Lee's. Past the barricade, an SCPD officer holds a clipboard. Quietly, Lee gives him both of our names. It occurs to me that I probably should've checked with Lightman before taking on an unofficial consulting position with the SCPD. He would have said no, which is, of course, the right answer. I don't particularly want to advertise my whereabouts to Dmitry Novak and his cohort, nor do I feel like opening myself up to subpoenas from DAs and defense attorneys, if and when a suspect is taken into custody.

It's too late to worry about that. The crime scene recorder has written down my name in his official-looking notepad. And Ann-Marie Marshall's presence has sent me spiraling back into a dark part of my past. I won't leave Suffolk County without talking to her, I decide. My uncertainty about what happened that night—and about the weight Dorsey gave to my testimony—has always eaten away at me. It's a fire that has slowly but steadily consumed me for years. Now that I'm home, I feel its burn more than ever. This may well be my last trip to Suffolk County. Once I close my father's estate, there will be no reason for me to return. I need to know more about Sean Gilroy, about what happened in those dark hours while I slept soundly in my tent in Sears Bellows County Park. Ann-Marie Marshall has talked to Gilroy more than anyone else. She's looked into his eyes; she's heard him tell his side of the story. If I talk to her, maybe I can finally put it behind me.

Lee and I walk across the sand and up into the dunes. It's nothing short of miraculous that this land has remained undeveloped all these years. It's beautiful. I hate thinking that about a crime scene, but it's true. There's water all around us. To the south, the ocean advances and retreats on the sand, the sound of the waves steady as a heartbeat. To the north, the bay sits dark and still, glimmering in the morning light.

Unlike most beaches in the Hamptons, this place is untouched. The dune grass grows high and unruly. In places, it comes up past my knees, nearly brushing my hips. Overhead, seagulls circle, dropping crabs onto the rocks to crack open the shells. One swoops off with a whole fish in its claws, victorious. I take a deep breath, filling my lungs with fresh salt air. If I'm going to be buried anywhere, I'd want it to be somewhere like here. Somewhere beautiful and wild.

The dunes hum with activity. Along the perimeter of the beach, Southampton Town Police are setting up more orange barricades, sure to attract attention. The coroner's van is in the parking lot at the base of the dunes. A physician's assistant chats with a tech beside it. A spark of light by the gravesite tells me the photographer is here. Officers are everywhere, sweeping the dune grass for evidence. They walk with the synchronized cadence of a chain gang. In the distance, a cadaver dog barks. For a moment, everyone freezes.

"Just a dead bird," someone calls out, and the dunes spring back to life.

A red flag sticks in the sand at the side of the road. Lee gestures for me to follow him in that direction. The dune is steep, maybe fifteen or twenty feet high. Once we reach its crest, I have to pause to catch my breath. The terrain along the top of the dune is thick with sumac and bramble, a challenge to navigate. This is the kind of place my father would warn me against exploring as a kid. Ticks thrive in grass like this. There's a wooden fence surrounding the area, presumably to keep people out. A stretch of ten feet or so has been knocked over. I walk over to it, crouch down. "SFPS" is stamped in small letters along the edge.

"Lee," I call out, beckoning him. He doubles back and kneels down beside me. I point to the lettering. "South Fork Preservation Society. Looks like this is another one of their restoration sites."

Lee shakes his head. "I'm telling you. Morales."

We stand and keep moving until we come to a break in the bramble. A grave has been scratched out of the sand, like a giant plover's nest. About six feet long and five feet wide. Stakes and crime scene tape form a rough-edged pentagon around it. At my feet are clumps of dune grass, torn up at the root.

I squat down, staring close at a pile of rocks. They are small and flat, about as thick and wide as the palm of my hand. Seven of them. Stacked one atop the other, like a deck of cards.

"A cairn," I murmur, turning my head to examine it closer.

"A trail marker?"

"Something like that. Cairns have been used for centuries, for lots of things. Trails, caches of food. They can be ceremonial, like for a burial site."

"Here." Lee hands me a pair of latex gloves. He puts on a pair himself, stretching them over his long, bony fingers.

"Look at this. This is deliberate. The stones are stacked so precisely. And I'm not sure these rocks are even from this area. They should be tested. Was there anything like this near the Sandoval site?"

"Not that I recall. But it's possible we missed it."

"It could have been disturbed before you got there, too. Maybe the hikers who found the body remember seeing it."

"You think it might still be there?"

I shrug. "It's worth going back to check it out." I

stand up, brush some sand off my jeans. "I have a friend from the Bureau. Sarah Patel. She works out of Miami. She's the head of a human trafficking task force. If we're looking at two young sex workers murdered a year apart, killed in this very particular way, I think you guys should consider bringing in her team. Either that or someone from the BAU."

"You're from the BAU."

"You know what I mean. This is not a case for local PD, Lee. You need to be cross-checking this stuff against national databases."

Lee kicks the sand with his toe. "I'll raise it again with Dorsey."

"Or you could just let me call Sarah Patel and let her decide."

"No." He shakes his head emphatically. "Absolutely not. Dorsey will flip out. He does not want outside involvement here. And it's his call, not Sarah Patel's."

I disagree, but there's no point in saying so. We're quiet for a minute. I clear my throat, breaking the tension. "Who did you say found this body?"

"Grace Bishop. She lives down the street. Married to Eliot Bishop."

"The Treasury Secretary?"

"Yep . . . she's on the board of the Preservation Society, actually. She might know about the restoration project here. She walks her dog on the beach every morning. Dog took off, came up here, dug up the body. Tore off a piece of the ankle bone. Grace had to wrestle it out of the dog's mouth. When I got here, she was hysterical."

"A human foot before seven a.m.? I'd be hysterical, too."

Lee blanches, and I wonder if he's going to lose his breakfast. He probably hasn't seen all that many murder victims in his time at the SCPD. Fewer than I have, anyway. Car accidents, sure. Maybe the occasional suicide. But there is something particularly unsettling about murder scenes. There is a darkness that clings to the air long after the killer has departed. I know it well.

This one feels particularly gruesome. The body in the grave is shrouded in burlap. It reminds me of the trip Dad and I would take every December to a nursery on the North Fork. We would pick out a Christmas tree—usually a small one, so that I could reach the top of it without too much help—and the nursery owner would wrap it in burlap just like this. Then Dad would hoist it over his shoulder and tie it to the top of our car. We'd drive home in silence, both of us knowing that Dad rarely had the energy to decorate the tree. During the holidays, Dad's drinking was worse than usual. Something like a tangle of Christmas lights was enough to set him off. He'd get frustrated, yell at me, throw something. Then he'd disappear, returning only when he was too drunk to notice that while he was gone I'd managed to unwind the lights, fix the broken bulbs, and wrap them around the tree by myself.

There is a tear at the bottom of the sack. Visible through it is a brown stump. The girl's anklebone, I'd guess. The dog had torn the foot clean off. The mangled remains of it lay like trash at the edge of the gravesite.

"Can I see her?"

Lee nods. He stoops over and pulls back the burlap. The smell intensifies. Lee reels, as though knocked back by it. The scent of human decay is something you never really get used to. It's a heavy, rancid odor that creeps into your pores and crawls beneath your skin. It feels unholy, as though it might infect you just by getting too close. The first time I saw a cadaver, I couldn't shake the smell for days. I kept showering and washing my hands, but the scent of it had burned itself on the inside of my nostrils like gunpowder. Out of the corner of my eye, I see Lee gulp air, his fingers pinching at his nose.

The body has putrefied and shriveled. The maggots are gone, at least, but there's still skin on her; she hasn't fully skeletonized. I'd guess the corpse is a few weeks old. Skin, like leather, is shrink-wrapped around the bone. Her teeth are bared, like an animal's. When I shift positions, the sunlight gleams off the metal plate in her jaw. *Lucky girl*, I think to myself. A plate like that is a pathologist's golden ticket to identification.

"The eyes," Lee groans. "God, that freaks me out."

The eye sockets are hollow. Part of her skull is missing, too. It looks as though she was nailed clean in the middle of her forehead. I feel a shiver of respect for the shooter. As a hunter, my father trained me to go for a one-shot kill, preferably to the head, so as to minimize suffering. This is about as perfect a shot as one could ask for.

After the shot to the head, the killer dissembled her limbs, and tied them to her torso with twine. It's a surreal, macabre presentation; gory and precise at the same time. In my experience, you could tell almost as much about a person by the way they died as anything else.

"Ria Sandoval was shot in the head, too, wasn't she?"

"Yep," Lee says, his voice hoarse. "Point-blank range. And then . . ." He gestures to the body. He swallows hard as though the word *dismembered* is lodged inside his throat.

"Strange way to kill a working girl."

"Why's that?"

"It's clean."

"You call this clean?" Lee stares at me incredulously.

"Professional, I mean. Like an execution."

"So maybe gang related?"

"Possibly. It's meticulous. Almost ritualistic."

The light catches something in the sand. I gesture to Lee. "There's something there. Metallic, I think."

Lee drops onto his knees. He pulls a pen out of his back pocket. With it, he scoops out a thin gold bracelet.

He holds it up to the light. "Cartier."

"Bag it."

"It's Grace Bishop's. Look. It has her initials on the inside." He takes an evidence bag and drops the bracelet inside. "We should get this back to her. Poor woman."

I bite my tongue and say nothing. It bothers me when the cops out here kowtow to the summer people. Especially Lee. I used to see him down here when we were both in high school. He threw beer cans at Meadow Lane with the rest of us. The bracelet should go into evidence. I'd hazard a guess that Grace Bishop has another one to wear while she waits to get it back. She probably doesn't even know it's gone. But it's not my case. Not my problem.

"I'll take it," I tell him. I hold out my hand for the bag. "I'd like to talk to her, anyway. You said she's on the board of the Preservation Society, right?"

"Yeah. And I think she knows Morales. Your dad talked to her about him last summer."

"Where's the pathologist? I'd like to speak to him before I go."

"It's a her. And she's here somewhere." Lee turns and points to a woman—a girl, really—trudging toward us. She's wearing jeans, hiking boots, and a backpack. Her thick blond hair is pulled back into a braid that trails down her back. She's unsettlingly attractive, with a long, lithe body and a perfect heart-shaped face. "That's her."

I stare at her, then look back at Lee.

"You're joking."

"I'm not. Jamie Milkowski. She's young but good."

"How young?"

"Just started this year."

"So it's her first serial. Maybe even her first murder. How exciting for her."

Lee gives me a look. "Everyone says she's brilliant. Stop being so judgmental, Flynn. You of all people should know that an attractive young woman can do her job just as well as a grizzled old man."

I ignore the compliment, but heat rises to my cheeks. "You can't have someone green on a case like this," I argue. "You know that. You have to send it into the city if you want this done right."

Lee sighs. Though he'd never admit it, I know he agrees
with me. Our jobs are learned through a slow and steady
accumulation of experience. There's science to crime scene
evaluation, but there's also artistry. The best teacher is a
dead body. If it were up to me, the body would be sent to
Nicole Prentice. Nikki is a nationally recognized forensic
anthropologist who leads a team at the New York City
Medical Examiner's Office. I've worked with her before.
She's the best. Of course, it isn't up to me, nor is it up to
Lee. It's Dorsey's decision and he will assuredly keep everything in-house for as long as possible. To do anything
else would read as a lack of confidence in the Suffolk
County team. It would also send a signal: this is not just a
murder. It's a serial. And it's time to call in the Feds.

"Dorsey wants the Suffolk County ME to give it a try.
If they're overwhelmed, or the body is really badly decomposed, they'll send it into the city for DNA analysis."
Lee speaks with finality, as though this has already been
discussed and decided.

"The body *is* decomposed. Jesus Christ, Lee. Sending
it to Suffolk County is just a waste of time."

Lee nods his chin. I turn around. Milkowski is standing behind me. She extends her hand. "Jamie Milkowski.
Suffolk County ME," she says, without a trace of animus.

"Nell Flynn. FBI."

"Glad you guys are here."

"No guys. Just me," I say.

"Nell is Marty Flynn's daughter," Lee explains. "I
asked her to consult on the case. She's with the Behavioral Analysis Unit."

"I'm sorry about your dad. He was a good man."

I nod, unable to muster up a response. I'm starting to regret being a part of this investigation.

"It's good you're here," Milkowski says diplomatically. "We could use the help. And I agree with you about sending the body into the city. If we could get Nikki Prentice to look at it, all the better."

"Sorry. I wasn't trying to be disrespectful."

"You were being honest." She gives me a short nod. "It's going to rain soon. We've got to clear the body out."

"Of course." I look up. The color of the sky has retracted as if in expectation of rain. Dark clouds gather in the distance. There's cool wetness in the air, cutting at my wrists and ankles. I wonder how many storms this body has weathered outside. How degraded she's been by the elements. As if she hadn't been degraded enough.

I shove off, allowing Milkowski some breathing room. I gesture for Lee to do the same. He lingers for a second, giving Milkowski a healthy once-over. Once he's in range, I flick him hard in the bicep.

"What the fuck?" He cradles his arm in his hand. "Ow."

"Do you really think a crime scene is the best place to stare at some girl's ass?"

"I wasn't staring."

"Lee." I give him a look.

"It was like a second's worth of staring," he argues. "Maybe two. Tops."

I turn my back to him and focus on the landscape. Down on the beach, I see two people poking around the barricades. They don't look like reporters, more like curious locals on a midmorning walk down the beach. Even though this park feels remote, I'm reminded that we're in a public place. The fallen fence isn't much of a deterrent. I'm not sure it's clear where the beach ends and the park begins. People have, no doubt, walked across these dunes. They may have smoked here, picnicked here, hiked here. That means anything we find—footprints, cigarette butts, hair—is likely useless.

The particular spot where the body is buried is tough to get to, at least. We're standing in very dense brush, the kind that only the most ambitious of dogs would bother to burrow through. It's the thickest patch of foliage in the surrounding area. Good for hiding bodies, but a hell of an effort to bury them.

I shield my eyes from the sun and stare down at the coroner's van. We're a quarter mile from the parking lot. I try to imagine a man carrying a body up here, and then pulling back the dune grass, which has deep, stubborn roots. After all that, he'd have to dig a hole deep enough to bury a body, so at least four or five feet deep and three or so feet wide. More if he wanted to be sure it would stay buried.

For a single man, it would be an extraordinary, almost herculean effort. It would take several hours. Even at night, he'd be in plain view of the parking area below. Why would anyone risk being seen by a passerby? There were plenty of secluded places in the area, more conducive to burying bodies. There's also the bay right there across the street. A couple of yards of twine and a cinder block would dispose of a body just as well, and with a lot less effort.

"The park's been closed for months. Because of the sand erosion," Lee says, as though in answer to my thoughts. "So there's no traffic in and out of here at night."

"But the beach is still public."

"True."

"A lot of parks around here are completely desolate."

"Right."

"So why here?"

"Maybe because the killer worked here and knew it well?"

"Well, then we need to find out if the Preservation Society had workers in here over the past few weeks. From the looks of that fence, they did."

"Yep. Will do."

"Did someone call in a botanist?"

"Not sure," Lee says. "We need a botanist?"

I bend at the knee, pull up a clump of dune grass. "It looks like someone did a reasonably careful job of unearthing these. The roots are still intact. If they were replanted over the gravesite, no one would see the difference. If it had been a rushed job or done by someone who didn't know what they were doing, he probably would have hacked through the roots instead of taking the time to dig them out."

"Interesting. This wasn't the kill site, either. No blood spatter. No signs of struggle. So this burial was deliberate. Whoever did this took his time and planned in advance."

I shake my head, frustrated. "It's just such a strange place to bury a body. Much safer to dump it in the water. Or out in the elements, where it will decay faster, like Ria Sandoval."

"Sandoval got found. Maybe he learned his lesson."

"Maybe. Or maybe this place has significance for him. Somewhere he could come back and visit. Maybe that's why the dune grass was so carefully replanted. It's a public place, but he's also trying to ensure that no one can find her. Except for him. That would explain the cairn, too."

"A trophy garden."

"It's not uncommon with serial killings."

"Morales is a landscaper," Lee says. "He would know about the roots."

"Right. He would have had time, too, to case out the site, especially if he'd been working on the dune restoration project here. He might've even prepped it. Dug the grave in advance."

Out of the corner of my eye, I catch a flash of movement. I look up. The house next door has a small balcony overlooking the park. The window is dark. Maybe I'm seeing things, but I could swear the movement came from there.

"Who lives there?" I ask, pointing to the balcony.

"James Meachem. Finance guy. Grace Bishop's house is on the other side."

"Has anyone talked to him yet?"

"He's not there. He's almost never there."

"Where is he?"

Lee shrugs. "He's got houses in Manhattan and Palm Beach. And an island down in the BVI."

"An island?"

"Yeah. A private island. Named after himself, someone said. Little Saint James. How do you like that?"

"Find him. A girl was found dead a hundred yards from his property line. We'll need a complete list of everyone who works in his household. If anyone was there, they might have seen or heard something."

"I'm on it."

"I'm going to go talk to Grace Bishop."

"You want company?"

"Let me talk to her alone first. Get a botanist. Track down James Meachem. Get a list of his household staff and start contacting them. I'll meet you back here. I gotta head home in an hour or so."

I stride past the barricades, scanning for Ann-Marie Marshall. I spot her up ahead, stepping into her Jeep. I hurry toward her, but I'm too late. She closes the door and drives off down Meadow Lane, her tires kicking up sand in my direction.

5.

I take some time prowling around the perimeter of James Meachem's house. The hedges surrounding the property are thick and high. The gate is made of industrial metal. Through the slats, I see a rolling lawn. In the distance, a house made of glass and steel sits high on the dunes. While the views from inside are, I'm sure, spectacular, there's a coldness to the place that unsettles me.

A mechanical buzz causes me to look up. A security camera, affixed to the gatepost, focuses on me. I take a step to the left. The camera moves. I give it a little wave. It vibrates, mimicking my movement. I'm tempted to give it the finger, but I restrain myself. Instead, I back down the driveway, aware that the camera is following me, capturing my image on someone's computer. When I reach the street and turn toward the Bishop property next door, the camera falls still. I wonder who, if anyone, is watching.

The Bishop house, too, is guarded by a gate. Most houses on Meadow Lane are. I walk over to the keypad and press a button to call the house.

"Nell Flynn to see Grace Bishop," I say into the speaker, after I hear someone pick up on the other end. "I'm with the Federal Bureau of Investigation."

The gate swings open. I see that the property is as grand as Meachem's but less antiseptic. The lawn is well landscaped. Hydrangea bushes and Rose of Sharon line the edges of the drive. There's a vegetable garden and an orchard. From between the trees, a woman emerges, removing gardening gloves from her hands. She wears a wide-brimmed hat, a rumpled linen shirt, and jeans. Her face is pink from exertion.

"Hello, there," she calls out. Her voice has a soft southern lilt to it. "I'm Grace."

We walk toward each other, meeting halfway between the orchard and the drive. Grace Bishop is a beautiful woman. Tall, slim, and elegant. When she extends her hand, I notice that she's wearing a simple gold band on her finger, and her nails are short and unvarnished. Not what I was expecting. I let my guard down just a little.

"I hope I'm not intruding, Mrs. Bishop."

"Call me Grace, please. You're not. I've just been working in the gardens to keep myself distracted. It's been such a horrible day."

"I know, I'm sorry. Would you mind if I asked you a few questions?"

"Not at all. Why don't you come sit? I could use a break, anyway." Delicate beads of sweat gather at her

hairline. She blots them away with the back of her wrist
and then gestures for me to follow her.

The house is a gambrel-style home with white wooden
shutters and porches that wrap all the way around it. Morning glories climb up the banisters. I can hear the distant
murmur of the ocean in the background. It's the kind of
house that you see in movies and magazines. It has the
grandness of an old home, but one that has been watched
over with a meticulous eye. Grace bends over a white
wicker couch on the front porch, upholstered in a cheerful
sunshine-yellow stripe, and begins to straighten the pil-
lows. Overhead, a coordinating awning flaps in the breeze.

"Can I get you something to drink? Lemonade? Iced
tea? Or maybe a sweet tea? I make a fierce sweet tea. You
can take the girl out of the South, but you can't take the
South out of the girl." She gives me a sad smile. I can see
how nervous she is. She flutters around the porch like a
hummingbird as she talks, fluffing upholstery and pulling brown leaves off the plants. I see this a lot with crime
witnesses. Finding a dead body is jarring, like a car accident or a mugging. It affects people physically. Some
people fall apart and need to rest. Others, like Grace, fly
off the adrenaline, unable to calm their shattered nerves.

"I'm fine. Thank you, though." I pull out the bag
containing her bracelet. "Detective Davis found this on
the beach. He asked me to return it to you."

"Oh!" she says. She stops moving. I hold it out for her.
She retrieves it gingerly, as though she's not quite sure
she's allowed to touch it.

"May I?"

"Yes, of course."

She slips the bracelet out of the glassine evidence bag and takes a seat. "Would you mind helping me with the clasp? I'm a little shaky today. Haven't been able to eat all morning."

"Happy to." I sit beside her and lean in, joining the two ends of the clasp around her fine, blue-veined wrist.

When I finish, she runs a finger across it. "It must have fallen off when I was wrestling with Jasper this morning," she says quietly. "I was looking for it everywhere. I was worried it went down the sink. The chain is getting old. It was a gift from my mother, just before she died. I've never taken it off. I'm so grateful to have it back."

"It must've been very upsetting for you. This morning, I mean."

Her face clouds over. "It was awful. Jasper's a hunting dog. Or at least, I think he is. He was a rescue. He reminds me of the coonhounds we had back in Texas. Long legs, great nose. Up to no good if you don't train them right."

"You grew up in Texas?"

"I did. On an old ranch south of San Antonio. My daddy was an oilman. Loved to hunt. I shot trap from the time I was six. Now I shoot at the Mattituck Gun Club. Do you know it?"

"I know it well," I say, surprised. You don't see a lot of Bentleys parked in the Mattituck Gun Club's lot. Mostly it's SUVs or pickups, like my father's. It's a locals' spot, frequented by cops and firemen and farmers. "I learned to shoot there."

"How old were you?"

"Young. Six or seven, maybe."

Grace nods approvingly. "My daddy always said a girl had to know how to protect herself in this world."

"Smart man."

"Between us, I like it a lot more than any of the stuffy country clubs we belong to."

"Do you take Jasper hunting?"

"Oh heavens, no. I don't believe in shooting birds or deer. It's cruel to kill a helpless thing. Just clay pigeons. I like to birdwatch, too. There's some terrific birdwatching out here on Long Island, especially when the migration starts. What did you ask me? Oh, Jasper. Right. I'm sorry. I'm scattered today. I do think someone taught him to retrieve. He's always darting off, getting into things. He'll come back with dead birds—once he even brought back a dead turtle! God, that smell was just awful, you can't imagine. He left it on the doorstep, proud as can be. It's his way of saying thank you, I think. He was just a pile of bones when I took him in. In the off-season, I let him off the leash on the beach. He likes the exercise. When I saw him digging, I just thought . . ." She lets out a deep, shuddering breath. "I shouldn't have let him up there. I know you're not supposed to. I mean, for God's sake, I'm on the board of the Preservation Society. I helped them put up the damn fence!"

"If you hadn't let him up there, we might never have found that girl's body."

She shakes her head. "Only an animal would do something like that. I hope you find him."

"We will."

"Do you work for the police department?"

"I'm with the FBI. I'm consulting on this case."

Grace's face relaxes. "Oh, good. I'm glad they brought you in. Please don't repeat this, but I don't have much faith in the police out here."

"What makes you say that?"

"There was a similar case last summer. Young girl. Shot clean between the eyes with a .22 and then cut up. Her body was wrapped in burlap, just like this one."

"The Pine Barrens case."

"Yes. I think some hikers found her. Can you imagine? What a surprise that must have been, all the way out in the middle of nowhere. I'll tell you, this morning gave me the fright of my life. At least I was close to home. Ran all the way back, dragging Jasper most of the way."

"I'm so sorry."

"They never did solve that case. I'm not sure they bothered to try."

I'm tempted to interject. To defend my father in some way or perhaps, at least, assure her that someone cared. I bite my tongue and nod politely. "Did you follow it?"

"I did a bit. The girl was left on a tract of land that the Preservation Society was restoring after a forest fire. An officer came to talk to me about Alfonso Morales. He's a landscaper who works for the Preservation Society. I told the officer he had the wrong man. Alfonso is a decent person. Humble. Hardworking. He wouldn't hurt a fly."

"You know Mr. Morales personally?"

"Well enough. I hired him. He works for me here on occasion." She gestures at the lawn and gardens beyond the edge of the porch.

"The Preservation Society was involved in the dune restoration out in Shinnecock County Park, wasn't it?"

"Yes. I spent a year raising money for that project and then another year convincing the Town of Southampton to let us do it. You'd be surprised how much pushback you can get from local government, even when you're doing something that benefits the whole community." She sighs and leans back against the sofa cushions, like the idea of the project still exhausts her.

"What does dune restoration entail?"

"Well, it's more complex than it sounds. Sand dunes are fragile ecosystems. They provide habitats to highly specialized fauna and flora. The vegetation that grows there has adapted to a rather brutal way of life. Changing temperatures. A moving substrate." She stops herself, blushing. "I'm sorry. This is terribly technical, isn't it?"

"I like technical answers."

"I've been studying this for years. It's so important to me, I sometimes forget that not everyone wants to be versed in coastal ecology."

"That's how I feel about serial killers."

Grace lets out a surprised laugh. "You know what amazes me? How boring most women allow themselves to become. I go to a lot of cocktail parties out here. And the wives, they all went to Harvard and Yale and Stanford. And then they marry a hedge fund manager and have children, and it's like they've been lobotomized. All they want to talk about is tennis tournaments and interior design. You're different. It's refreshing."

"As are you."

"Well, yes. I suppose I am. But I wasn't able to have children. I had to find other things to nurture."

"I'm sorry." I frown, embarrassed to have wandered into such personal territory.

She waves me off. "Oh, it's all right, I'm very open about it. So is Eliot. One of the things we agreed on, when we finally realized it wasn't going to happen for us, was that we would make our lives meaningful in other ways."

"Your conservation work is meaningful."

"It keeps me busy. What Eliot does, that's the important stuff."

"He's the Secretary of the Treasury?"

"Yes. He retired from finance a few years ago. He wanted to give back. It's a bit of a challenge, him being in DC so much. But we're making it work. I wish he was here now, though." She stares off at the lawn, and I notice her chin tremble.

"When did the dune restoration begin?" I ask, trying to get us back on track.

"The town finally agreed to close the park at the end of June. They balked about it at first—summer is the high season, you know—but we convinced them. Everyone kicks and screams when we limit their usage of parkland, but humans do so much damage." Her face darkens. She looks as if she might cry.

"They really do, don't they?" I say gently.

"They don't even realize they're doing it. It goes beyond litter and bonfires. I suppose I'm part of the problem. I let Jasper run loose there when I shouldn't've. Of all people, I should know better." She covers her face with her hands and sniffs.

I give her a second. "Did Mr. Morales work on the restoration in the park?"

"Yes. I can get a list for you, if you like. Of everyone who worked on that site."

"That would be helpful, thank you."

"Do you happen to know if Mr. Morales worked for James Meachem?"

She winces, looking momentarily pained. "I know he does, in fact. We share a boundary line with Mr. Meachem. I suggested perhaps we plant some trees along it, to give us both more privacy. Alfonso and his crew took care of that. I believe Mr. Meachem hired them to work on the rest of his property as well."

"Mr. Morales isn't here now, is he?"

"No, no. I just bring him in during the summer, when I need extra help. In the off-season, he works at one of the nurseries on the North Fork."

"Do you know which one?"

Grace hesitates. She blinks, looks down at her hands. I'm certain she knows, but she doesn't want to get him in trouble. "I can't remember now."

"That's okay. You don't happen to know where Mr. Meachem is, do you?"

"He isn't here. He comes and goes."

"He must have staff, then. To care for the house while he's out of town?"

"I imagine he does. With a house that size, one really must. But I don't really know. I've never been over there." I catch a faint whiff of disdain in her voice.

"Have you met him?"

"I have. But we don't socialize. There's a reason I planted trees between us."

"Why do you say that?"

Grace's jaw flexes almost imperceptibly. "He has parties. They go on for days sometimes. The noise is unbearable. Very high-profile men attend. Politicians, CEOs. And there are girls. Beautiful. And young. Apparently, that's his thing."

"He entertains young girls?"

She arches her brow. "I think they're entertaining him."

"I see."

"We have a house down in Palm Beach. He has a reputation down there, too. Ask around. You'll hear stories. Rich as he is, they won't let him into any of the clubs. Not here, and not down there. Because of his—how shall I say it—*proclivities*."

"Have you ever called the police? About his parties, I mean."

"Oh, the police won't do anything."

"Why do you say that?"

"Everyone out here knows about him. Including the police. And they just turn a blind eye. He's a powerful man. He has powerful friends. Down in Palm Beach, people whisper that he has the commissioner on his payroll. And he has all sorts of people at his parties. Judges, senators. People who can stop investigations if they want to."

"And out here? Do you think he has friends in the police department?"

"Between us?"

"Of course."

"I'm certain of it."

I hear footsteps on the driveway. I turn and see Lee making his way toward us.

"That's Detective Davis," I tell Grace. "Have you met him?"

"Briefly, this morning."

She stands, the mood broken. Her lips form a tight smile. "Hello again, Detective. Thank you for returning my bracelet."

"Of course. Sorry to interrupt."

"You're not. Is there anything I can do for you?"

"No, ma'am. I was just coming to get Agent Flynn." He taps his watch. I glance down and realize it's almost two o'clock. Howard will be dropping by any minute, if he isn't there already.

"Thank you for your time, Mrs. Bishop," I say, hopping up. I extend my hand and she grasps it, giving it a firm shake. "You've been very helpful."

"Anything I can do. Remember what I said. Call me if you have any questions. I'm happy to help with the investigation in any way I can."

"I will. Thank you."

As I follow Lee down the Bishops' driveway, I can feel Grace watching us from the porch.

6.

Howard Kidd is waiting for me on the front steps of the house.

He holds a briefcase in one hand. The afternoon sunlight glints off the top of his head. The tip of his nose is red from the cold, and he hunches inside his Barbour coat, the collar flipped up to keep him warm. He looks worried, like a kid whose mother has forgotten to pick him up at a birthday party. I wonder how long I've kept him waiting. When he sees us pull into the driveway, he gives us a big, relieved wave.

"There are moments," Lee says as he pulls the car to a stop, "when I'm grateful I never practiced law."

I snort. "Oh, poor Howie. I'm sure there are some highlights of his job."

"His job is about death and taxes. And watching families fight over money."

"Well, the good news here is that there isn't any."

"Money? Or family?"

"Either." I open the car door and hop out onto the gravel. "Talk later?"

"Sure. I'll call you. Thanks for your help this morning, Nell."

"No problem." I watch Lee pull into reverse and back out onto Dune Road. I wonder if I did, in fact, help with anything. It's possible I just complicated the case further. I may not hear from Lee Davis again. The thought deflates me a little.

I turn to Howard and feign a smile. I'm not in the mood to talk to him—to anyone, really—but I've put this off long enough. "Come on inside. Can I get you some coffee? Hot tea?"

"Tea would be nice. Thanks."

"Got cold all of a sudden, huh?"

"Yeah. Fall sneaks up on you out here."

"Sure does."

I put my key into the rusted lock and jiggle it, fighting with the door until it opens. Howard follows me into the house. I'm suddenly acutely aware of how dusty it is, how in need of repair. Dad was always spartan in his tastes, but he was compulsively neat, too. He could fix anything and did. It wasn't always pretty, but the house was functional and organized. At least, that's how I remember it.

My mother, more of a free spirit, was content to live with clutter. She would break out paints and brushes and unspool a giant roll of paper across the living room floor. She would play music and we would paint, neither of us caring if we dripped on the wood, on our hands, on our clothes. She cooked that way, too: lots of bowls and mess, flour on the floor, the kitchen alive with the scent of baking bread in the oven and the tang of chilaquiles on the stove. She would hum while she worked; she would taste things straight from the pot, spoon to mouth. I would sit at her feet spinning leaves in a salad bowl or sorting spices by color on the rack.

They fought often about the mess. My father liked to come home to a clean, quiet house. My mother argued that she was not running a military base, she was trying to raise a child. She wanted me to color and spill, to cook and make forts out of blankets and couch cushions without worrying about what it did to the furniture. At night, when they thought I was sleeping, I would creep out of my bed and sit at the top of the stairs and listen to them argue. I felt horribly guilty. I was my mother's co-conspirator, after all. I knew that she often napped with me when she could've been doing the laundry, because I slept better when curled up in her arms, and that she let me stay longer at the beach or park instead of rushing home to make dinner, just to make me happy. These were our secrets. She'd never tell. My father's ire was reserved for her and her alone. Sometimes after they fought, he would bang out of the house and I would hear the buzz of his motorcycle fade in the night air. Other times, they would open a bottle of wine, turn on music, and dance, her head resting gently against his chest. I told myself that this was love. It was as messy and imperfect as the house my mother kept. It was an uneasy marriage, but a passionate one. It wasn't until I was in high school that I realized marriages weren't all this way. I couldn't picture Tom Street's parents fighting the way mine did. I couldn't imagine them dancing barefoot, either. They were always polite to each other, more like business partners than lovers. I wasn't sure which kind of marriage was worse.

After my mother died, the paints disappeared. So did the baking supplies. My toys were collected from the living room floor and put in baskets in my room. It was clear to me that this was where they were meant to stay. There wasn't music in our house anymore. My mother's clothes vanished from her closet. My memories of her began to fade, at an alarmingly fast rate. I searched the house for traces of her—in the medicine cabinet, in the crawl space below the kitchen—but found nothing. She would come back to me only in snatches: I would smell her perfume on a woman at a party or catch a whiff of empanadas baking at a restaurant and I'd think of her. I'd see a woman in a bright red bathing suit at the beach and feel a physical pang, as though my mother were a phantom limb. My father never spoke of her and I never dared ask. Our house was stripped clean of her existence, except for the urn with her ashes in the closet. The house took on my father's character: practical, organized, precise. My mother simply evaporated, as though she'd never lived there at all.

Something slipped. I don't know when. Maybe it happened in the weeks before his death; maybe he'd been living like this for the last ten years. My father never really had company, so it's possible that the house just slowly, quietly decayed around him. Did he not see the cracks spreading in the walls, the film building up on the windows? There's so much dust in the air that you can see suspended particles of it floating in patches of sunlight. Piles of clutter have accumulated, too. Nothing, perhaps, that Howard would notice. But I notice. I would have thought Dad would've, too. The stack of old newspapers in the corner would've bothered him; so would the cache of unopened bills on the kitchen counter. It all feels unlike him, the man who used to make his bed so tightly each morning that sometimes I wondered if he had slept in it at all.

"Sorry about the mess," I mumble, and hurry toward the kitchen to put the teapot on the stove. "I know it's cold in here. I can get a fire going. The boiler's not in the best shape."

"The tea is just fine."

"Take a seat wherever you like."

Howard looks around and settles on an armchair. As I dig a box of tea out of the cabinet, he unsnaps the buckle on his briefcase. From it, he removes a stack of papers, and then another, and another. He lines them up neatly on the coffee table. Most of them are flagged in multiple places, presumably where I need to sign or initial something. For a man who died with no family, no substantial assets but for this house, and what I imagine is a clean debt record, my father sure did leave a lot of paperwork.

"You preparing for a merger over there, Howie?"

He chuckles. "Sorry. I know this looks like a lot."

I pour two cups of tea. They are in mismatched mugs: an SCPD mug for Howard, a chipped "Kiss Me, I'm Irish" mug for me. There is no sugar, so I don't offer any. I hope Howard likes stale English Breakfast, because that's what he's getting.

"Thanks," he says. He wraps his hands around the mug and lets the steam rise toward his face.

"So. Where do I need to sign?"

Howard looks up at me and frowns. "Well, there are things we need to discuss first. Before we get to signing."

I lean back against the couch. "All right."

"Did you and your father discuss estate planning?"

"No."

"His assets?"

"You mean this house?"

"Well, the house, yes. But your father's estate was substantial."

"Substantial? I know this land is probably worth something. But beyond that . . ." I trail off, unable to think of anything else that Dad might have owned.

"There are other assets. An offshore account, for one."

I raise my eyebrows. "An offshore account? You mean, in the Caymans or something?"

"Yes. Cayman International Bank. I don't know how much is in it. But right before your father died, he brought it up. He wanted to be sure you knew how to access it."

"I'm sorry. I'm confused. I mean, he was a cop. What was he doing with money in an offshore account?"

Howie shakes his head. "He didn't tell me and I didn't want to know. I promised him I'd get you this." He hands me a business card.

Justin Moran, the card reads. *Senior Vice President, Cayman International Bank.*

"I'm sure if you contact him, he can help you."

I stare at the card, trying to make sense of it. I can't imagine why my father had an offshore account. A familiar sensation seeps into my body. Dread.

My eyes shut. I'm seven again. I'm sitting in the back seat of my father's car. Outside, police lights flash in the murky morning light. My father heated up leftover rice and beans for breakfast and my stomach is sour, heavy. My father and Dorsey are talking. Their lips are moving; their faces are pale and pinched. Something has happened, something bad. What, I don't quite understand.

I press my tongue against the backs of my front teeth. I'm still surprised by the absence of one. The place where the root used to be is tender and raw. My tongue retracts as the metallic taste of blood fills my mouth.

"Nell?"

My eyes snap open. Howie is staring at me, his brow furrowed. "What else is there?" I ask. "Besides the account."

Howard raises an eyebrow. He seems surprised that I don't have more questions. "The house goes to you."

"Fine."

"If you want help with listing it, I can put you in touch with a broker. We'll also need to have the contents appraised at some point."

I gesture at the coffee table and the ancient couch beyond. "That should take all of fifteen minutes. That's it?"

Howie coughs uncomfortably. "Were you aware that
he was considering redrafting his will when he died?"

"No," I say, a little stunned. I set my tea down on the
table between us. "Meaning, he wasn't going to leave me
the house?"

"No. The house was always yours. But he took out a
two-year lease on an apartment in Riverhead last summer."

"An apartment?"

"Yes. Here's the address." He slides a piece of paper
across the table. "He didn't say much about it. He has a
separate bank account set up, which he said covers rent,
utilities, all of that. He wanted to make sure that the
person who lives there can stay, even if something happened to him."

I squirm uncomfortably in my seat. Howie, I notice,
busies himself shuffling papers. We've entered awkward
territory and both of us know it. "The person . . . like a
tenant?"

"I get the sense that she was more than that."

"Do you know her name?"

"No. I thought maybe you might."

I sigh, frustrated. "This is the first I'm hearing of an
apartment. Or the person who lives there."

"Maybe he was seeing someone and he didn't want to
upset you."

"I'm not a child, Howie. If Dad had a girlfriend, he
could have told me."

"I have a daughter your age. I can understand how that kind of thing would be sensitive."

"So what am I supposed to do?"

"Well, that's up to you. But Marty was clear. He wanted this woman to be taken care of. Hence the re-structuring of the will."

"But it wasn't restructured."

"No. We had this conversation maybe a week or so before he died. Everything is yours. I'm just trying to be up front with you. There was another person in your father's life that he wanted to provide for in some way. You have no legal obligation to her. His will is valid, and unless this woman comes forward and contests it—and frankly, even then, given that they weren't married, I don't think she really has grounds to—everything will go to you. But I'd be remiss in not telling you his intentions."

I sit back and cross my arms. I wonder if it's too early for a drink. "Well, shit, Howie. This sounds complicated."

"I'm sorry, Nell. I really am. I hope you don't think he was trying to take money away from you. I just think he was trying to do right by this woman."

"If he had someone in his life, I would've been happy for him. My mother's been dead for twenty-one years. I didn't expect him to become a monk."

"Were you two in touch?"

I sigh. "Not really. We had a falling-out ten years ago. When I was in high school."

"He mentioned that."

I raise my eyebrows. "What did he say?"

"He said he pushed you to go to college out of state.

He didn't want you to end up trapped here in Suffolk County like he did. He said you never forgave him."

I nod, stung by the notion that he felt trapped here, by my mother. By me. "I did forgive him. We talked now and then, but it was always a little bit strained between us. We're both stubborn. I think we both expected an apology, and neither one of us was willing to give one."

"That's a shame."

"I know. He'd call a few times a year to wish me a happy birthday or a merry Christmas, but that was about it. We never really got into personal life–type stuff."

"Your dad was a very private man."

"He certainly was."

"Maybe one of his friends on the force knew her?"

"Glenn Dorsey planned the whole memorial service yesterday. He never mentioned a girlfriend. I think he would have, if this woman had been so important to Dad."

"Maybe he didn't know about her, either."

"So you don't have her contact information?"

Howie shakes his head. "I'm sorry. Just the address of the apartment. He gave me a copy of the lease agreement—it's all in there. The account is at Suffolk County Bank. I'd contact them. As I said, the will specifies that you get his entire estate. And the will is valid. So the account is yours. It's up to you what you choose to do with it."

I close my eyes and let my head fall back against the sofa. I am suddenly excruciatingly tired. My bones ache. My head feels like it's made of lead. I wonder if I just stay here long enough, maybe I will drift away into sleep.

Howie gets the message. He taps a stack of papers against the table, stands up. My eyes flicker open. "I'm sorry. It's been a helluva day."

"I'm sure. Why don't you rest. I've left everything there for you to look over. If you have questions, call me. We can talk more when you've had a chance to read through everything."

I stand up, extend my hand. "Thanks, Howie. I appreciate it."

He gives me a quick hug instead. "Nell, I've been doing this a lot of years. Estates are complicated in every family. Some things about your dad's life might come as a surprise. But your dad cared about you. You were the most important person in his life. Don't doubt that for a second. Every time he was in my office, you were all he talked about."

I shrug, unsure of how to respond. My father always felt like an enigma to me, even when we lived beneath the same roof. I wondered often if I knew him at all; whether he had the capacity or desire to really know me. Now it strikes me that we'll never get the chance. The thought fills me with a hard, uncomfortable sadness. I bite down on my lip. The pain keeps me from tears.

"Do you see anyone?" Howie asks. "A therapist, I mean. I can recommend some names if that would be helpful."

"I'll be fine. Thank you, though."

Howie nods. He picks up his briefcase and we walk together to the front door. He gives me an awkward, stilted handshake goodbye. As soon as he's gone, I go to the kitchen and pour myself a drink. I finish it in a few large gulps, pour another. I settle in on the couch. The alcohol courses through my veins, warming me. On impulse, I dial Dr. Ginnis's phone number.

"Andrew Ginnis." He answers on the first ring, startling me into momentary silence. I assumed it would go straight to voicemail. I was prepared to leave him a message. I'm not yet ready to talk.

"It's Nell Flynn," I say finally. My voice is flat and hard, like it's him who called me and not the other way around. "I work with Sam Lightman at the BAU."

"I remember. We met a few weeks ago."

"I know I should've followed up with you. My father passed away. I've been in Long Island for the funeral."

"I'm sorry to hear that. You've had a tough month."

"People keep saying that."

"Do you want to talk about it?"

I take a sip of scotch before replying. "You mean now? Shouldn't I set up an appointment first?"

"If you like. It's up to you."

I hesitate. A part of me wants to hang up, return to my scotch. But if I don't talk to Ginnis today, I'll just delay the inevitable. And there's something oddly soothing about his voice. It's warm, like he's an old friend.

"Where do I start?"

"Wherever you'd like."

"We scattered his ashes yesterday. He was only fifty-two."

"That's sad. How did he die, if you don't mind my asking?"

"Motorcycle accident. He had been drinking. It was late and the road was wet. At least, that's what I've been told."

"You don't believe that?"

"I don't know what to believe. I didn't really know him. I haven't been home in ten years. Even when I was home, we hardly spoke."

"And your mother? Is she alive?"

"No. She died when I was young. It was just me and him."

"I'm sorry."

"My father was a marine. A cop. The kind of man who woke up every day at five a.m. to go for a run. He'd run in the rain, in the snow. He ran when he was sick or if he hadn't slept the night before. He was obsessively disciplined. Except for alcohol; that was his weakness. But he was tough as they come. And deeply principled. At least, I thought he was. Today I found out that he had money stashed in an offshore account. And he rented an apartment I didn't know about, either. A woman lives there. His girlfriend, I guess."

"Does it upset you that he was seeing someone?"

I take a gulp of scotch and consider the question. "It upsets me that I knew so little about his life."

"Are you worried that he harmed himself?"

"Maybe. Or that someone harmed him." I say this aloud for the first time. The words are strange, foreign. "I don't know. It's possible I'm being paranoid."

"Why would someone harm him?"

"He was a homicide detective. He was investigating a case when he died. A young girl, an escort. She was murdered last summer. Today they found a second body. Another young girl, buried the same way as the first."

Ginnis doesn't reply. I realize that I'm rambling. My words are starting to run together. Maybe I've had too much to drink. Maybe I'm tired. Probably both.

"You think I sound crazy, don't you?" I ask, though it's more of a statement than a question.

"I didn't say that."

"I know how it sounds. He's just a cop. It's just a murder investigation."

"Something about it troubles you."

"I have a bad feeling." I stand up and the blood rushes to my head. I sit back down, resting my head on the arm of the couch. The room spins a little, and then stops. "I don't know why I'm telling you all of this. I'm sorry."

"Don't be sorry. It's why I'm here."

"Can I ask you something? Off the record."

"There is no record, Nell. Everything you and I discuss is confidential."

"Except that you're paid for by the Bureau."

"That doesn't mean they get to listen in on what we discuss. Doctor-patient privilege exists between us. I take that very seriously."

"You have to write a report on me, don't you? How can you do that and still maintain privilege?"

"I will write a report," he says carefully, "about your mental fitness for your job. Not about what we discuss in session. Do you understand the difference?"

"It seems like a fine line."

Ginnis sighs. I'm being difficult, and we both know it. "Don't worry about the report. My job is to help you cope with trauma. Not to type up some form for the Office of Professional Responsibility." The way he says it, with just a hint of disdain, makes me smile just a little.

"To be honest with you, the most traumatic thing that's happened to me all month is coming back here. To Suffolk County."

"A lot of people feel that way about returning home. Especially under such sad circumstances."

"It's brought up a lot of old memories. Some not so pleasant."

"Do you want to talk about those memories?"

"I—I don't know yet."

"That's fair."

"If I were to tell you something that might implicate someone else in a crime, do you have to report it?"

"It depends."

"On what?"

"Well, on a lot of things. But foremost, whether or not I think someone is in danger. If I could prevent harm to someone by breaking privilege, I would. Does that make sense?"

I mull this over. The ice in my drink clinks against the bottom of the glass. I roll my head toward the counter, eyeing the bottle. It's more than half-empty: a surprise. I've drunk more than I thought. I'm not in any shape to be confiding in anyone. Especially not a therapist who reports to my boss.

"I think I should stop talking and set up an appointment."

"That's fine. Get some rest. Call me when you can, Nell. I'm here."

7.

I don't rest. Not well, anyway. I toss and turn until the room begins to brighten around the edges. When it's officially morning, I hop behind the wheel of my father's pickup and drive to Riverhead. It's early and the town is still asleep. I'm still half-asleep myself, propped up only by the two cups of black coffee I drank as my breakfast. The stores are closed and there's hardly any traffic. I find a parking spot on Main Street, directly across from the address Howard gave me.

Dad's apartment is on the top floor of 97 Main, a small, boxy building sandwiched between an Irish pub called O'Malley's and a dusty drugstore with vacant-eyed Victorian dolls lining the window. It's a three-story building with one apartment per floor. The landlord lives on the ground floor. Dad has been renting out the third floor since June of last summer. From what I can see, the second floor is vacant. The windows are boarded over.

It's not a particularly charming place, but then, Dad didn't care much for aesthetics. He did like seclusion, however, and so I can see how he'd appreciate a third-story apartment with no neighbors, no one living directly below or above, and a discreet entrance through a parking lot behind the building.

The rent on this apartment is a thousand dollars a month, which is not exorbitant for a two-bedroom apartment in Suffolk County, but it's not insubstantial, either. I can't imagine why my father would have committed such a large percentage of his income to a second residence, especially one that's a fifteen-minute drive from his own. Maybe he used it as an office. But why, then, would he keep an office in his house, as well? Maybe he used it on nights when he wanted to drink at O'Malley's and stumble upstairs instead of driving home. That seems plausible but extravagant, and my father was not an extravagant man.

The most obvious answer is that he had a girlfriend. Maybe he wasn't ready to cohabitate with her but still felt some sense of obligation or commitment. Or maybe he'd been planning to move in and put the house on the market and just hadn't gotten around to it yet. Still, I found it strange that there's no trace of her—or any other visitor, really—at the house on Dune Road. No extra toothbrush in the medicine cabinet, no women's nightclothes in the bureau, not even a bottle of wine or soda in the fridge. Just my father's things: my father's bourbon, my father's scotch. My father's clothes, my father's arsenal of weapons. My father's house, and his alone.

The landlord, I hope, has some answers. Dad's separate account at Suffolk County Bank has a balance of $25,000, more than enough to cover a year's worth of rent and other expenses. After turning it over in my head all night, I've decided the right thing to do is track down this woman and give her the money. If for some reason I can't find her—or if I do and she seems like a terrible person—I can donate it to charity. But if Dad didn't intend for me to have it, then I don't want it.

Anyway, I don't need more money. I hardly spend what I make, and Dad left me plenty, between his life insurance policy and the house. And that's to say nothing of the Cayman Islands account, which I have yet to explore. I still haven't decided if I'll ever explore it. Doing so could cost me my job. Last night, as I drank my fifth and final scotch of the evening, I sat in front of the fire and debated tossing the card with the contact information for Justin Moran into the flames.

I didn't toss it. I still might. For now, it's tucked inside the drawer of my nightstand. I have more pressing matters to attend to today. My father's apartment. His girlfriend. His bike. His case. His life. I'm tired and it's not even eight o'clock.

I ring the landlord's bell and listen to the symphony of barking this sets off inside apartment 1. I feel bad disturbing someone at such an early hour, but not so bad that I stop myself from doing it. It's going to be a long day, possibly even a long week, filled with dead bodies and mystery. Given that I can't sleep, I might as well get a jump on things.

I hear feet shuffling, and the dogs quiet down. The locks click: there are three, which seems like a lot. The door opens a crack, the deadbolt chain still in place. A gray-haired man in pajamas and a bathrobe peers at me through the two-inch opening.

"What do you want?" He glares at me. The dogs weave around his feet.

"Good morning," I say, as brightly as possible. "Are you Lester Simms?"

"Yeah. That's me."

"I'm Nell Flynn. My father, Martin Flynn, was your tenant on the third floor."

The man frowns and strokes his chin. "I wouldn't say he was my tenant."

"Isn't this 97 Main Street? I have the lease agreement here." I open my purse and withdraw a folder.

"He pays the rent all right. I just don't see much of him."

"Well, if he wasn't there, who was?"

"Not sure I see how that's any of your business."

"My father is dead, and I'm the sole beneficiary and the executor of his will. So if you don't mind, I'd really appreciate it if you'd let me in and we can discuss this privately."

The door shuts, and for a second, I wonder if Lester Simms is off to call the police. But then I hear the deadbolt chain slide open, and the door creaks on its hinges and the dogs click their nails on the floor in excitement. As I step inside, one of them rears up and places its paws on my midsection. It's a big animal, with a muzzle the size of a horse's, and the force of its full body weight nearly knocks me on my ass.

Lester grabs the dog by the leash and gives it a firm yank. "No, Brutus," he chides, so sharply that the dog cowers in response. "Sorry about that. He doesn't bite, just a little excitable, especially before his morning walk. Come in. Ignore the mess."

He gestures at a small wooden table in the kitchen. "You want some coffee? It's made."

"Sure, thanks."

"How do you take it?"

"Just black is fine."

He nods and pours us each a mug. "Sorry to hear about your dad. When did he pass?"

"About ten days ago."

"He was a cop, right?"

"Suffolk County PD. Homicide."

"Killed in the line of duty?"

"No, nothing like that. Motorcycle accident."

Lester looks disappointed but nods nonetheless. "A damn shame."

"How well did you know my father?"

"I didn't, not really. He came around last summer, said he wanted to rent the place. He said he was going to use it as an office. Maybe last July it was. Can't remember now."

"Just as an office?"

"Yeah. That's what he said. He'd come and go, maybe once or twice a week that I could tell. About a month later, he asked me to make another set of keys. Said he had a friend that needed to stay there. Asked if that was all right by me."

"Was it?" I take a sip of my coffee. Lester makes better joe than I do, which probably says more about me than it does about him.

He shrugs. "Doesn't matter to me what my tenants do as long as they're quiet and keep the place up and pay the rent on time. Maria's a good woman. Hardly see her, but she makes me muffins sometimes and leaves them outside my door. And last winter, I broke my hip and she helped me out. Walked the dogs, brought in the mail, made sure the trash got taken out, that kind of thing."

"Maria—do you know her last name?"

"Cruz, I think. A Cuban girl. You don't know her?"

"No. I know my father wanted her to be able to stay in the apartment. I thought I'd introduce myself and see if we can work something out."

Lester raises his eyebrows. "Well, you're welcome to keep paying the rent. But Maria, she's gone. Moved out about two weeks ago."

"Moved out? You sure?"

"Yeah, I'm sure. I was taking my dogs for a walk and I saw her carrying this big duffel bag into a cab. I asked her if she needed help and she said she was fine. She gave me a hug and then gave me back her key. She was crying, I remember that. I asked her where she was going and she just shook her head. She said once that she had family down in Miami. Maybe she went there. She never got much mail, so I guess she didn't see fit to leave a forwarding address. Anyway, the lease is still good."

"When exactly did she leave? Do you remember?"

"Hmm, let's see. I think it was a Sunday night? Yeah, that's right. I was watching my show and then my sister called. She calls every Sunday. Usually to carp at me about something. So what's that, ten, eleven days ago?"

"Eleven," I say, my breath caught in my chest. The day before my father died. "Do you have the key to the apartment? I'd really like to see it. And I'd like to try to find Maria, if that's possible."

Lester shuffles over to the kitchen counter. He digs through a basket filled with mail. After a minute, he produces a key. He holds it up and I wince. The key hangs from a chain I gave to my father the Christmas before I left. A small Swiss Army knife is attached to one end. His initials, MDF, are engraved on the side.

"All yours," Lester says.

"Thanks. Can I keep this for a few days?"

"Sure. Long as you pay next month's rent."

"Fair enough. Hold on. I'll write you a check now."

8.

Apartment 3 has a thick metal door. There are two deadbolts on it, a feature my father certainly appreciated, and steel bars on the window. A rudimentary security system, but an effective one.

Maria, it appears, has indeed moved out. There are no personal possessions in the apartment: no art hanging on the walls, no clothes in the closest, no toiletries in the bathroom. The only signs of recent life are the lightly wrinkled sheets on the bed and a few pots and cups in the dishwasher. A sour smell emanates from the refrigerator. I open it to find an expired container of milk, orange juice, and three boxes of stale Chinese takeout. I close the door quickly and make a mental note to take out the trash before I leave. The apartment's mine now, at least for another month. It's the least I can do.

In the living room, there is a desk. In the top drawer, I find an assortment of pens and pencils, paper clips, and printer paper. There's an envelope with forty dollars in it; she must have left in a hurry. A Polaroid is pushed to the very back. I withdraw it and stare at the image. It's of two young women, their arms looped affectionately around each other's shoulders. They look young—younger than I am, anyway—and both are beautiful. It's possible they're sisters. They have the same long black hair, olive skin, high cheekbones. I wonder if one of them is Maria.

My phone buzzes in my pocket. I set the photo down. When I see it's Lee, I answer right away.

"Good morning," he says, his voice too chipper for a man in the midst of a murder investigation. "Did you get some rest last night?"

"Not really. You?"

"Not a wink." He laughs. "But I have some good news. We have an ID on the body."

"That was fast."

"I told you, Milkowski's good."

I don't respond.

"She traced the number on the plate in the vic's jaw. It's a match with the girl who went missing around Labor Day. Adriana Marques. Eighteen years old. Local girl from Riverhead. Very similar profile to Ria Sandoval. Did some escorting, advertised on Craigslist and Backpage. They even look alike. Long, dark hair. Petite, attractive."

My finger traces the girls in the Polaroid. "Any family?"

"Limited. Mom passed away, Dad's serving time upstate. Adriana lived with her older sister, Elena Marques. Elena was the one who called her in missing."

"Boyfriend?"

"She has an ex. He's a real piece of work. Low-level gangbanger, affiliated with MS-13."

"Lovely. Check his alibi."

"He's serving time at Mid-State Correctional for aggravated assault. Been in since June."

"Okay. So he's in the clear. But maybe there's some kind of gang connection here."

"When the sister reported Adriana missing, she mentioned that she'd seen a dark red pickup parked outside their house. More than once."

"So?"

"So that's what Morales drives."

"Should we track Morales down?"

"Dorsey wants me to go talk to the sister first. Before this thing blows up in the news. Thought it might be good if you came along."

"Notifying next of kin. My favorite part of the job."

"Are you home? I can pick you up on my way."

"I'm actually in Riverhead. I'm at the coffee shop on Main Street. Why don't you meet me here?"

"Sure thing. I'm on my way. Oh, and get me a donut if you can. And a cup of coffee."

"You know you're a walking cliché, right?"

Lee chuckles. "Look, I'm trying my best to fit in. See you in a few."

TWENTY MINUTES LATER, Lee pulls up in front of Main Street Coffee. I'm standing on the sidewalk, donut and coffee in hand. Lee reaches across the passenger seat and pushes open the door for me. He looks like hell, I can't help but notice. I'm sure he's thinking the same about me.

"You're a lifesaver," he says, reaching for the coffee.

"I know."

"Thanks for coming. This is the toughest part of the job."

"Always is."

"Doesn't get any easier, does it?"

"Telling the family? No, I don't think so. If it feels easy, it's probably time for a vacation."

I see a local number pop up on my phone. "Hang on a second. Let me take this."

Lee nods, as if to say, *Go ahead*.

"Nell Flynn."

"Nell, it's Cole Haines, down at impound. Not sure if you remember me, but I used to go fishing with your dad now and then."

"Yes, of course. Good to hear your voice, Cole."

"I'm sorry about what happened. Marcy and me were just devastated when we heard."

"Thank you. That's kind of you to say."

"Your father was a good man, Nell. A real good man."

I clear my throat, hoping to speed this along. "About his bike," I prompt.

"Right. The bike. It took a hard beating. Looked like he drove it headlong into a tree or something. I told them to take it to the crime lab, you know, just in case. Maybe there was brake trouble. If it were me, I'd be suing the manufacturer."

"Why didn't they? Take it to the lab, I mean."

"Got me. It's just been sitting here. And then Dorsey called me today and tells me to take it to the junkyard."

I frown. "You didn't junk it yet, did you?"

"No, ma'am. I got your message and I figured you should take a look and decide for yourself. I mean, I'm happy to dispose of it, if that's your preference. But if there's insurance money to be had—"

"I'll come by later. Thanks, Cole. I appreciate it."

"Of course. See you soon."

"Who was that?" Lee asks when I hang up.

"Cole Haines, down at impound. He's got my dad's bike."

"Ah, jeez. I'm sorry. You want me to handle it?"

"Nah, I got it." I look away, aware that I'm not telling him everything.

Lee stuffs a quarter of the donut in his mouth and returns the rest to the bag. He puts the car in reverse and pulls out onto Main Street. The radio springs to life. The static crackle, the staccato code that the dispatcher used to direct traffic, washes over me in a tidal wave of nostalgia. It's like an old language I once spoke fluently and haven't heard in years. I press my forehead against the glass, watching the Main Street storefronts rush by. When I was a kid, my father would let me ride in the front seat of his cruiser. He'd turn on the radio and tell me what all the codes meant: 10-16 was domestic trouble; 10-33 was emergency; 10-79 was notify the coroner. He'd quiz me later. I never forgot.

Elena Marques lives on a dead-end street bordering

the Riverhead Cemetery. I stare out the window as the headstones roll past. It isn't a particularly pretty final resting place. There is a chicken-wire fence surrounding the cemetery, and the lawn is brown in some places, as if the sprinklers are spread just a little bit too far apart.

I've been here before. A field trip in junior high school. We were each given butcher paper and charcoal. Our history teacher, Mr. McManus, told us to do a rubbing of the most interesting tombstone we could find. I picked one from 1862. An eighteen-year-old named John Downs who had died in battle at Gloverston, Virginia. A member of Company D, 12th Regiment. I brought it home and showed my father. He ripped it in half and told me it was disrespectful to do that to someone's grave, especially someone who'd served our country. He'd been drinking; I could smell the whisky on his breath. His eyes got dark when he drank, and his voice went cold. I hadn't yet learned to avoid him when he got like that. He gripped my arm so hard that a bruise swelled. First purple, then a sickly green. I was too embarrassed to explain to Mr. McManus what happened to my rubbing, so I bought butcher paper and charcoal with some money I'd saved up and I skipped gym class and biked to the nearest cemetery to make a new one. I started wearing long sleeves after that. I kept wearing them for months, even after the bruise had faded.

A sign at the entrance reads "Riverhead Cemetery, Founded in 1859." Below that, a smaller sign announces: "Internment Plots Available." I wonder if this is where they'll bury Adriana. I think about my mother's ashes, stashed in an urn in my father's closet. He never could part with it. With her. We had a haphazard memorial service at St. Agnes nearly two months after her death, arranged mostly by her friends. I was too young at the time to know this was strange or that my fascination with old cemeteries wasn't normal. On Long Island, they're mostly quiet, beautiful places. Some of them date back to the 1600s. Sometimes I'd bike over to the one in town after school. A lot of the stones were old and worn, and in the spring, cherry blossoms coated the grass in pink. I'd sit on a bench and read until sunset. It never occurred to me that having somewhere to go to mourn my mother might have been helpful, or that keeping her ashes in our house didn't allow my father and me much closure. It strikes me now, for the first time since I returned to Suffolk County, that I probably should do something with my mother's remains, too.

Lee pulls up in front of a small, dun-colored house across the street from the cemetery. The lawn, such as it is, slopes downward to the street, as though the land itself is frowning. A child squats in the driveway. She wears a purple T-shirt, clear jelly sandals, and pants with Elmo on the knees. Her hair is wild and curly, bound up in two uneven pigtails that stick out in opposing directions. She stares intently at the ground, picking up stones one by one and dropping them into a red plastic cup, the kind kids drink out of at high school parties. She freezes when she hears us step out of the car, staring up at us as though we've caught her shoplifting. I smile and give her a little wave. She doesn't respond. A glob of drool pools on her lip. She watches us pass with big, blinking eyes.

Before we ring the bell, a woman opens the door. She wears a long skirt and a white tank top that shows off her olive skin. Her hair is pulled back in a knot at the nape of her neck. Though her face is beautiful, there is a heaviness to it. Half-moons swell beneath her eyes. She stares at us wearily.

"Excuse me," she says, and steps around Lee. "*Isabel! Ven aquí por favor.*"

The small child looks up from the gravel. Reluctantly, she drops a final rock into her cup and comes running. The woman crouches down, scoops her up. She wipes the girl's mouth with the edge of her thumb. In the house, a television is blaring. The frenetic, electric sounds of cartoons compete with news streaming in from a radio that sits perched on a windowsill. She sets the girl down and pats her on the bum. "Go with Diego, please."

The girl toddles out of sight. The woman turns back to us, her expression grim. "Can I help you?"

"Are you Elena Marques?"

"Yeah. What's this about?"

"I'm Detective Davis with the Suffolk County Police Department. This is Agent Flynn with the FBI. May we come in?"

Elena hesitates. She knows why we've come. For a moment, I think she might turn us away. But then she pushes the door open and motions for us to enter.

"Are you with missing persons?" she asks.

"Not exactly," Lee replies.

The living room is small and messy. Dented screens cover the windows, allowing in little light. A dining room table is still covered in breakfast detritus: cereal bowls with spoons in them, half-full glasses of orange juice, a plate with the ends of buttered toast. I count four bowls. I wonder who else lives here and how old they are. I wonder if they've heard about the body in Shinnecock County Park. Elena moves a basket of laundry from the sofa and gestures for us to sit. She perches on an armchair across from us.

"It's Adriana," she says, her voice cold. "The body they found in the dunes. I heard it on the news. It's her, isn't it?"

"I'm so sorry, Ms. Marques," Lee says. He nods slowly. "It's her."

She looks me in the eye. "That's why you're here. They don't send in an FBI agent for some missing girl."

"I'm so sorry for your loss. I know how hard this is to hear," I say.

She shakes her head. "No, you don't. None of you people care. When I went down to the police station to file the missing persons report, do you know what the cop asked me? If my sister was a working girl. That was the first thing. And when I said, 'Yeah, she did some of that,' he closed his notebook. Like there was nothing more to say about her. Like she wasn't a fucking person."

"That's not right," I say, cringing.

"There was a girl who went missing last summer," Lee offers. I can see how nervous he is. His leg jitters up and down as he talks. I want to put my hand on his thigh to make it stop. "A sex worker. He may have just been trying to establish a pattern."

"Oh, there's a pattern. Brown girls no one gives a fuck about."

"We give a fuck," Lee says, a bit plaintively.

"What do you think would have happened if my sister was a white girl from Southampton? I tell you what, the whole fucking National Guard would've turned out to look for her. Don't tell me I'm wrong."

The toddler, Isabel, appears in the doorway. She has a pacifier in her mouth, which she sucks on furiously. She runs to Elena. Elena picks her up. The girl lays her head on Elena's shoulder.

"She's tired. No one slept last night."

"It's all right. If you need to go—"

Elena shakes her head and grips the girl tighter. She looks away from us and lets out a small, gasping sob. We are all quiet. The girl doesn't seem to notice that Elena is shaking with tears. Her eyelids droop as she presses her head against her mother's shoulder, allowing herself to be rocked by the gentle rhythm of Elena's heaving breast.

A minute passes. Maybe two. Isabel's eyes flicker open. She sits up, pushes herself off of Elena's lap, and goes running back down the hall.

Once she's gone, Elena dabs at her eyes with the corner of her sleeve. "Isabel loved my sister so much. Adriana watched her every afternoon. She doesn't know that her aunt is gone. I don't know how to explain it to her."

"How old is she?" I ask.

"Almost two."

"Do you have other children?"

"I have a seven-year-old boy. Rafael."

"Tell them the truth."

She frowns at me. "They're too young. They won't understand something like this."

"I was seven when my mother was murdered. I was grateful when someone finally told me she was dead. Children understand more than you think. And they appreciate straightforwardness."

This information disarms her. Her face crumples. I realize I've said too much. "Was Adriana murdered?" she whispers.

"It looks that way. I'm so sorry. We'll know more once we have the medical examiner's report."

"What happened to her?"

"It's still early," Lee says, hedging. He could tell her, of course. About the gunshot to the head. The dismemberment. The burlap and twine. But he won't. We've both been trained to break the information to the victim's family slowly, one bit at a time. She doesn't need to know details, certainly not now. If we withhold them from the public, she may not hear them for a while. "We'll have more information from the ME's office soon. It would be helpful if you could give us a DNA sample. I can swab the inside of your cheek. To confirm the identity of the body."

Her head lifts slightly. I want to kick Lee for giving her a flicker of hope. "So it might not be her? It might be a mistake?" she says, her voice ringing with desperation.

"No. It's her. She had a metal plate in her jaw. It had a number etched on it, and we were able to run that through the system. The DNA—it's just a way to reconfirm. I'm sorry. I should've . . . it's her."

"I want to see her. Can you take me to her?"

"Not yet. Soon. She's with our doctors now."

"Why can't I see her? She's my sister. She's family. You can't keep me from her."

"Ms. Marques," I say, as gently as possible, "the only way we will figure out what happened to your sister is if we let the doctors do their full examination. Okay? The best thing you can do right now is answer our questions."

She stares at me, her eyes wide and vacant, like she doesn't fully hear me. She turns her head to the door and then back to me. Reluctantly, she sinks back into her chair.

"I need a glass of water," she says, her voice hoarse.

Lee bounces up. "I'll get it," he offers, and ricochets off toward the kitchen.

"Can you tell me about the day your sister went missing?" I ask, once he's gone.

Elena shrugs through tears. "It was the Friday of Labor Day weekend. She said she was going to a party. I knew she was working a job, though. I always knew."

"How did you know?"

"Do I look stupid to you?"

"Not at all. But the details help me understand."

She sighs. "A car would pick her up. An Escalade."

"The same car?"

"Usually, yeah. She said he was a friend. He'd wait for

her down the block. Sometimes she'd come back late. Other times, she'd be gone all night and come back in the morning."

"Would you recognize the driver if I showed you a photo?"

"Oh, yeah. Once I went out there and gave him a piece of my mind. Told him to get off my property. I said I'd call the police. He laughed. He said, 'Go ahead.' Like he was daring me. Asshole."

"Was his car white?"

"Yeah. White. Rims. Flashy, you know? The night she went missing it was a different car. A black sedan. Like a town car."

"Same driver?"

"I don't know. I didn't see his face."

"That's okay. This is all really helpful."

Lee returns and hands Elena a glass of water.

"Thanks," she says. She takes a small sip. Her hands shake; I can see the water vibrating inside the glass. She holds it tightly as though she's afraid it might slip from her grasp.

"Did you ever call the police? About the guy in the white car?"

"No. I didn't want Adriana to get in trouble."

"But you didn't want her escorting," Lee counters.

"Of course not. Would you want your sister doing that?" She stops, takes a breath, and begins slowly. "Look, it's easy money. Put up an ad on Craigslist, Backpage, and that's it, the phone starts ringing. Adriana, she

had her regulars. I would hear her talking to them sometimes, like they was her boyfriend. 'Hey baby, how was
your trip?' That kind of shit. She was young, you know?
She trusted people. She was always like that, even back in
school."

"She was a kind person," I say.

"Yeah, she had a big heart. She wanted to be a nurse.
She was real sensitive. Like, you could put her with anyone and she would be their best friend by the end of the
night. Everyone always talked to her about their prob-
lems."

"Did she finish school?"

Elena shakes her head. "She had some learning issues.
Made school tough for her. And our household wasn't all
that stable growing up. I mean, it was fine. We had what
we needed. But our dad wasn't around and our mom, she
wasn't all there, you know what I'm saying? I pretty
much raised Adriana myself. I kept telling her to get her
GED. But she wanted to be out on her own, to make
some money and then go back. Once that lowlife she was
dating got shipped upstate, she didn't have a lot of options. She moved in with me. We fought about her getting a job. A real job. Not this shit. We fought about a lot
of things."

She sighs then, a bone-tired shudder of a sigh, and
drops her face into her hands. "I just kept hoping she'd
stop," she whispers.

"When she went on a job, did you ask her where she was
going?" Lee asks. "Or to text you when she got there?"

Elena bristles at Lee's question. Her eyes narrow. "Yeah, I did," she says, defensive. "Sometimes she would. Sometimes she wouldn't. Look, she was eighteen. I couldn't control her. All I could do was give her a place to stay. We all need to work, Detective."

"I get it. I'm sorry, I wasn't suggesting—"

"She helped out a lot around here. She'd buy groceries, bring home pizza. And she watched Isabel, too, so we didn't need as much day care. She was making good money. Her clients were loaded. Even if she was spending too much on herself, looking the way she did, she still brought a lot of cash home."

"What do you mean, looking the way she did?"

"You know. Hair done, nails done. Fancy clothes. After she started up working these parties, she got real focused on her appearance. You can see." She gestures toward a door across the hall. "That's her room, right there."

Her hackles are up. I can see by the way she's sitting: ramrod straight, shoulders up around her ears. She grips the glass so hard I worry she might break it. Lee doesn't seem to notice. He opens his mouth. Before he pisses her off further, I interject. "Lee, why don't you go check out Adriana's room. I want to ask Ms. Marques a few more questions."

Lee nods, grateful to have something else to do. Once he's gone, Elena's body softens a touch. She slumps back into her chair. I can see the energy draining out of her. Her eyelids flicker, like they want to close and stay that way.

"Adriana left around eight that night," she says. "The kids were eating dinner. I wanted her to eat with us, but she said she had to go. She seemed rushed, like she hadn't had much notice or whatever. She was dressed up. High heels, tight dress."

"Did she have a purse with her?"

"She had a bag. A tote bag. Maybe she was planning to spend the night."

"Did you see her get in the car?"

"Yeah. I followed her outside. I called out to her as she was getting in the car, but she didn't hear me."

"I know the car was different, but do you think it might have been the same driver?"

"I don't know. The windows were tinted."

"Can you close your eyes? Picture the car, driving away. Can you tell me anything about it?"

She blinks. Then she closes her eyes, squeezes them shut. "The license plate was yellow."

"Good. What else?"

"Maybe there's a five in it." Her eyes open again. She shakes her head, frustrated. "Or an *S*. I don't know, I'm not good at this stuff."

"You're doing great. And you'd never seen that car before?"

"No."

"When did you realize she was missing?"

"I work a Saturday shift, cleaning at the hospital in Southampton. I leave around six thirty in the morning. Everyone was asleep. Adriana's door was closed. I assumed she was in there. I didn't think to check." She puts her hand to her face. I wait quietly as her body convulses with a wave of tears.

"It's not your fault," I whisper. The words feel empty as they leave my mouth.

"I'm her big sister," she says, her voice reaching a hysterical pitch. "I should've checked to make sure she came home."

I reach across the table and pick up a box of tissues. I hand it to her. "When did you get back on Saturday?" I ask quietly, once she's blown her nose.

"Around six at night. Kids were watching a show when I got back. And I asked Diego—he's my boyfriend—where's Adriana? He hadn't seen her all day. That's when I got nervous. Her room was empty. I called her cell twice. No answer. Just went straight to voicemail."

"Had she ever been gone more than one night?"

"No. Not that I remember. But it was the weekend. Diego said maybe she's out having fun, not to bother her. He thinks I hover too much, you know. That I treat her like a kid. So I let it go. I didn't sleep at all that night. I just felt like something was wrong. You know that feeling? You just get it in your bones. When she wasn't back in the morning, I called the police."

"Do you remember who you spoke to?"

"No. I just called 911, and they transferred me to the station. And then some guy said I had to come down and file a report. So I did. That's when I talked to the jerk who asked if Adriana was a working girl. I could just tell he didn't give a fuck about her, about me, about any of us."

"You mentioned in your report that there had been a car—a red truck—parked outside your house."

She nods slowly, like she's remembering something she'd forgotten about. "Yeah. There was. A pickup."

"Right before your sister went missing?"

"Yeah. Like, literally, the day before."

"Did you see anyone in the car?"

"Yeah, the guy just sat there. Didn't see his face. He was wearing a baseball cap. He never got out. It was like he was watching our house. It gave me the creeps."

"Have you seen that car since?"

"No. Maybe it was nothing. I don't know." She hesitates then, like she wants to tell me something.

"Ms. Marques," I say quietly, "if there's anything else you think is important, you can tell me. I won't share it with anyone else. But it might help me find out who did this to your sister."

She looks at me then, her eyes welling with tears. "I think Adriana was pregnant."

"Why did you think that?"

She shrugs. "Just, you know. Intuition. She'd been tired a lot. And a couple of times, I heard her throwing up in the mornings."

"Did you ask her about it?"

"No. I wasn't sure. She wasn't showing or anything. I figured she'd tell me when she was ready."

"Did she seem upset in the days before she went missing? Secretive? Anything out of the ordinary?"

Elena chews her lip, considering. "Honestly? She seemed happy."

"Happy?"

"Yeah. Like a cloud had finally lifted."

"Maybe she was excited about the baby."

She nods. "I thought so. She was on the phone more. Whispering to someone. Usually late at night. Once, she used the house phone and so I picked up the extension. I was curious. It was a man's voice. He was telling her that she had to be discreet. Because of his position. Something like that."

"What did she say?"

"That she understood. That she would never do anything to hurt him. Then he said, 'I'll take care of you. I'll take care of everything,' and she started to cry."

"Did you ask her about it?"

"No. I didn't want her to feel like I was invading her privacy. She wouldn't have told me, anyway."

"That's okay. We can get your phone records and see who she was talking to. Did you speak to anyone else from the police department? After you filed the missing persons, I mean."

"A cop came by the house later that night. A tall white guy. Dark hair, kind of a buzz cut. Like a military guy. He looked around Adriana's room. Asked me a few questions about her. He was odd. Real quiet. Seemed nervous, too, like he was looking for something."

"Looking for something?"

"Yeah. He kept looking around her desk. And in her closet."

"Did he take anything?"

"He found a phone in her desk. I was surprised. She

always took her phone with her. This one didn't look like hers. I told him that, but he took it anyway."

I feel my throat tighten. In the background, a child begins to wail.

"Do you remember his name?"

She frowns. She looks up at me then. "You know," she says, "I think his name was Flynn, same as you."

9.

My ears buzz. The sound of crying intensifies. Elena stands up. "I'm sorry," she says. "Isabel needs me."

I nod, still dazed by her mention of my father. "Of course. Go ahead."

Elena disappears down the hall. I stand up slowly, feeling light-headed. I need to get home, back to my father's office. I want to see if I can find Adriana's phone.

I hesitate outside the door to her bedroom. Should I ask Lee about my father's visit here after Adriana went missing? I decide against it. He would have mentioned it if he thought it was important. My guess is he doesn't know about it. But why would my father keep secrets from his partner?

Her room is a small space, just big enough to hold a twin bed and a small desk. Books are stacked in the corner. I tilt my head, read the titles. An anatomy textbook.

A Guide to Practical Nutrition. A brochure from the nursing program at St. Joseph's College. A flyer for an informational session on campus, August 28. She'd circled the date in thick black pen.

There is one window in the room, right above the desk. It looks out at the wall of the neighboring house. Outside, a woman is pulling clothes off a line. The wind has picked up. It ruffles her hair, her skirt. The clothes flap, threatening to fly away. She glances up and makes eye contact with me. She frowns, turns. She snatches up the last of the laundry and hurries back inside.

I close my eyes and try to picture the window at the Meachem house, the one with the balcony overlooking the dunes. Someone in that house knows something. And Grace Bishop knows more than she was willing to say. If not about the night Adriana was murdered, then about the girls, coming and going. About the parties. About the men who frequent them. About James Meachem himself. Grace is his neighbor, not just here but down in Palm Beach. Neighbors often know more than anyone would suspect. I need to talk to her again.

Through the wall, I can hear Elena singing to Isabel. It's a melancholic melody, slow and written in a minor key. I recognize it from childhood, though I can't recall the words. My skin prickles listening to it. I can almost hear my mother's voice. The crying diminishes and then stops. I picture Isabel clinging to her mother's torso. I wonder if she did that with Adriana, too. According to Elena, Adriana doted on the girl. Maybe she thought a baby of her own would bring her a fresh start, a new life.

Especially if the baby's father was wealthy, powerful. Instead, it might've been the reason she'd been murdered.

Over Adriana's bed is a corkboard. Tacked to it are photographs, a ticket stub, a few business cards. I stare at the photos. I pick out Adriana instantly. She's the kind of girl who burns brighter than the others around her. Her smile is wide and well formed; her face, perfectly symmetrical. She's a more delicate version of her sister. Small-boned, with high, round cheekbones and large, luminous eyes. She glows with youth. Her skin is a rich, smooth hazelnut; her hair is thick and glossy obsidian. She wears it down in most photographs, parted in the middle. When she smiles, her cheeks dimple and that makes her look warm and approachable.

I pause, lean in. One photograph shows Adriana and Elena together on the beach. The water is calm; it looks like the bay and not the ocean. I wonder if it's Meschutt Beach in Hampton Bays, where my parents used to take me when I was little. I remember the buoys out in the water, marking where it is safe to swim. My father could walk all the way out to them with me on his shoulders. My mother would hang back, watching us and waving, her figure casting long shadows on the sand.

In the photo, the sisters are standing at the water's edge, their arms linked together. It must be the end of summer. The light is pale and bright. The water gleams with it. Adriana in particular is deeply tanned. Her head is tilted back, her eyes are closed, her lips are parted in laughter. Her hair is pulled back in a braid, with tendrils escaping around her face. She is happy. Happy and alive.

She looks like Elena, I think. *She looks like my mother.*

An image wells up fresh as a bruise. My mother is holding my hands in hers. We're at Meschutt Beach. There are shells underfoot; we've been collecting them and putting them in a pail with my name painted on it. They make a satisfying *clink* each time they hit the bottom of the pail. I feel them cutting the soft undersides of my toes.

"*Uno*," my mother says, her black eyes finding mine. She had thick, beautiful eyelashes, my mother. When she held me close, I could feel them fluttering against my cheek.

She is trying to be serious now, but it isn't working. We both are laughing.

"*Dos*," I say.

"*Tres*." On three, she whirls me around. She is the axis, turning, turning. My body flies horizontal to the earth. Our hands lock tightly; if I let go, I will land hard on the sand and the pebbles and the crushed shells. It will hurt to fall. I don't let go. She won't let me.

I whirl around, giddy, hysterical, until her arms give out and she stops. Both of us collapse, laughing on the sand. We roll over then and stare up at the blank sky, her ear next to mine, our chests heaving from exertion and laughter.

I remove the photo from the board and hold it up to the light. I can't shake the feeling I've seen Adriana before. Why? My memories are beginning to blur, like film strips shuffled together. Have I seen her before, or is it just my mother I'm remembering? Now that I'm home,

I see my mother everywhere. Crossing the street in town. Walking along the beach. I dream about her, too, more than I have in years.

"She was pretty," Lee says from behind, startling me. "It's sad, isn't it?"

"It would be sad if she weren't." My words come out sharper than I intended.

"I know. I didn't mean—"

"I know what you meant." I turn back to the board. When Lee isn't looking, I tuck the photo in my pocket. My heart is racing. Why did my father come here? Had he linked this case to Pine Barrens before he died? And if he had, then how? I need to know what he knew. I want to be able to see what he saw. Did he have the same feeling I did? That there was something familiar about Adriana, something that drew him to her on instinct?

A business card is tacked at the very bottom of the corkboard. It is a small black square. In the corner, printed in silver, it reads "GC Limo Services." A cell phone number is listed in small print. I reach into my pocket, withdraw my gloves. As carefully as I can, I remove the card. The silver lettering catches the light as I slip it inside an evidence bag.

Lee is standing in front of the closet. He turns, a small white handbag dangling from one finger. It has a gold chain, a quilted front. "Hey. Look at this. Chanel. How much do you think this thing costs?"

"A couple thousand? Maybe more."

Lee raises his eyebrows. "I will never understand women."

"That makes two of us."

I walk over to the closet. It looks as though two people live here. Half the clothes are what you'd expect from a teenager. Jeans and T-shirts are piled on the floor in loosely folded stacks. Sneakers are pushed toward the back; a single, fur-lined Ugg boot lies abandoned in the corner. A row of teetering heels are arranged in front of the sneakers. Some are still in boxes. I bend down, open a box. Out of the tissue paper, I pick up a red-soled stiletto. The bottoms are still smooth. The heel is dagger-sharp, as long as my hand from my wrist to the tip of my fingers.

"Never worn."

"A gift?"

"Maybe." I stand and page through the dresses. "A lot of expensive clothes in here. There's no way she could afford this kind of stuff."

"She had rich clients."

"I'd say so."

I pull out a hanging bag from Bergdorf Goodman. I unzip it. Inside is a white cocktail dress, size two. It's a demure dress, with capped sleeves and a flared skirt. The kind of thing you see on women in the society pages. It still has a price tag dangling from the sleeve: "$2,200."

Lee whistles.

"Rich clients with expensive taste. I bet someone picked this out for her. I can't see this girl going into the city for a day of shopping at Bergdorf Goodman. And even if she did, she wouldn't pick out this dress." I hold up a pair of well-worn Converse sneakers. "This is what she wears on her own time."

"We can talk to the store and find out who bought it."

I nod. "I wonder if she was going somewhere."

"Going where?"

"Look." I point to the label. "It's mostly resort collection."

"What the hell is that?"

"What rich women wear on vacation. You know. Bright colors. Tropical prints. Strappy sandals."

"How do you know that?"

"I read."

Lee snorts. "What, *Vogue*? Didn't take you for such a fashion plate, Flynn."

I ignore him. I pull a pair of white silk pants out of the closet. I hold them up for Lee's inspection. "This. This is resort. It's like someone went to Bergdorf's and bought a whole wardrobe. Not just evening clothes. Daywear, too. I'm telling you. She was going somewhere. Somewhere expensive. With someone who wanted her to look the part."

"Or maybe she was just going to parties in the Hamptons."

"Maybe," I concede. "Ria Sandoval used a driver named Giovanni Calabrese, right? The night she disappeared?"

"Yeah."

"Adriana used him, too. Not the night she went missing, but before that. Her sister said she was picked up by a bald guy in a white Escalade. That can't be a coincidence, right? I think we should pay him a visit."

"We should, but it'll have to wait." Lee holds up his

phone. "Dorsey said as soon as we were done here, we should meet him down at the ME's. The press is all over this case already. He needs to give a statement."

"Okay. Let's bag everything up. Clothes, too."

Lee nods. As I move to help him, I reach into the pocket of my jacket, my fingers curling around the photograph.

Then it hits me. I have seen Adriana before. It's not just that she looks like my mother. She is one of the two girls in the Polaroid picture I found in the desk at 97 Main Street.

10.

The drive from Riverhead to Hauppauge is thirty-five minutes, give or take. At this time of day, most of the traffic is headed away from the city, not toward it. As we get in the car, I decide I'm better off going it alone. I want to speak to Grace Bishop again. She clammed up the moment Lee appeared. She doesn't trust any member of the SCPD, and I'm starting to understand why. I'd also like to collect my father's bike and search through his office without Lee hovering over my shoulder.

"Can you drop me at my truck on Main Street? I'll meet you at the ME's."

"Sure thing. You want to follow me there?"

"I have one stop to make. You go ahead. I don't want to hold you up."

"Is it on the way? I don't want Milkowski to start without you."

I sigh. Lee is going to be harder to shake than I

thought. And I don't want to miss the coroner's report, either. My solo investigation will have to wait. "Yeah," I say. "It's on the way. I just need to swing by impound. Sign some paperwork on my dad's bike. Won't take more than a few minutes."

He checks his watch, then gives me a short nod. "Yeah, fine. No worries. Let's do that and we'll head to the ME's together."

Fifteen minutes later, we're both pulling into the impound lot in Westhampton. I park my truck; Lee does the same.

He rolls down his window. "You want me to come with?"

"No. Hang out. I'll be back in a few." I lock the door behind me. Especially after talking to Elena Marques, I have the ever-growing nagging sensation that something is off about my father's death. I picture his ashes in the breeze. It's too late to force an autopsy, but it may not be too late to examine the bike.

Cole walks out to greet me. He looks the same as I remember: burly and red-faced, with meaty hands and a ponytail. He's grown his beard out some, and it's flecked with gray. At the SCPD Christmas party, he always used to dress like Santa so the kids could sit on his lap and pose for pictures.

"Hey, Cole," I call out, trying to appear cheerful.

"Hey, Nell." He pulls me in for a hug. When he steps back, he gives me a smile. "You look good, kid. You could maybe stand to eat a pizza or two, but you look good."

"You look well yourself."

He laughs. "This is the first year I don't need to use a fake beard to play Santa. Not that I mind, though. That thing itched like hell."

"You were always a great Santa."

He wags his finger at me. "You were such a little smart-ass. You'd come sit on my lap and look me in the eye and go, 'Hey, Cole.' Just to let me know you knew what was up."

I smile. "Listen, I don't mean to rush you, but Lee Davis is waiting for me, so I gotta make this quick."

Cole raises his eyebrows. "Lee Davis? He was your dad's partner, right?"

"Yup."

"Nice guy. He married yet?"

"No." I pause, and then, catching Cole's drift, I add: "Oh, no, no. I'm helping him out with a case. We're old friends."

"Mm-hmm."

"Seriously, Cole. Strictly business."

"Right, of course. Come with me. I'll show you the bike."

We walk past rows of cars. Some are junked, waiting to be sent to the salvage yard. Others are in decent condition. Those will either be picked up by their owners or, if they are part of an ongoing investigation, sent to the crime lab.

At the far end of the row, past a rusted heap of metal that looks like it's been outside for more than one rainstorm, lies the mangled remains of my father's Harley-Davidson Road King.

"There ya go." Cole shrugs. "Now, I don't know what all your dad was doing the night he died, but damn. You can't do that kind of damage unless you're pushing eighty, ninety miles an hour."

"Yeah, or maybe the brakes gave out."

"Thought occurred to me. Listen, I'm happy to send it over to the crime lab to find out. I'm sure they'd expedite it. Anything for your family."

"No." I shake my head. "No crime lab."

Cole frowns. "You sure?"

I press my lips together hard, considering what to say here. I don't want it to go to the crime lab, but I don't want to make Cole suspicious, either. "Listen, between you and me, I was a little worried about my dad," I say finally. "You know, mentally. He was pretty depressed. I heard he was seeing someone, and she'd left him."

Cole raises his eyebrows. "Really."

"Yep. So I'm wondering if he did this to himself. From the looks of it, he might've. I'd like to know, one way or another. Make peace with what happened."

"Of course. I get it. Would you want my brother to take a look? Ty's good with repairs."

I nod, relieved. "That's a great idea. Dad always trusted Ty with his bikes. You think he'd mind?"

"Not at all. Ty loved your pop. And he knows his way around a bike, that's for sure. I'll have him pick it up today."

"You think you could keep this between us? I really don't want Dorsey and the guys to find out. They'd be gutted."

"I hear ya." Cole draws a line across his mouth, like he's zipping it shut. "This will stay between the three of us. I promise."

"Thanks, Cole. Really appreciate the help."

I give Cole a final hug and make my way back to the lot. I stop in front of my dad's truck, appraising it. I swallow hard. It's covered in a coat of dust, but in sunlight, the body is an unmistakable deep red.

I knock on Lee's window, letting him know I'm ready to go. He rolls it down.

"Everything in order?" He's listening to an oldies station, which he quickly flips off. He gives me a genuine smile, and for a minute, I feel conflicted. I don't think he would have pulled me into this mess if he thought my father's death was even a touch suspicious. Lee doesn't seem to have that kind of cunning. But then, maybe that's why he was sent over. To babysit me until I go back to where I came from.

"Yeah, sorry about that. Just some paperwork."

He nods and starts the engine. "Well, I'm glad it all got sorted. Let's head out. You can follow me to the ME's."

We cruise down the highway at a decent clip, my truck tailing Lee's car. We pass the Pine Barrens Preserve, where Ria's body was found, and then Yaphank, where the Suffolk County Police Department is headquartered. After that, the road becomes a blur of scrubby pines and exits for towns I have long since forgotten. When I was young, I loved their strange, mystical names. They reminded me that these had once been beautiful places, filled with lakes and forests teeming with wildlife, instead of the strip malls and gas stations and dusty commercial centers that have since taken root. Ronkonkoma comes from an Algonquian expression meaning "Boundary Lake." Copiague meant "Place of Shelter." Hauppauge, where we were headed, meant "Land of Sweet Water." Or at least, so it tells you on the faded sign we pass on our way into town.

The Suffolk County Medical Examiner's Office is located in a dated white office building off the side of the highway. Outside of it, there are a few sparse trees and a lawn that is mostly dead. The parking lot is less than half-full. If I had to guess, I would have said it looked like the headquarters for a company that had recently filed for Chapter 11. It seems perverse to force forensic pathologists to do their work in a place so devoid of life. At least in the city, the examiners get to walk outside to bustling sidewalks and honking cabs and subway cars jam-packed with people. Here, there is only the quiet hum of cars passing by and the squawk of geese overhead.

I feel a drop of rain on my shoulder as I step out of the truck. The air is thick with moisture. In the distance, thunder rumbles.

"There goes the crime scene." Lee sighs. He slams his door shut and beckons for me to follow him.

As we step inside the building, the sky opens up. I hear the faint hush of rain as we push through the revolving doors. We check in at the front desk with a bored security guard who stares blindly at our IDs. We jot our names down in a guest ledger. I scribble mine, just a big *N* followed by a line. Lee nods to the guard, who swipes us in through the turnstiles. We take the elevator down to the basement level.

Lee leads me down a series of winding hallways lit with fluorescent track lighting that gives everyone a sickly greenish pallor. I am momentarily grateful that I don't work in an office building, especially one like this. I have an office, of course, but I'm rarely there. Most of my work happens out in the field, and the field changes with each case. Most of the time, I work out of a motel room with nothing but a suitcase and a laptop, with periodic stops into whatever shithole conference room local law enforcement has grudgingly handed over for the course of an investigation. If it sounds like I'm complaining, I'm not. I like moving around. I like the solitude of working on the road, and the challenge of doing it in sparse working conditions. It gets my adrenaline pumping. The idea of going to the same building every single day of the week, parking my car in the same space, riding the elevator with the same people, and ordering the same lunch from the building cafeteria makes my skin crawl. I think I'd last a week in a job like that. My father, even less.

Lee either knows everyone at the ME's or he's the kind of person who nods amiably at random passersby. I find his good cheer enviable, if a touch irritating. Most homicide cops I've come across, my father included, have a bleak outlook on humans, generally. They tend to be fiercely loyal to the few people they've elected to bring into the fold and regard everyone else with suspicion. Maybe Lee hasn't worked homicide long enough yet to lose faith in humanity. Or maybe there are just unshakably positive people, and Lee happens to be one of them. Either way, it's hard for me to picture him and Dad spending their days together, tied to each other like Oscar and Felix from *The Odd Couple*. I can't decide who would have annoyed who more.

As we step into the elevator, Lee starts to hum along with the music piped in through a tinny overhead speaker. It's an instrumental version of "Every Breath You Take."

"You know that song is about a stalker, right?"

"It's by the Police." He laughs. "It's a classic. Come on, Flynn. Don't tell me you're not a karaoke fan. This is my song."

"Not really my thing."

"*I'll be watching you,*" Lee responds. He points his finger toward me, like a gun. I can't tell if he's being goofy, ironic, or maybe just a touch threatening. I grit my teeth. Either way, he's getting on my nerves.

"Maybe after this, I can take a peek at your dad's office?" Lee asks. The doors ding open. I don't answer. I push past him into the hall, even though I don't know which way to turn once I get there.

"Hey. Slow down, kid. We're going right in there." Lee points at a stainless-steel door across from the elevator. On it is a placard that reads "MEDICAL EXAM ROOM 1."

"Please stop calling me that."

"Calling you what?"

"Kid. I'm fucking twenty-eight years old."

Lee raises his hands. "Sorry," he says quietly. "Nell. Got it."

He looks wounded, and I feel embarrassed to have snapped. He opens the door to the exam room and ushers me inside. "Thanks," I mutter as I pass him. He nods, silent.

Over the course of my career at the Bureau, I've spent a lot of time talking to pathologists and coroners and crime lab techs. Rarely, though, am I present for autopsies. By the time my unit has been called in, the bodies are cold. Even when new bodies hit the ground during the course of the investigation, we typically hang back from the autopsies themselves, giving the uniforms and techs the space they need to do their jobs. Only after the autopsy do we rush in and get in everybody's way.

Lee has probably been to more autopsies than I have. Someone from the crime scene always has to go, just to confirm that the body on the table is, in fact, the correct one. This is the kind of scut work that typically gets handed off to rookies and suckers, while the more senior detectives just wait for the postmortem report. Given that Lee is a bit of both, I imagine he's done more than his fair share.

No matter how many autopsies you've witnessed, it's hard to numb yourself to them. This one in particular has me on edge. Maybe because the girl looks so much like my mother. Or maybe because I know my father was involved with the case, maybe more intimately than anyone but me suspects. Whatever it is, every nerve in my body crackles like a live wire. As we enter the room, nausea washes over me. I bury my nose in the neck of my sweater, trying to stifle my gag reflex.

The smell hits you first. The distinct mix of death and cleaning agents will cause even the most iron-clad stomach to flip-flop. The rooms are typically windowless and dark, lit only by the unforgiving glare of overhead lighting. There are often stains on the floor and sinks, which you try not to focus on but can't ignore. The tables themselves are ridged on one side, like the drainage end of a butcher's block. Along one wall is a stainless-steel workspace for dissection, appropriately termed a grossing station. It has a ventilated hood like an industrial oven. In some of the bigger and more state-of-the-art facilities, like the one Nikki Prentice runs in the city, there are whole grossing rooms. I've seen some worse facilities in my day, but this one is on the low end of the spectrum. The room is small and poorly ventilated. There isn't any of the fancy new technology I've grown accustomed to: digital imaging and video conferencing, for example. Overhead, a persistent drip from some unseen crack in the wall sounds like a metronome. I wonder when it was this place last got an influx of funding.

The sounds are what you remember once you leave. The whine and sputter of drills as they cut through flesh and bone. Under that, music. A lot of pathologists and techs play music while they work. I know one in New York who listens to salsa; another in Key West who plays Jimmy Buffett's *Son of a Son of a Sailor* on repeat. I get that it's their job. I also get that, for some, the music brings joy into an otherwise grim space or, at least, drowns out the whine of the bone saws. For me, it creates a cognitive dissonance that shakes me to my core. After the Key West job, I've never been able to hear "Cheeseburger in Paradise" without wanting to throw up.

Milkowski is playing classical. *Moonlight Sonata*, which at least feels appropriately somber. It echoes from a small speaker in the corner of the room, barely audible over the slap of our footsteps on the tiled floor. She wears a white lab coat, latex gloves, and a mask over her mouth. When we enter the room, she is standing on a stool so as to get a better look at the vic's torso. In her hand is a smallish saw.

She looks up and sees us by the door. "Detectives, come on in. I was wondering when you'd get here."

"Sorry we're late. Had a stop to make on the way," Lee says without further explanation.

Milkowski pulls her mask down, revealing a thin, no-nonsense smile. "That's fine. Just about wrapping up here."

"Nice work on the ID," Lee says. He holds up the DNA sample he took from Elena. "We swabbed the sister to confirm."

"Leave it there." Milkowski points to a gleaming countertop that looks as though it's been recently rinsed. She peers at us expectantly until we gather around the table.

"Adriana Marques, eighteen-year-old female. Five feet six inches, looked to be about one hundred twenty pounds or so. Her jaw was broken two years ago, hence the metal plate. She's young but has not had an easy life." She points to her skull. "She has a predominantly healed hairline fracture here. Her right pointer finger was broken in two places and did not heal properly. Both are old injuries, unrelated to cause of death."

"And cause of death?"

"One shot, close range, to the head. It's a clean shot, well placed. She died instantly."

"Sounds professional."

"Whoever killed her is experienced with firearms. A less confident shooter would aim for the body. I would hypothesize, too, that the vic knew her assailant, or at least trusted that person enough to allow them to approach her. You don't shoot someone in the head unless you are in close enough range to do so effectively."

"Could have been a john," I say. "Someone she'd seen before or saw regularly. Someone she trusted." What I don't say is this: it could've been my father.

"Or a friend or family member," Lee adds. "We know her ex-boyfriend had MS-13 affiliation."

"Any defensive wounds?" I can't take my eyes off her dismembered body. It's been reassembled on the slab like a Barbie doll that's been pulled apart by a child who can't figure out how to put it back together again. I've seen disembodied limbs before, but never a fully deconstructed cadaver, all in one place. Usually, if someone takes the time to dismember a body, they do it so they can dispose of the parts separately, thereby lowering the risk of identification. Why take the time to hack someone up, only to bury them in a neatly wrapped package in a shallow grave in a reasonably well-trafficked public park?

"No defensive wounds that I could see. Most tellingly, she's got long, artificial nails. The kind that break off easily. These were all intact. If there had been a struggle, I'd expect to see one or more broken off. There are no signs of sexual assault, either, though it's hard to be definitive, given the level of decomp."

"If she wasn't sexually assaulted, and there was no struggle, then why were her wrists bound together?"

Milkowski nods. "Good question. And it wasn't just her hands. Her ankles were bound as well. By the time the body was discovered, the twine used to bind the ankles had snapped. But we found remnants of it on the scene, and there are markings on the ankles consistent with tight binding."

I shake my head. "That doesn't make sense. Who willingly allows themselves to be bound hand and foot?"

"A hooker?" Lee says.

I shoot him a sharp look.

"Sorry," he says quickly, "*sex worker*."

"I was thinking that maybe she was unconscious," I say coldly. I turn my back to him and face Milkowski.

She shakes her head. "She was bound postmortem."

"Really? But why?"

"I don't know. There are abrasions to the wrists and ankles but no evident bleeding."

I close my eyes. A memory bubbles up. My father and I are standing in the cold. It is night. The stars are brilliant overhead. There is snow on the ground, fresh and wet. There is a hole in the sole of one of my boots. I can feel the ooze of cold, wet mud seeping in, saturating my thick, woolen sock, creeping slowly up the fabric until it surrounds my ankle. My foot is growing numb. I shift my weight, trying to alleviate the discomfort. It's no use. There are still flakes drifting down. It must have just stopped snowing. The air smells rich, of balsam and pine needles. When I exhale, my breath crystalizes in front of me.

"That one," Dad says. He points to a small fir, as wide as it is tall. Overhead, clouds rush past the moon. The stars are faint points of light in a sea of darkness. "Nell, what do you think?"

I hesitate. I love the tree. I want it. I can see it with the star on top, brightening the corner of our living room. We haven't had a tree since Pop died. It's been two years. Two Christmases with a few small gifts, wrapped in newspaper, piled on my chair at breakfast time. Two years of watching the ornaments collect dust in the crawl space beneath the house. Two years of TV dinners on aluminum trays and a hastily purchased pie from the local supermarket. I miss the red poinsettias that my mother made from felt. I miss popping corn with her so we could string it into garlands and drape them across the boughs. I miss the smell of ham in the oven and feeling my fingers press into the dough she would roll out and turn, like magic, into piecrust.

I want the tree.

But I see the ax in my father's hands and the impatient look on the nursery owner's face. The tree is small, no bigger than me. It should grow. Its boughs are bright green, not a faded blue-gray like some of the other, larger trees that have begun to lose their vitality. I know someone will cut it down eventually. Probably this season. But it doesn't have to be me.

I shake my head. "Taller," I say.

As we walk past, I look back at the little tree. Its branches curve upward, like the tiers of a pagoda. As if it's smiling, just for me.

We choose another, more mature tree. Slim with long, less impressive branches. There are hundreds more like it at this nursery alone; thousands, probably, across Long Island. That's why I pick it. It isn't special. It won't be missed.

My father fells the tree. The first hard blow of the ax reverberates through the branches. Pine needles flurry to the ground. It takes several more swings before the tree gives way. I feel my stomach lurch when it does. The nursery owner holds it down while Dad ties up the branches with twine. Together, they wrap it in burlap. Dad carries it himself, over one shoulder. His strides are long and purposeful. I try to jump from one footprint to the next, leaving no tracks of my own.

"It's how they tie trees," I say. "You secure the branches first to make it easier to wrap up."

"Alfonso Morales." We all turn at the sound of Glenn Dorsey's voice. It feels like ages since we were on his boat with my father's ashes. "He spent all of August working on the dune restoration project at Shinnecock County

Park. I confirmed it with the South Fork Preservation Society. I'm telling you, he's good for it."

Lee nods. "I knew it."

"There are a few other things I wanted to mention," Milkowski says. There's a slight edge in her voice, like a teacher trying to keep her students' attention. "First, the victim was struck across the abdomen repeatedly, also post-mortem. By a wooden object. We were able to withdraw a splinter, which has been sent to the lab for analysis."

"Like a baseball bat?" Lee asks.

"Thinner. I'd say more like a broomstick."

"Or a rake," I posit.

Milkowski nods. "Yes, could be a rake. A baseball bat would have done more damage. But it's worth noting. It seems like an angry thing to do, to hit a body postmor-tem. A crime of passion, perhaps."

"Was she pregnant?" I ask. Everyone turns and stares at me.

Milkowski raises her eyebrows. "If she was, it was very early. I can run some tests."

"Let's do that."

"What makes you think she was pregnant?" Lee asks me.

I shrug. "Just a hunch."

"We also found trace amounts of cigarette ash on the body," Milkowski adds. "So you're looking for a smoker."

"Can we find out the brand or anything?"

"I doubt it, but let's give the lab a chance."

"Morales smokes like a fucking chimney," Lee says.

"Anything else?" I ask.

"From the angle of the bullet wound, I'd say the shooter was several inches taller than Ms. Marques. And left-handed."

"You said she was about five six?"

"Yeah. I'd say you're looking for someone between five ten and, say, six one."

"How tall is Morales? Do we know if he's a righty or a lefty?"

No one responds. Milkowski opens her mouth to reply but is cut off by Dorsey.

"We need to get moving," he says. "The press is all over this story. We cannot not let this guy slip through the cracks again."

"What's our next move, Chief?"

"Let's head back to the station. We've got an incident room going. Let's circle up there."

I hang back until both men have cleared the room. Then I turn and hand Milkowski my card.

"Hey," I say quietly, "looked like you had more to say."

She gives me a terse shrug. "They're in a hurry."

"If you want to chat, feel free to call me. My cell number is on there."

She nods and tucks the card into her pocket. "I'll do my best to find out if she was pregnant," she says. "It may not be possible."

"Do what you can do." We exchange glances, as if sealing a silent pact between us. I hustle out the door and down the hall until I'm in lockstep with Lee.

———

IN THE PARKING LOT, Dorsey claps Lee on the shoulder. "You wrap this up fast, son, and you'll be a hero. A win like this will be big for the department. And for you."

"I'll do my best, Chief."

"It's too bad we didn't find enough on Morales last summer."

"Not enough to stick."

Dorsey makes a displeased clicking sound and then digs a tin of Skoal out of his pocket. He doesn't take a pinch, just holds it in his fist like a security blanket. He's been trying to quit since I left the island ten years ago. Doesn't look like he's made much progress. "Well, get it done this time." He shakes his head. "Damn shame about this girl. Shouldn't have been this way."

"You want us to pick up Morales now?"

"Let's get a warrant first. Do this once and do it right."

"You think we have probable cause?"

"I'll call Judge Mahoney. He's a good man. He won't hold us up. He knows what we're up against here. He sees what these people are doing to our community." He taps the side of Lee's cruiser. "Let's meet back at the station."

11.

An incident room has been set up in one of the conference rooms at SCPD headquarters. Two white boards sit side by side at the front of the room. One is labeled "PINE BARRENS (Ria Sandoval)." The other, "SHINNECOCK COUNTY PARK (Adriana Marques)." Photos are taped to each. Squint and the victims—both young, slender, lovely—are interchangeable. They are practically the same age, the same weight, the same height. The same long black hair and glamour-girl smiles; the same olive skin and luminous dark eyes. The crime scenes, too, are nearly identical. Adriana's twine-tied, burlap-wrapped body looks just like Ria's. Their burial sites, both on preserved land, have the same remote, eerie feel. They both went missing on a hot, summer Friday, almost exactly one year apart. Some say it takes three or more isolated murders to make for a serial killer. But if this isn't the work of a meticulous, thoughtful, seasoned serial killer, I don't know what is.

And that's when I realize: there are very likely others.

"No mistakes," I say aloud, to no one in particular.

"What did you say?" Lee asks.

"The Sandoval murder was so clean. One shot to the head: the dismemberment, the presentation. The location is technically perfect: a shallow grave in a remote location, unlikely to be uncovered. Another month and the body would have decayed to the point of unrecognizability. It makes me think Sandoval wasn't his first kill."

"So there are others."

"I'd guess so. Did you search for old cold cases with similar MOs?"

"Yes. We went back as far as we could. Nothing in the tristate area."

"You might want to expand that search. Maybe the killer moved here recently."

"An immigrant."

"I didn't say that."

"Maybe he's killed before and we haven't found the bodies."

"Possible."

A photo catches my eye. I move closer. My breath quickens.

"Lee."

"What?"

"Look." I point. The photograph depicts Ria Sandoval's burial site in the Pine Barrens. The grave is in the center of the picture, her burlap-shrouded body still inside. I'm not looking at the grave, though. I'm looking at the edge of the frame, to a small pile of rocks that, on first glance, are easy to miss.

"Holy shit."

"Do we have a loupe? Or a magnifying glass?"

"Yeah." Lee turns. "Donnelly," he barks at a young guy passing in the hallway. "Get us a magnifying glass. Now!"

Donnelly nods and hustles down the hall. We wait for him to reappear. Officers have begun trickling into the incident room. Most of homicide, it seems, wants to be briefed on this case. There are a few rookies, too, who have, no doubt, been rounded up to do some of the basic procedural work. This has to be one of the largest, most brutal cases Suffolk County has seen in years. The kind of case that requires all hands on deck. All internal hands, anyway. Dorsey's reticence to bring in outside assistance rubs me the wrong way, and not just because I'm a Fed. It seems shortsighted at best, destructive and suspicious at worst. Either way, every second that ticks by is a lost one. The longer he drags his feet, the farther away the killer gets. Given that Dorsey seems to only have one suspect in mind, he'd better be damn sure he's right.

Donnelly returns with a magnifying glass. Lee holds it up and peers through it.

"A cairn," he says. I feel my skin prickle. "Damn. I don't know how we missed it. What do you think it means?"

"I think it rules out the possibility of a copycat. If you

guys didn't know it was there, it wasn't a detail that was released to the press."

"What do you think it means to the killer, though?"

"Either it's a marker so he can come back and visit the site later on, or it has some kind of psychological significance for him. He's someone who camps and hikes regularly, or maybe it's something he remembers from his childhood." *Someone like Dad.* Someone who grew up camping in state parks in Suffolk County, who continued to camp in them until very recently.

Lee frowns, considering. "What if it's a marker to someone else?"

"What do you mean?"

"What if it's a team? One person digs the grave, the other buries the body there."

"That's an interesting theory."

"The Shinnecock site in particular is so hard to get to. Even if he had all night, it's a helluva job to dig that grave and then drag a body from the parking lot all the way up there. It's possible that's why the bodies were dismembered, too. Makes them easier to transport."

"So maybe Morales is involved, but he has a partner."

Lee raises his eyebrows. "That would explain a lot. According to Milkowski, the shooter is tall and left-handed. Morales is neither. He's a pretty small guy, actually. Maybe he was just responsible for disposing of the bodies. We have to get into your dad's office. I need to figure out what he knew and when."

The room has filled in behind us. I glance around,

assessing the crowd. Most of them are staring expectantly at Lee. As the lead detective on the case, he's the one who will be running the briefing. "Are you waiting on someone?" I ask.

"Dorsey. He's on the phone with Judge Mahoney now, trying to get a warrant."

Lee seems nervous, like a kid preparing for a high school debate. He flips through a notebook, his mouth moving as he reviews the facts of the two cases. I soften a little. There's something disarming about Lee. A kind of earnestness that makes me want to trust him, despite my best instincts.

"Can I ask you something?" I say quietly. "Something personal?"

"Sure," he says, distracted.

"Was my dad seeing someone?"

"Seeing someone? What do you mean?"

"Did he have a girlfriend?"

Lee looks up, surprised. "I don't know. We didn't really talk about that stuff."

"He never mentioned a woman named Maria?"

"No. But your dad was a private guy. And I wasn't like his best friend or anything."

"You guys spent ten hours a day together in a squad car."

"Fair. But most of that was him telling me to shut the fuck up or silently judging my taste in music."

"You do have terrible taste in music."

He holds up a finger, warning me. "You don't get to say that until we do karaoke together."

"I'll think about it. Could you do me a favor?"

"Sure. Shoot."

"My dad was paying rent on an apartment in River-head. A woman named Maria Cruz lived there. She moved out a few weeks ago, but I want to try to track her down. If she was important to my dad, I'd like to get to know her."

"You want me to run background on her?"

"That would be great. I just don't know how to find her. The apartment was at 97 Main Street in Riverhead. Maybe that's a place to start." I don't mention the fact that I found a photograph of Adriana Marques in the apartment.

"You got it." Lee grins. "Your dad was a real lady-killer, you know."

"What?" I frown, unnerved.

"The ladies loved him. He was a good-looking guy, Nell. And the cop thing, some women like that. Whenever we went out, someone would try to buy him a drink." Lee laughs. "He usually said thank you, took the drink, and then brushed them off."

"Well, maybe that's because he had someone in his life already."

Lee shrugs. "I'll see what I can find out. He's the one you should ask, though." He points to the door. "Dorsey and your dad were thick as thieves."

Dorsey walks into the room, shuts the door behind him. Everyone falls silent. He signals to Lee, prompting him to begin.

Lee clears his throat and stands up. "As you all know,

Marty Flynn and I worked the Sandoval case together. I've invited Marty's daughter, Nell, to join us today. Nell's with the Behavioral Analysis Unit at the FBI. We're lucky to have her with us. Her expertise will, no doubt, be a great asset here."

Heads swivel in my direction. Greetings ripple across the room. I give the crowd a short nod and busy myself with a pen and paper, pretending to take notes.

"I'll try to keep this short since the clock is ticking here. Sandoval's body was found last August. The only lead Detective Flynn and I were able to come up with for the Sandoval killing was a landscaper named Alfonso Morales. He lived across the street from our victim. He also worked on the tract of land where her body was found." Lee points to a map of Long Island. A big red *X* has been drawn in the center of the Pine Barrens Preserve. "We searched his home in Brentwood and his vehicle, a dark red GMC pickup truck. We found burlap and twine, similar to that used to wrap the victim's body, in his truck, and burlap fibers on his rug at home. A truck fitting that description was seen in the parking lot of the motel where Ria Sandoval was last seen. We interviewed Mr. Morales on two separate occasions. He had significant abrasions on his arms and legs, consistent with a struggle. We weren't able to find enough evidence to concretely link him to the killing, however, so eventually we had to turn him loose."

I watch Lee glance over at Dorsey. Dorsey's face remains placid and unreadable. Lee flushes for a second and then continues. "With this new case—the body found yesterday in Shinnecock County Park—Morales remains at the top of our suspect list. He was working at Shinnecock County Park at the time Marques went missing. He also did work on the property bordering the park. As you can see from the evidence compiled here on the board, these cases mirror each other almost exactly. We are working under the assumption that one killer is responsible for both murders. Morales seems like the natural fit."

A detective in the front raises his hand. "What's Morales's connection to the second victim?"

"We haven't found a direct connection between Morales and Adriana Marques. Not yet. Adriana's sister, Elena, mentioned that she saw a maroon truck outside her house in the days leading up to her sister's disappearance. The description matches the truck driven by Mr. Morales, the same one that was seen at the motel the night of Ria Sandoval's disappearance."

I shift uncomfortably in my seat. It also matches the description of my father's truck, the one that I've been driving all morning. The one that's currently on display in the SCPD lot outside.

"We also found trace amounts of cigarette ash on and around Marques's body. Morales is a habitual smoker, so that fits."

"The medical examiner pointed out that whoever shot the victim was tall and left-handed," I say. "Morales doesn't fit that profile."

If Lee is annoyed with me for pointing out this inconsistency, he doesn't show it. "No," he says. "He doesn't.

Morales is about five seven. He's right-handed. So another possibility is that we're looking for a team. Morales could've had a partner who shot the victim, and then Morales himself disposed of the bodies on his worksites."

"Any idea how or why he targeted Marques specifically?"

"Both vics were escorts who advertised their services online. Morales could've connected with both victims that way."

Ron Anastas clears his throat and we all turn toward him. I haven't seen him since we spread Dad's ashes over the bay. He looks exhausted: pale-faced and gripping a large cup of coffee. It occurs to me that since Dad is gone, Anastas is likely the most senior detective in homicide. I always thought he was nice enough but not terribly sharp. Still, he's deeply loyal to Dorsey. I imagine this means he'll be running homicide for the foreseeable future. "We got a call early this morning from a woman named Sally Hayes," he says. "Hayes is employed as a housekeeper by James Meachem, the man whose property borders the park. We've been contacting everyone who works there. Her husband is the caretaker for the house. Meachem is traveling abroad, and the Hayeses have been staying in Mr. Meachem's guesthouse for the past month, overseeing some renovations on the property. According to Mrs. Hayes, she saw a red truck pull into the parking lot of Shinnecock County Park a few weeks ago. It was nighttime, and she wasn't able to get a look at the driver. But she felt certain that she saw someone digging in the dunes. At the time, she dismissed it, thinking it was just the Preservation Society working overtime on the restoration project. But when she saw the news this morning, she called it in."

"She was certain the truck was red?" I chew on my lip, wondering if anyone else is thinking the same thing I am.

"Yeah. She said she saw it drive past the front gate. Meachem's got security lights out there. Mind you, this was late. Around eleven, she said. An odd time to be doing any dune restoration. I was going to go by there later and show her some photos, see if I could get her to ID Morales's truck."

I think about the motion sensor on the security camera outside Meachem's gate. It might've tracked a car going by, especially late at night, when everything else around it was still. I wonder how I can get my hands on those security tapes. Check to make sure it's Morales's red truck that drove by and not anyone else's. If it was Dad's truck, I want to be the first to know.

"Sounds like Morales is our guy," DaSilva announces.

"We think so." Lee nods in agreement. "We're waiting on a warrant. But let's keep our eyes and ears open. Remember, Morales could've had a partner here. The phones have been ringing off the hook. We're going to need everyone's help. All right, that's it. Let's get back to work."

The crowd disperses, breaking into small groups and loose chatter. Lee lets out a deep exhale, like he's relieved to be done.

A young cop strides into the room. "Chief," he says, addressing Dorsey, "Judge Mahoney got back to us. We've got the warrant."

"Do we know where Morales is?" Dorsey asks.

Lee checks his watch. "Still at Harald Farms is my guess. That is, unless he's decided to run."

Dorsey points at Lee and me. "You two. Let's go, before we lose this guy again."

12.

At Riverhead, Long Island splits into two tines. The Peconic River widens between them. The North Fork is farm country. Acres of berries, zinnias, lavender, and grapevines roll from the bay to the sound. The towns are mostly one-street, blink-and-you'll-miss-it affairs. The sky is wide and the roads are quiet. It's not uncommon to see horses and cows at pasture, a stone's throw from the highway. The barns are dilapidated and workaday, nothing like the picture-perfect restored farmhouses you'll find in Sagaponack and Bridgehampton. The paint peels from the wood. Shingles fall from the roofs like old teeth. No one replaces them. I find the barns here beautiful. As they decay, they become a part of the landscape, a touchpoint for a time when Suffolk County was more than just a summer playground for the über-rich.

Just past Riverhead is Aquebogue, a small hamlet

known for wineries and farm stands and not much else. One of the most popular stands belongs to Harald Farms Nursery. In the fall, it's a bustling operation. Apples, corn, pumpkins, cucumbers, and tomatoes are piled high in wooden crates bearing the Harald Farms logo. The crates are aesthetically arranged and the stand itself decorated according to season. Now, at the end of September, scarecrows are everywhere. Candy apples and jams are wrapped in cellophane and sold at a markup. On weekends, you'll find hayrides and a corn maze out back to entertain children, and a small, man-made stream where they can pan for prepurchased bags of fossils and gemstones.

It's the kind of spot that attracts weekenders from the South Fork and day tourists from the city. Harald Farms itself is sprawling and picturesque and conveniently located along 495, the island's central artery. Behind the counter there's a white-haired woman wearing a gingham apron and a cheerful, apple-shaped nametag that reads "NANETTE." The scent of fresh apple cider donuts suffuses the air. There is a refrigerator behind her stuffed with expensive cheese and a display of local wines from nearby vineyards.

Because of the rain, the stand is mostly empty. It's twilight, and people are heading home to prepare for the storm. There are a few stragglers ringing up final purchases, but no one is browsing the stalls. A man in an apron is hauling crates of produce back inside. Another is lowering the awnings. A gust of wind rushes through the open sides of the stand, sending a chill through my body. I wish I were wearing wellies and a raincoat instead of a vest and sneakers.

The wind catches the banner that hangs from the rafters. It reads "Harald Farms Fall Festival, October 1." The woman at the counter lets out a dismayed yelp as the banner floats, lifeless, to the floor.

Lee and Dorsey hustle over to help her collect it. My phone rings. It's the medical examiner's office in Hauppauge. I walk out back behind the stand before answering.

"Hello?" I answer, my voice low.

"It's Jamie Milkowski."

"Hi," I say, surprised. "What's up?"

"You were right. Marques was pregnant."

"Really." My pulse quickens. "How far along?"

"Not far. First trimester, I'd guess. Do you think it has something to do with her murder?"

"I don't know. But it opens up a new possible motive for why she was killed. Her sister thought she had a boyfriend. A wealthy one. Thanks for checking it out so quickly."

"It's my job. Listen, between us, I don't feel like this investigation is being handled all that well by the department. I mean, if this is a serial investigation, I would expect to have access to a full crime lab."

"Agreed."

"Instead, it's just me. And honestly, I don't get the sense that anyone much cares what I have to say to begin with."

"You don't happen to have access to the medical records from the Sandoval case, do you?"

"No. That's the other thing. The facilities here are
shit. Everything is falling apart. Last fall, there was a
flood in the records room and it destroyed a lot of the
files, including the ones on Sandoval."

"That's not good."

"I want to send the body into the city. I know you
mentioned Nikki Prentice. Is she a friend of yours?"

"Yes. A professional friend, but someone I trust.
We've worked together a few times. She has impeccable
judgment."

"Do you think, if I were to ask for her help off the
record, she'd be willing?"

"Off the record, meaning what?"

"Meaning, I've been told specifically that no one outside the Suffolk County Medical Examiner's Office
should be brought in on this case."

"Did Dorsey tell you that?"

"Yes. He was very clear. So it would be . . . on the
down-low, so to speak."

The way she says it, in her rigid academic cadence,
almost makes me chuckle. "Gotcha. Listen, give Nikki a
call. Explain the situation. Tell her you're a friend of
mine and that I recommended you speak to her. She's
discreet. If she can help, she will."

"Okay. Thanks. I appreciate it."

"Keep me posted."

"Likewise."

I hang up and glance around, orienting myself.

There's a driveway wide enough to accommodate a tractor and a flatbed truck. Three workers are in the driveway, slinging bags of peat onto the flatbed. They wear sweatshirts and baseball caps and seem impervious to the rain.

I move toward them, close enough to hear the men speaking to one another. They're mostly quiet, occasionally piping up with a directive in Spanish. It's hard work, and I can hear them breathing beneath the weight of the bags. None are Morales. I walk past just to be sure. They don't notice me. Over the years, I've found that being a small, nondescript person has its benefits. I'm often overlooked. Unlike Lee and Dorsey, who might as well be wearing their SCPD badges on their foreheads, the men in the driveway don't eye me with suspicion. They nod politely when I walk past them for a second time and watch only for a moment as I head toward the end of the drive.

I can see the outline of a few parked trucks. As I get closer, the rain picks up. I hunch down, driving my hands into my pockets. My jeans stick to my skin. My sneakers are soaked through. Lightning sparks in the sky, followed by a deep roll of thunder. The storm that everyone's been talking about has finally arrived.

A shout behind me pierces the air. I turn. A man sprints out of the back of the farm stand, toward the drive. Lee and Dorsey run after him, their feet slapping against the wet, muddy grass. I dash behind the nearest truck. My lungs burn. My shoulder throbs.

Fuck you, Lightman, I think to myself. *You were right about PT.*

I unzip my vest, pull out my weapon. My foot slips in the mud and I stumble, righting myself against the side of the truck. I blink back rain.

Then I see him. A body emerges from between the cars. His right arm is outstretched in front of him. In his hand, he holds a gun.

He is looking backward, toward Dorsey and Lee. I could shoot now and take him out. I don't. Instead, I sprint. Three big leaps. He hears me and turns, but it's too late. I've caught him off guard. I tackle him to the ground. He's small, not much taller than me, with a wiry build. The gun is knocked from his hand. I pin him down, face in the mud. He twists and jerks, but I have him. My knee is in his back. My weapon is trained to his head.

"Don't fucking move," I tell him through clenched teeth.

"*Esa perra*," he mutters. *That bitch.* He turns his head just enough so I can see him spit.

We hold that position for what feels like an eternal stretch of time, each of us straining hard against the other. The rain is coming down in sheets. My hair hangs around my face, making it hard for me to see. Finally, I hear footsteps behind us.

"Holy fuck, Flynn. Nice work," Lee exclaims.

"Some help would be good."

Morales squirms beneath me. I push harder into his ribs. He breathes heavy, fighting hard against the weight of my body.

Dorsey drops to his knees beside me. He slips cuffs on

Morales. I roll back off him, my face turned up toward the rain. I close my eyes and lie there, my body shivering against the gravel, my shoulder alive with pain, until I feel Lee's hands beneath me, pulling me back onto my feet.

13.

"You okay, kid? You sure you don't need to see a doctor?"

I'm not in a position to remind Lee to stop calling me *kid*. He's offered to drive me home and I've accepted; I can barely keep my eyes open, much less handle a car in my condition. I'm slumped in the passenger seat. My dad's truck is still in the parking lot at Harald Farms. Dorsey promised one of the guys would get it back to me. No one seems to notice that it fits the description of the truck that was seen at the motel where Sandoval disappeared, the truck that Elena Marques saw in front of her house, and the one that Sally Hayes, James Meachem's housekeeper, remembered seeing at Shinnecock County Park at night. Or maybe they do notice. That's the possibility that scares me most of all.

My eyes slip closed. The pain is excruciating. I focus

on the drumbeat of rain on the roof of the car. Pain radiates from my shoulder to my fingertips. I've done something to my shoulder that can't be undone with Tylenol and a drink. I need a doctor and soon. But not now. I have too much to do. I need to get into Dad's office. I want to talk to Grace Bishop. And I need to check back in with Milkowski. Every second counts.

"I'm all right," I mutter. "Nothing scotch can't fix."

"That was a helluva move you pulled out there." Lee shakes his head. "I can't believe that son of a bitch was armed."

"He may have just been scared."

Lee shoots me a look. "You going soft on me?"

"Not soft. Just realistic. He's undocumented. He's been questioned before. He's probably terrified of the police."

"He should be terrified."

"Everything you have on this guy is circumstantial. Maybe enough for probable cause. Maybe. But definitely not enough to convince a jury."

"He worked at both sites."

"So did a bunch of other people, I'm sure."

"The bodies were both wrapped in burlap, which we found in his car."

"The same burlap that you yourself said is commercially available all over the North Fork."

"He smokes."

"Come on. How many smokers do you think there are in Suffolk County alone?"

"His pickup was seen in front of the motel where Sandoval went missing, again in front of the Marques home, and late at night at Shinnecock County Park."

"No. A red truck was seen in those three locations. You don't know if it was Morales's truck. You're extrapolating." The seatbelt tugs against my shoulder. I move it behind me so at least it's not pulling across my wound. "Honestly, the most significant thing you have on him is that he was armed and resisted arrest."

Lee lets out an exasperated sigh. "Anastas is on his way over to search Morales's house. And Dorsey is questioning him. We'll get what we need."

I shift again, unable to find a comfortable position. I turn my body away from Lee and stare out at the rain. The definitive way he says this unsettles me. It echoes something Ann-Marie Marshall wrote in an op-ed from twenty years ago: *The police worked Gilroy over until they got what they needed.*

"You know there's a lot of evidence that's pointing away from him, too, right?"

"What, the height thing?"

"Yes, the height thing. Milkowski seemed pretty convinced the shooter was taller than Marques. Morales is my height. She thinks the shooter was left-handed. From what I saw out there, Morales is definitely right-handed. And think about the clothes in her closet. Morales wasn't sending Chanel bags and Louboutin shoes to his victim."

"So? Some other john did. That doesn't mean anything."

"I'm going to bet that Morales didn't send a town car to pick her up the night she went missing, either."

"You don't know that. Maybe Calabrese owns that town car, and he picked her up in that instead of his Escalade."

"Possible. But we should talk to Calabrese. At the very least, doesn't it bother you that an ex-con is using his limo company as a front for a prostitution ring and two of his girls have ended up dead? And then there's James Meachem, who has wild parties with young escorts and happens to live next to the park where one of the bodies was buried. I feel like we lifted up a rock and a million creepers crawled out from underneath it."

"All of that bothers me. But right now, Morales is a prime suspect in two murders. He just tried to resist arrest while brandishing what I'm sure is an unlicensed handgun. So personally, I think we should focus on him before we start up on prostitution rings and dirty johns. Let's see what Dorsey pulls out of Morales in questioning and we'll go from there."

I grit my teeth, wondering why he's so determined to pin this on Morales. Maybe I'm not the only one who sees my father as a viable suspect, too. The thought makes my blood run cold. What if Dorsey's so determined to close the case without implicating Dad that he's pinning it on an innocent man? It would explain why he's so unwilling to bring in the Feds, except for me, Marty's own daughter.

"You know, I've been driving a red truck all day," I

say, unable to help myself. "One that belonged to a tall, left-handed expert shooter."

One who visited Adriana's home two weeks before his own death. One who was married to a woman who looked exactly like the victims.

Lee frowns. I can tell from the look on his face that this is not a possibility he's considered. "What are you saying? That your dad did this?"

"It's possible. Honestly, he fits Milkowski's profile better than Morales."

"Nell, come on. He was a cop, for Christ's sake."

"He had a serious temper. He had a drinking problem. And this isn't the first time he'd be suspected of murdering someone."

Lee makes an exasperated sound. He thinks I'm playing devil's advocate, and his patience is wearing thin. "This is not the fucking BAU. We don't spend months crafting unsub profiles here. It's the Homicide Division of the Suffolk County Police Department. We have a finite number of officers and resources. We need to stay on point. And that means not entertaining outlandish theories about one of our own."

"Forgive me. I thought you actually wanted to solve these murders, not just squeeze a confession out of the first person of interest. Isn't that why you were so eager to get into my dad's office?"

"You should take it easy tonight, okay? Get some rest. Have a drink. I need to be on hand for the interrogation. I'll keep you posted."

"Why did you get me involved in this case if you didn't actually want my opinion?"

Lee pulls into my driveway and cuts the engine. He doesn't answer my question. "You want me to walk you in?"

"It's not the prom. Thanks for the ride." I hop out into the rain, shutting the car door a little harder than I intended.

14.

Outside, the sky is dark. Salt rain pours in rivulets from the gutters. The temperature has dropped significantly since the morning. My hands tremble so hard I have trouble fitting the key into the lock. Lee waits, his engine idling, his headlights illuminating the front porch, until the door closes behind me. Then he pulls out of the driveway, so hard that his tires spin on the gravel. I watch his taillights disappear through the glass.

I flick the lights on. Nothing. The power is out.

"Fuck," I say aloud, my voice echoing in the hallway. Power outages are not uncommon for Dune Road during a storm. Most of our neighbors have installed backup generators, but Dad was too cheap for that. Anyway, he was unfazed by darkness. There are flashlights stocked throughout the house. Canned food in the pantry. And enough wood to start a fire. *I'm fine*, I tell myself, though there's a weight in my gut that insists otherwise.

I get to work on the fireplace, laying newspaper and kindling and logs. Soon, the living room fills with crackling heat and enough light to brighten the room. In the bathroom, I strip off my wet clothes. There's no point in taking a shower; it won't warm me up. I need to get into my father's office. I've been thinking about it ever since Elena Marques mentioned his name. I dry myself with a towel. My clothes are filthy with mud; my hair is caked in it. Blood stains the stiff fabric. I pull the bandage off my shoulder, feeling the sting of cool air against the open wound.

Once I've changed, I find a large flashlight, a step stool. My father kept the key to his office hidden in a coffee can in a cabinet. I know this because once, when I was a teenager, I spent two days systematically searching the house until I found it. I was always more resourceful than he gave me credit for; more keen-eyed and more stubborn. I learned, after all, from the best.

The key is unmarked, suspended on a rusted wire ring. I cross the living room and slip the key into the lock. I flinch when I push open the door. Even now, it feels wrong to go into Dad's office. It was his private space, specifically off-limits to me. If he was inside and I so much as knocked on the door, I better have had a damn good reason.

I have a damn good reason now. I can't shake the feeling that my father's death is inextricably bound up in these murders. What if he killed those girls? The possibility eats at me. Maybe he killed them and then killed himself. Or maybe this is all more complicated than I could

imagine, and I won't understand it until I step back and
start seeing a bigger picture.

The air in Dad's office is stale. The sound of dripping
emanates from the ceiling. I point the beam of my flashlight around the corners of the room but can't isolate the
source of the leak. The light falls to a framed photograph
on my father's desk. I walk over, pick it up, examine it
closely. Dad and Glenn Dorsey. They stand side by side
on Dorsey's boat, the blue expanse of Long Island Sound
glittering in the background. The sky is cloudless and
serene. It is the end of summer. They are tan and grinning ear to ear. Dorsey is wearing Oakley sunglasses. An
SCPD baseball cap casts a shadow across my father's face.

Together, they hold up the body of a giant striped
bass. I remember when they caught it: at seventy-eight
pounds, it was one of the largest caught in this area.
They made the local paper. This was a few years back,
when Dad and I were in a relatively communicative period. He was proud of it, of them. He cut out the article
and sent it to me in the mail.

A striped bass is a beautiful thing, and this one is
particularly grand, both in scale and proportion. Its
silver-scaled body gleams in the late afternoon sun. Its
mouth gapes wide in protest; its eye is round and still.
When I was young, I used to ask my father to throw back
the fish we caught. I hated watching them squirm on the
boat deck, gasping to be back in the water. Even more, I
hated killing them.

Dad told me it was cruel to catch and release. The fish
were injured, he told me. Damaged goods. They'd have

trouble surviving in the wild. It was better to end it for them, he said, quickly and cleanly. The humane thing to do. Dad had a small club designed for the job, called a priest. He'd strike the fish hard on the skull, just behind the eyes, killing them instantly or at least rendering them unconscious.

My mother thought fishing and hunting were both barbaric. She wrinkled her nose in protest whenever my father took out the rods. I still remember the first time he taught me to shoot. They fought about it in the kitchen, the staccato sounds of my mother's anger rising to the rafters. I still don't know why she relented. Dad called up to me, told me to hurry up and get a move on. I scurried down the steps. When I passed her, she hugged me hard and then released me. "Go with your father," she whispered, "have fun." She patted me on the back, as if to tell me that it was okay. I turned around as Dad pulled the truck out of the drive, looking for her through the rear window. She was watching us from the kitchen window, her arms crossed against her chest, her mouth hardened into a straight line.

Dad and Dorsey were both avid hunters. They enjoyed the sport of it, the thrill of the hunt, the victory of the catch. But were they just hunting fish and deer and birds? Or had they moved on to larger prey? Were they putting damaged girls down, freeing them from the burden of surviving alone in the wild?

I put the picture of them facedown on the desk. I can't look at it anymore. I turn my attention to the file cabinet beneath it. It has a padlock on it, the kind that unclicks once you align four numbers correctly. I drop to my knees and begin to fidget with it. I try various iterations of my father's birthday, then my own. Nothing works. When, as a last-ditch effort, I try my mother's birthday, I feel the lock give in my hand. I pop it open. Jackpot.

Dad's files are meticulously organized, each one labeled in his obsessively precise block-lettered handwriting. I flip through them, scroll past one labeled "WILL" and another that reads "BANK STATEMENTS." I stop when I see a large accordion file labeled "GC LIMO SERVICES."

I withdraw the file. It's heavier than the rest. When I open it, a photograph slips out and flutters to the floor. I pick it up and stare at it, bile rising in my throat. It's a photograph of Adriana Marques.

The photograph is taken from a distance with a telephoto lens. Adriana is entering what looks like a warehouse. She's dressed for a party. She's wearing a tight blue dress that crisscrosses her body like a bandage, stiletto pumps, a large golden cross nestled in the hollow of her neck. Her lips are painted a deep shade of red. She looks back over her shoulder, her eyebrows furrowed. She knows someone is watching her. I turn the photograph over. On the back, my father has written: "A. Marques, 18, entering GC Limo Services on 8/29/18." Two days before Adriana disappeared.

I pull open the folder. At the bottom is a burner phone. I have to believe it's the one I've been looking for, the one Dad removed from Adriana's room just after she was reported missing. Beside that is a gold cross, just like the one Adriana is wearing in the photograph.

I stand up. Blood rushes to my head. I close my eyes, steadying myself. I'm not well. It takes work for me to remain upright. My body screams for rest. *I have to keep going*, I tell myself. If I lie down now, I may never get back up again.

Why did he have her necklace?

When I open my eyes, I focus on the large map of Long Island. It runs the length of the office wall. It's new; at least, it wasn't there when I was a kid. I wonder why he put it up. I walk toward it, looking for any markings. Maybe the locations of the bodies had some kind of significance. My eyes linger for a moment on Sears Bellows County Park, where Dad and I camped the night my mother was murdered. I study the small green expanse before forcing myself to look away.

It strikes me for the first time that Long Island is shaped like a body. I wonder why I've never seen this before. It seems clear as day to me now: a woman, floating lifeless in the water. Brooklyn composes her head. Her face turns southward toward the ocean. Smithtown Bay rests in the small of her back. Her legs—the North and South Forks of the island—part at Riverhead. Between them flows Peconic Bay, where Dorsey and Dad would take me boating as a kid.

We'd pack lunch in a cooler—sandwiches and juice and beer—and take off in Dorsey's boat, the same one we took out to scatter Dad's ashes. It's called *Bout Time*, an ironic name, now that I think of it. I still remember the spray of salt water on my face, and the way Dorsey would smile when I climbed up onto his lap so that I could pretend to steer. I'd wrap my hands around the wheel. For a few seconds, he'd let go and I'd feel free.

I walk up to the map and stare at the Pine Barrens Preserve. My eyes move south, to Shinnecock County Park, then back up to Sears Bellows County Park. The place we were camping when my mother was murdered.

Three state parks. All green, all wild, all a short drive from this house.

I sit down on the floor. The weekend my mother was murdered—that whole summer, in fact—comes to me in snapshots. They're scattered, out of order. The details change. Sometimes I remember that it was raining when we arrived; other times I think the rain started later, once we were tucked inside our tent. In dreams, my father is always wearing army green, though later, I saw a photograph of us as we were packing up the car and he's in a blue jacket. In my line of work, you learn quickly that memories—particularly traumatic ones—are mercurial. The longer you live with them, the more fallible you realize them to be.

We hiked for nearly an hour to get to the spot where we would pitch our tent for the night. It was drizzling and I was cold. We passed other places where it would be easy to stop, but my father marched on like he had a drill sergeant hot on his heels. I knew better than to complain or to question his choices. To keep up with him I had to trot, my little legs moving twice as fast as his just to stay on pace.

I stumbled over a tree branch and he stopped. My kneecap smarted and I clutched it, fighting back tears. Beneath my fingers, blood began to rise from where I'd cut the skin.

"Are you okay?" Dad asked, and knelt down beside me. He leaned over and kissed me on the knee, a rare act of physical affection.

"I'm fine. Where are we going?"

"There's a pond a few minutes that way. I think you'll like it. If you're tired, we can turn back. It's up to you."

"How much farther?"

Dad turned then and pointed to something on the edge of the trail. "See that?" he said. "It's called a cairn. It helps hikers find their way. It means we're almost there."

I nodded and stood. "Okay," I said. "Let's go."

The cairn.

My whole body shivers now. I gather my legs up in my arms, rocking myself. Now I know why the cairn we found by Adriana's grave struck such a chord. It stirred up this old memory, one I'd buried in the dark recesses of my mind. There was a cairn near Ria's gravesite, too. Maybe it's just a coincidence. Or maybe it's further proof of what I've begun to suspect is true: my father killed both girls.

He may have killed my mother, too.

15.

On the wall across from the map, there is a large white board, like the one in the incident room at SCPD headquarters. I stand up and rifle through the desk drawer until I find a dry-erase marker. With it, I start scribbling at the top.

> JAMES MEACHEM
> ALFONSO MORALES
> GIOVANNI CALABRESE
> GLENN DORSEY

At the bottom of the list, I add:

> MARTIN FLYNN

In the center of the board, I write the names of the two victims.

I draw a line between Meachem and Morales. Another between Dorsey and Flynn. Giovanni Calabrese is connected to both victims. Morales is connected to both Sandoval and Meachem. My father is connected to Adriana Marques, to Glenn Dorsey, and possibly to Calabrese, though I don't have proof of that yet.

I take the picture of Adriana and tape it up to the white board. A damning piece of evidence. Next to it, I put up the Polaroid. I take out the gold cross and examine it, turning it over in my hands. It's such an intimate object. I wonder if it was a gift from someone. Was it something she wore every day or just on special occasions? Did it bring her protection? Luck?

I hang it over the corner of the board so that it drapes over the photograph of her wearing it. It troubles me that my father had it. If he was just watching her from afar, how did it come into his possession? I step back, frowning. So many puzzle pieces, none of which seem to fit. The white board looks like a spider's web, connecting Suffolk County's richest residents to its poorest. Maybe the lines mean nothing. Maybe Morales did kill two girls and bury them on Preservation Society land. But then why was my father following Adriana Marques? Why is Dorsey so quick to pin the murders on Morales, when there are as many facts leading away from him as there are toward him? And why has no one even considered Calabrese as a suspect?

I pick up the phone and dial my old friend Sarah Patel's number. I need Bureau backup. I could call Lightman, but that might piss him off. Sarah's always been a bit of a renegade, and with the Human Trafficking Task Force under her command, she'll be able to get a team up and running in a matter of hours.

"Nell," she says, sounding pleasantly surprised. "It's been a while. How are you?"

"I'm fine. Actually, fuck that. I'm a mess." In the background, I can hear the chatter of people, the bump of a bass. I wonder if she's at a restaurant or a party. I feel suddenly embarrassed by my candor. For someone who is usually guarded to the point of social isolation, I've been spilling my guts a lot since I landed in Suffolk County. "I'm sorry. Is this an okay time? I know I'm calling you out of the blue."

"Of course it's okay. I'm happy to hear your voice. What's up? Where are you?"

"I'm out on Long Island."

"Why?"

"My dad died. Motorcycle crash."

"Oh, Nell. I'm so sorry." Her voice softens. The background noise on her end of the phone fades away. I hear the *thunk* of a door closing.

"He was a cop, right?"

"Yeah. Homicide. He was working a case when he died. A big one. And that's why I called. I want to close it, but I need help."

"What can I do?"

"Last summer, hikers found the body of a seventeen-year-old girl, shot and dismembered, left out in a public park. Her name was Ria Sandoval. She grew up in Brentwood, originally from El Salvador. It was my father's case. He never closed it. Another victim was found yesterday. Similar profile. Mexican girl from Riverhead. Shot, dismembered. Someone buried her out in the dunes at Shinnecock County Park."

"Oh, damn. I think I just saw this on the news. They arrested a guy, no?"

"Yeah. A Salvadoran guy. Local landscaper. Undocumented."

"You don't buy it."

"Both of these girls were sex workers. They used the same driver, an ex-con named Giovanni Calabrese. I think they were part of a ring, one with some very high-end clientele."

"Sounds up my alley."

"The second body was a stone's throw from this billionaire's house. Guy named James Meachem. I know this is a stretch, but—"

"Oh, I know Meachem."

"You do." I exhale, feeling a rush of excitement.

"He's a known predator. Likes young girls. And he likes to provide young girls for his friends. And they pay him back in kind."

"They protect him?"

"They don't just protect him. They invest in his fund. They do favors for him. Meachem came from nothing. Grew up in the Bronx. Dropped out of college without a degree. And now he's worth a billion dollars. No one can figure out how he got to where he is or why all these powerful people trust him with their money. But I've always suspected it's because he has enough dirt on them to keep them coming back. His fund runs on extortion, but at a very high level."

"His neighbor here told me he has cops on the take."

"Oh, for sure. Not just cops. Judges. Senators. For a while, we were chasing down a story about him and the vice president."

"Seriously? What's the story?"

"Well, allegedly Meachem has cameras in the bedrooms at his house in Palm Beach. According to one girl we talked to, he has a tape of the VP with a fifteen-year-old undocumented Nicaraguan girl. Not a good look for our super-conservative, Bible-thumping, very much married vice president."

"Have you seen the tape?"

"No. We tried, believe me. But we've talked to girls who have been at his house. They all know that they're being recorded. One girl ID'd various men who she said frequented Meachem's parties. She gave us a detailed, credible account, naming a number of high-ranking politicians. The vice president included. We began to build a whole case around her. And then she vanished."

"Vanished?"

"Yeah. No trace."

"Do you think she was murdered?"

"Honestly, yes. If Meachem found out she was cooperating with us, then he'd certainly have reason to get rid of her. So would a whole host of other people. But without a body . . ." She trails off, and I can almost hear her shrugging.

"And the investigation? What happened?"

"It fell apart after that. We had to move on to other, equally sleazy traffickers. There's no shortage of them, unfortunately. There is, however, a shortage of people on my team. So we do what we can. I wish there was more we could've done there. Maybe one day."

"Could you pull records of every Jane Doe found in the Palm Beach area over the last few years? Check to see if any of them were shot and dismembered, and then wrapped in burlap. If Meachem is having someone kill off the girls who have worked for him, he's not going to stop at the ones from Suffolk County."

Sarah pauses. "I will. But Nell, I don't think Meachem is your guy in this case. I think he's a complete scumbag, don't get me wrong. And absolutely capable of murder. But burying a girl in your backyard seems like a very stupid thing to do, and Meachem is not a stupid guy."

"Maybe he panicked," I suggest. "Maybe she was trying to blackmail him and he just snapped."

"Then why not toss her in the ocean with a cinder block tied to her ankle?"

"I know. Fuck. You're right. It doesn't make sense."

"Are you absolutely certain that both victims were in contact with Meachem?"

"I mean, I suspect they were. But I can't prove it."

"Well, get on that. Once you prove that this ring exists and that Meachem is a frequent client, it will be a lot easier to build a case against him."

"He's involved, Sarah. I just feel it. I need to know if

he was paying off cops in Suffolk County. His neighbor suggested as much. If he was, that helps explain why no one did anything to investigate Sandoval's death."

"Are we talking Suffolk County cops?"

"Yeah."

"Your dad was a Suffolk County cop."

"Correct."

"So these are your father's friends? Men you grew up with?"

Maybe my father, too, I almost say but stop myself.

"Yes."

"You sure you want to go down this particular rabbit hole?"

"Yes. I have to. I need to know."

Sarah pauses. "We're watching Meachem down here. We're waiting for him to screw up. He'll get his. You have my word on that."

"It's not just about Meachem. It's about Adriana and Ria. These are girls like us, Sarah. I want people to know their names. I want to know who killed them. They deserve that, at least."

"Does Lightman know you're doing this?"

"No. I can't ask the Bureau to come in officially. Not without tipping off the SCPD. That's why I'm coming to you." I decline to tell her that I'm also technically on medical leave and that Lightman would have my head if he knew what I was up to.

"Okay," she says, though I can hear the reluctance in her voice. She thinks we're in murky waters here. She's not wrong. "Let's start with the guy you think is running this ring."

"Giovanni Calabrese. Runs a limo company out of Wyandanch called GC Limo Services. He drove both victims around."

"If someone is paying off cops, it's probably him."

"So we need to find some way into his operation."

"Do we know any of the girls in this ring besides the two victims?"

It takes me a moment, but I remember. "There is one. Ria Sandoval, the first victim, had a friend named Luz Molina. She also worked for Calabrese."

"Well, go find her. She could be our in."

"She might be too scared to help us."

"She should be scared. If someone's killing off Calabrese's girls, she might be next."

"I'm on it," I say, already moving toward the door.

"Hey, Nell?"

"Yep?"

"Be careful. Watch your back. Meachem is smart and he's dangerous. Please stay in touch. I can't have you disappearing on me, too."

"I can handle myself."

"I know you can. But Meachem's got an army of people at his disposal. And you're alone."

"Not anymore. I've got you."

16.

The rain blows sideways past the glass doors. The windows rattle like teeth in their casings. I'm in the bedroom, struggling to pull a sweater over my injured shoulder, when I hear the rumble of tires on gravel. I peer outside; an SCPD cruiser has pulled into my driveway. Behind it is my father's red truck. The lights switch off. The driver hops out of the front seat. He's wearing a raincoat with the collar turned up and a hat. He glances up at the window; it's Ron Anastas. I inhale sharply and duck beneath the sill, my heart ticking like an overwound watch. The curtain beside me shivers. I wonder if he saw me. The front bell rings. I shut my eyes, willing him to leave. The door isn't locked. He could just turn the handle and let himself in. He's with a partner; I'm alone. My hand slides slowly to my weapon. I turn my head, listening.

Nothing. Finally, I hear the crunch of steps. A car door slams. Then the cruiser pulls away from the house, the sound of it evaporating against the heavy beat of rain on the roof. A minute ticks by, then two. Thunder rumbles in the distance. I stand up and look out into the rain. I let out a sharp exhale. For now, at least, they're gone.

Dune Road, sandwiched as it is between the bay and the ocean, often floods during storms. I imagine it will close soon, and if it does, I'll be trapped here until the storm passes. I can't afford to wait. I hurry down the stairs and take the photograph of my father and Dorsey off his desk. I find Dad's raincoat in the front closet, so large it comes almost to my knees. It feels strange to wear his clothes and drive his car while I'm investigating him. I don't have much of a choice. I need to know who my father was. I flip up the hood and head out into the storm.

The keys to my father's pickup are on the driver's seat. I hop in and start it up. As soon as I pull out of my driveway, I notice that the edges of Dune Road are filling with water. In places, my tires are almost submerged. The bay is closing in. A police cruiser passes as I turn onto the bridge. It's heading in the opposite direction. I feel a shiver of discomfort, an urge to slouch behind the wheel. There's no going back now.

Hank O'Gorman's place has a name—the Marina Bar & Grill—but no one ever calls it that. Folks just say Hank O'Gorman's place, or simply Hank's. It is as advertised: a bar and a grill, nothing more, nothing less, with sawdust on the floor and an old pool table in the back,

which everyone knows is tilted just slightly to the left.
There's a dartboard filled with holes and a jukebox that
plays only classic rock, mostly Lynyrd Skynyrd and AC/
DC. If there's a draw to Hank's, it's Hank himself. A
retired cop, Hank is big and bearded, with flaming red
hair and full-sleeve tattoos. He's hard to miss. Six nights
out of seven, he shakes up drinks behind the bar. More
often than not, he lets his boys from the SCPD drink for
free. I've never seen a non-local in the joint and I think
Hank wants it that way. There's no sign for the Marina
Bar & Grill along the highway; there's not even one over
the door. If I didn't know better, I would've thought it
was just an old shack, a part of the marina itself.

There are a couple of cars in the lot. The lights are on.
I hear the faint pulse of music from inside. When I let
myself in, a bell rings overhead, announcing my entry to
the mostly empty room. The wind whistles behind me. I
run a hand through my hair, shaking off the rain.

There is a lone man at the bar, bent over a glass of
scotch. In the back, a couple huddles in a booth. A television in the corner of the room is set to local news. A
storm whirls angrily toward the coast of Long Island. In
the corner of the screen, statistics flash. Predicted rain-
fall. Wind speeds. Beach closures. "Suffolk County," the
weatherman says, "will be hit the hardest. Folks along
the waterfront should prepare for evacuation."

Hank emerges from the kitchen. He looks just the
same as I remember. He's large enough that he should be
intimidating, but he has a kind way about him. He wears
an apron over a plaid button-down that says "Kiss the

Chef" on the front. When he sees me, his face lights up into a big smile, revealing the gap between his front teeth. He leans over the bar for an awkward hug, clapping me on the back with a bearlike paw.

"Nell Flynn. I was hoping I'd get to catch a glimpse of you. Dorsey said you were in town."

"It's good to see you, Hank. I've been meaning to stop by."

"I'm sorry about your dad. I'll miss seeing him around here."

"Thanks. This was his spot, you know."

"Yeah, I know." Hank presses his lips together as though he wants to say more. I never asked Dorsey where, exactly, Dad was coming from on the night he died. I assumed he'd been here, drinking at Hank's bar the way he did most nights. But it doesn't really matter. I don't want Hank to think I blame him for Dad's death. If Hank hadn't served him that night, he would have found liquor elsewhere. Liquor always managed to find him. Anyway, I'm starting to wonder if his drinking factored into his crash to begin with. It may have been an intentional act by a man with a guilty conscience.

"You were a good friend to him, Hank. I appreciate that."

"He was here the night he died. Did Dorsey tell you that?"

"I didn't ask. It was just an accident. His tires were worn. Roads were wet."

"He wasn't drinking. I mean, nothing more than a Coke. He was supposed to meet DaSilva, but he never showed up, and so your dad just watched the game with me. Anyway, I wanted you to know that. He was on the wagon. Took it real serious, too."

That catches me by surprise. "Really? Since when?"

Hank shrugs. "Few months. He didn't tell you? Quit cold turkey. He'd come in and just sip a Coke at the bar. I think he liked being around people instead of sitting around an empty house. I always figured that was your influence."

"No. We never spoke about his drinking."

"Well, I think you had something to do with it. He told me once he wanted to stop for you. I was proud of him that he finally did it."

"I heard a rumor he was seeing someone. A woman named Maria. Did he ever bring her by?"

Hank raises his eyebrows. "No. Who told you that?"

"An old friend."

"Your dad was in here most nights. Either alone or with the guys from SCPD. If he had a lady friend, I never met her."

"No worries. Just figured I'd ask."

"What can I get you? On the house."

I pause. It feels wrong, on the heels of discussing my father's sobriety, to order a drink. But it's been a hell of a day. My shoulder is smarting; my nerves are still raw. "Macallan neat," I say. I pull out my wallet. "And please, I got it. You can start up a tab."

Hank waves me off. "Your money's no good here."

He slides down the bar to fill the other patron's glass. As I wait for my scotch, I glance around. No sign of Luz.

Looks like Hank's working the joint himself tonight, which makes sense given the weather. I can hear the wind howling outside. It's reached a fever pitch. I'm surprised this place is still open. Then again, Hank lives in an apartment upstairs, so it's not like he has far to go when he decides to close up. And at least, for the moment, they have electricity.

The television switches from the weather forecast to local news. I sit up when I see a shot of Alfonso Morales being led out of the back of Dorsey's car in cuffs. His head is down. He hunches into the collar of his coat, shielding his face from the camera.

"This afternoon, members of the Suffolk County Police Department made a stunning arrest at Harald Farms Nursery in Aquebogue," a reporter says. "Alfonso Morales, an employee of the nursery, was seen running from officers, brandishing a weapon. A local resident, Mary Cassevetes, captured the exchange on her phone."

The screen cut to shaky, zoomed-in footage of Morales sprinting through the field behind the farm stand. It startles me to see my own outline appear in the distance, crouched behind a truck in the parking lot. I'm shrouded in shadow; no one could identify me. But still, there I am, on the local news. I cringe, imagining Lightman's reaction if he found out. I can practically hear him yelling at me through the phone: *What are you doing out there playing cops and robbers at a local nursery? You're on my fucking TV! Why don't you just mail Dmitry Novak a goddamn Christmas card with your return address on it?*

Just before I tackle Morales, the footage cuts off. The

reporter appears on-screen again. "What you've just witnessed is live footage from this afternoon from Harald Farms Nursery in Aquebogue, where police officers apprehended an armed suspect, a man who is wanted in connection with the murders of two young women here in Suffolk County."

There it is. The media has tied the two murders together. Ria Sandoval is no longer a cold case. She is one victim in a serial string.

Hank reappears with my Macallan. "Wild story, right?" He nods up at the television. "You hear about this? They found a girl yesterday morning buried out at Shinnecock County Park. Her body was all cut up. I guess they arrested the guy."

"It's why I'm here, actually."

Hank raises his eyebrows. "Oh yeah?"

"Dorsey has me consulting on the case. Dad was working on it when he died."

"Sounds like they're figuring it out."

"There was a case last summer. A girl buried out in the Pine Barrens. Her name was Ria Sandoval."

"Yeah, I remember. Her friend works here. Luz Molina."

"Looks like it might be the same guy."

"Oh, shit." Hank shakes his head. "Luz asked to leave early today. I was kind of an ass to her about it. I didn't realize what was going on."

"What time did she leave?"

"Around four, I'd guess? She gets in at noon. Supposed to stay until closing."

"I don't think she left because of Morales, if that's any consolation. He wasn't arrested until after five. How long has she worked here?"

"About a year. She's a good kid. Hard worker. I really shouldn't have given her a hard time about leaving early. She's usually reliable. I was just in a pissy mood because of the storm."

"You said she's been here a year? So she must have started working here right after they found Ria's body?"

"Yeah." Hank glances down the bar. The man at the other end looks half-asleep. He's slumped over his drink; his head rests heavy in his hands. Hank drops his voice low. "Between us, Dorsey asked me if I could hire her. Luz was caught up in the escorting thing, and after everything with her friend, she was scared out of her mind. Dorsey felt bad for her. Asked if I could do him a solid and give her some work. Just, you know, under the table. She needed the money."

"What does she do for you?"

"Cleans up, waitresses. Last week she put in all the storm windows. Whatever I need, really."

"How does she know Dorsey?"

"Through the investigation, I guess. Wait, was this the guy who lives across the street from her? The landscaper? Dorsey told me about him. He showed me a picture once, told me to keep an eye out for him."

"Yeah. Alfonso Morales."

"Well, I'll be damned. That fucking animal. If they'd locked him up last summer, that girl might still be alive." He paused then, and his cheeks flushed a deeper shade of red. "I don't mean no disrespect. I'm sure your dad did everything he could have to get the guy."

"None taken. Listen, you know where I can find Luz? I'd like to talk to her."

"Sure. I got her info in the back somewhere." He tops up my drink. "It's getting real nasty out there. If I were you, I'd stay awhile. No sense driving at night in these conditions. And definitely not out to Brentwood. That place ain't safe after dark."

17.

From Hank's, I drive straight to Brentwood. There are two police cars parked outside of Morales's house. The flashing red lights make me nervous. I hide my face as best I can inside the hood of my coat and hurry up the path to Luz's front door.

She's there, in the window. Watching the police. Watching me. I ring the bell and wait. She disappears from sight. For a minute, nothing. But then I hear footsteps, and the clicking of locks. Luz opens the door. A gust of wind blows her hair off her face. She's barefoot, wearing only pajama pants and a light pink sweatshirt. She crosses her arms against her chest, hunching in the cold. She looks so young. A wide-eyed, frightened kid. Inside, in a back room, a baby is crying.

"Are you Luz?" I ask.

She nods, silent.

"My name is Nell Flynn. I'm with the FBI. I was hop-

ing I could ask you some questions about your friend.
Ria Sandoval."

I show her my ID. She studies it and then peers over
my shoulder, toward the Morales house. "Have they arrested him?"

"Yes. Earlier today."

She chews her lip, considering. "Then why do you need
to talk to me?"

Rain cascades down the hood of my jacket, slipping off
its slick surface, pooling on the cracked cement beneath
my feet. I tremble from the chill. My shoulder aches. Luz
stands firmly at the door. She seems wary of me and more
so of the police. I'm starting to feel that way myself.

"This is a serial murder investigation," I explain. "It's
not just about Ria. There was another body found at
Shinnecock County Park yesterday."

"I heard about it."

"A girl named Adriana Marques. Morales is a suspect
in both murders. The police are questioning him now."

Luz's eyes widen. The color drains from her face. "Adriana? The girl from Riverhead?"

"Did you know her?"

"Oh my God," she whispers.

"I'm so sorry. I didn't realize you knew them both."

"They think he killed Adriana, too?"

"It's one theory. It would be helpful if I could ask you
some questions about Ria. I'm trying to understand how
these cases are connected."

She stares at me, her eyes bright with fear. "How did
she die? Was it the same thing as Ria?"

"It was similar."

She bends at the waist. For a second, I think she might throw up. She closes her eyes, and her palm covers her mouth.

I glance over my shoulder at the police cars across the street. Two men in SCPD vests emerge from Morales's house. I turn back around, hoping they don't notice me. "Do you think I could come inside?"

Luz's eyes open. "You said you're with the FBI? Not the police? I don't want to talk to the police again."

"You don't have to. Everything you say to me will be between us."

"If I tell you something important, something helpful about Ria and Adriana, can you help me and my brother get out of here?"

"Where do you want to go?"

"Anywhere. Just away from here. Off this island. Somewhere safe. I can't talk to you unless I know we'll be okay afterward." Her eyes are wide, pleading.

"Okay," I say slowly. "I will do everything I can to make sure you and your brother are safe."

"No, you need to promise. We have to leave."

"I promise. Witness protection, if that's what it takes. You have my word."

She frowns at me, considering. Finally, she says: "We can talk. Somewhere else, though. My family is home. They're sleeping."

"It's late. I can come back tomorrow."

"No." She nods her head toward the blinking lights. "It's better if we talk now."

We end up driving. It's late, close to midnight. Most places are closed. Luz doesn't want to run the risk of being seen with me, so we stay in the car, heading east along the highway. She seems, for the moment, relieved to be away from her house. Her shoulders drop from around her ears once we turn off her street and the lights of the police cars fade in the distance.

"Do you want to listen to music?" I gesture at the radio. Rain drums on the roof, and the wipers work furiously to clear the windshield. Luz leans forward and flicks it on. She turns through a few stations, rap to pop to classical, not settling on anything. Finally, she stops on 103.9, the local news station.

"Here's my problem," an excited male voice says. "If you look at Suffolk County as a whole, violent crime is on the rise. But if you take out those neighborhoods that are predominantly Latino—Brentwood, for example— it's actually a very peaceful county."

"But what's the solution?" another voice asks. "Do we divide the county? Do we deport people? A lot of counties have affluent pockets and not-so-affluent pockets. Look at Manhattan, for example."

"Right, but Suffolk County is huge. We have one police force for the whole eastern half of the island. And if they have to spend all their time and resources on a few select neighborhoods—"

"But they aren't spending their time there. I think you could argue they are spending a disproportionate amount of time and energy servicing the wealthier parts of the county, while at Brentwood High, we're seeing shootings every other week and no one is doing anything about it."

"I think if you were to actively deport everyone in Suffolk County who is here illegally, you'd see a different picture."

I reach to turn off the radio, but Luz beats me to it.

"You live with your uncle, right?" I ask, trying to sound cheerful.

She nods, silent.

"How old is your brother?"

"Miguel is fourteen. Fifteen next month."

"Miguel is a nice name. My grandfather's name."

She turns toward me. "Really?"

"Yeah. Miguel Santos. From Juarez, Mexico. My grandmother was pregnant and they wanted my mom to be born here, so they crossed the border and never looked back."

"And was she?"

"Yep. Born in Texas. They moved out to Central Islip when she was teenager. Just a few blocks from here, actually."

"No shit." Luz covers her mouth. "Sorry. I just—I didn't think you were Latina."

"Most people don't. With a last name like Flynn . . ." I shrug.

"So your grandparents, did they stay?"

"They did. Overstayed, in fact. Got visas that eventually expired. Never did sort out the documentation. Didn't matter, in the end. My grandfather was a proud

American. They had a flag on their front lawn. Every year they'd have a barbecue on July Fourth."

Luz stares out at the rain. She's biting mercilessly on a hangnail. I want to put my hand on her shoulder and tell her it's going to be okay, but I can't promise her that. My grandparents lived and died in a different time. Their lives weren't easy. Not even close. They both worked two jobs, sometimes three. They had no health insurance, no education, no safety net. There was never enough money. Sometimes there wasn't enough to fill the fridge. But the threat of deportation didn't hang over them the way I know it does for Luz.

"Ria was from San Salvador. That's how we became friends."

"Did you know her back home?"

"No. We met at school. I knew she lived down the street. She was different. Really smart. We both studied hard. We wanted to make enough money to get out of here."

"I get it. My mom cleaned houses during the day and went to school at night. You do what you need to do."

"That's what Ria used to say."

"The police report mentioned that Ria did some escorting to make ends meet. Same with Adriana Marques. You wouldn't happen to know anything about that, would you?"

Luz stays silent.

"They both advertised on Craigslist and Backpage at first. But that stopped after they met Giovanni Calabrese."

More silence.

"You wouldn't know where I can find him, would you?"

"He didn't kill them, if that's what you're thinking."

"How do you know?"

"Because I know Gio. He cared about Ria. Adriana, too. And they made him a lot of money."

"Because he drove them to and from jobs?"

She sighs. "It was more than that. Before Gio, Ria was putting up ads on the Internet. She'd go meet a client at a hotel or at his house. Sometimes just in his car. It wasn't safe. But Gio made sure she was okay. He didn't let anyone push her around and he made sure she always got paid. Eventually, Gio was just working for a few clients. He was really picky about the girls he hired. His clients, they like classy girls. They're willing to pay. Adriana and Ria were two of his best earners."

"What happened the night she went missing? He dropped her off in a parking lot of a motel. That doesn't sound so safe to me."

"That wasn't his fault. It was what she wanted. I was with her that night. We were supposed to work a party in Southampton for one of the regular clients. But at the last minute, someone called her. A guy she'd met at a party. He said he wanted to see her privately."

"Wait, you were in the car with them?" I try to keep my voice level.

"Yeah." A tear rolls down her cheek. "I never told anyone that because I didn't want to get in trouble. I don't know anything, anyway. I didn't see who she was meeting. We left her in the parking lot. I never saw her again."

"It's okay. It's not your fault."

"I shouldn't have let her stay there alone."

"You couldn't have known."

She shakes her head. "Gio was upset. He wanted her to come to the party with us. We both felt like something was off. I can't explain it. I just had a bad feeling."

"Where was the party?"

"In Southampton. This rich guy's house. He parties a lot, and Gio always brings him girls. And we got paid really well. A thousand dollars a night."

"Do you know his name?"

She shakes her head.

"If I took you to the house, would you recognize it?"

She looks up at me, her eyes wide. "I don't want to go back to that house."

"Not inside. I'll just drive you down the street and you can point. Okay? There's no one home, I promise."

Luz doesn't answer. She's crying quietly. Her cheeks glisten with tears. "After Ria died, I told them I'd never go back there again."

"Who is 'them,' Luz?"

"Gio. And the others."

"Can you tell me their names?"

She shakes her head.

"Was it Glenn Dorsey, Luz? I know he was the one who got you the job at Hank's."

"I can't talk about it."

"Luz, listen to me. Two of Gio's girls are dead. If there are cops involved, I need to know. It's the only way to make sure that you and the other girls who work for him aren't in danger."

"You need to get Miguel and me out of here. You need to swear."

"I will. But please, help me. Help me and I'll help you."

She turns and we lock eyes. "Two years ago, Glenn Dorsey busted Ria. She'd been advertising online. When he brought her in, he gave her a choice: he'd either turn her over to ICE or she could go work for Gio."

My face instantly flushes. My foot hits the brake, slowing the car. "Wait. *Dorsey* connected Ria to Gio? You're sure? Glenn Dorsey." I feel breathless as I say his name. I think about his arm around me in the parking lot after we scattered Dad's ashes. I rested my head against him, wishing we'd stay in touch. I told him I loved him.

I feel bile rise in my throat. It was bad enough to think that Dorsey was taking kickbacks from a pimp. It hadn't occurred to me that he was a pimp himself, preying on girls who had no other option but to obey him.

"Yeah, I'm sure. That's how most of the girls found their way in."

"And Gio pays Dorsey to bring him girls?"

"Dorsey does *everything*," she says, her eyebrows raised emphatically. She seems frustrated, like I don't fully understand. "Dorsey brings in the girls. He makes sure we don't get in trouble. He gets security at the parties, too. Some of the clients are really high-profile. They like having cops around. It makes them feel like they won't get caught." Her lips curl downward in disgust.

"Were there other cops involved?"

"Sure."

"Do you know their names?"

She pauses, thinking. "There were a few. Ron some-thing. He'd come around sometimes. And DaSilva. Short guy, red face? He was like the muscle. He worked secu-rity at the parties. He was a real asshole to the girls. Al-ways kind of threatening us, you know? Like he enjoyed seeing us scared."

"Anyone else you remember in particular?"

"There was another guy. I can't remember his name. Tall, quiet. Rode a motorcycle."

"Marty Flynn."

"Yeah. That sounds right. He came around some."

I turn onto Meadow Lane. Most of the houses are dark. The wind howls and rocks the body of the truck. In the distance, I can see the lights on the Ponquogue Bridge. At the end of the road, Shinnecock County Park sits, an expanse of blackness, an open mouth.

"This is it." Luz sits up. "This is the street."

We drive to the end and stop. I point up at Meachem's property. A flash of lightning illuminates the house.

"There?" I ask.

"Yeah. That's the house. The man who throws the parties lives there."

"Thank you, Luz. You've been so helpful. Can I ask you one more thing?"

"Sure."

"I need you to introduce me to Calabrese."

"What? Why?"

"He won't know I'm FBI, I promise. I need to get inside his office so I can figure out who pays him and who he pays in return."

"How am I supposed to do that? I haven't seen him in a year."

"Tell him you have a friend. A friend who might be interested in working for him. A friend who's really desperate for cash."

She looks at me, appraising. "I don't know. He's really picky about his girls. Most of them are young."

"You introduce us. Leave the rest to me."

She tucks her knees up under her chin and says nothing.

"By the time I meet with him, I promise you, you and Miguel will already be off the island. I'll get you on a plane the minute the meeting is set."

"Can you do that?"

"I can," I tell her, trying to sound more confident than I am. "And I will."

She nods slowly. "I'll do it. But please. You've got to understand. If you leave me here, they'll kill me, just like they did to those other girls."

"I know. They'll kill us both. That's why we have to be smart and move fast. We hunt them before they hunt us."

18.

By the time I get home, Dune Road is open again. The electricity still isn't on, so I lie down in front of the fire. My body is shot through with fatigue. I gather up some work, force myself to read. Soon, I fall into a restless sleep, punctuated by strange and violent dreams.

I cry out, waking myself. I'd been dreaming of my mother again. We were on the beach, just her and me. The sky was dark; the ocean churned and spat up foam. It was cold, too cold for the beach. The sand beneath my feet felt like ice. I don't know why we were there. I wanted to go back inside the house. My mother was in a bathing suit. She ran toward the ocean. I called out to her, warning her, trying to stop her from going in. She would die of cold; the tide would pull her under. I screamed but my words were lost on the wind. She turned back toward me and smiled, laughing. Then she sprang forward, her arms coming together as she dove, disappearing into a giant, frothing wave.

I sit up. I'm on the couch. The living room is freezing; the fire's gone out. My bare feet stick out from beneath the blanket. I pull them in toward me, rubbing them between my hands. When I stretch my arms, my shoulder pulses with pain. My father's bank statements are scattered on the floor. I must've fallen asleep reading them. I pick them up, shuffling them into some kind of order. I spent most of the night reviewing them. They seem to match up with his salary from the Suffolk County Police Department. There are no suspicious transactions. No large deposits or withdrawals. The only thing out of the ordinary was the apartment in Riverhead, paid for out of a separate account. Even that, though, was paid for from my father's salary. If he was receiving off-books payments from Giovanni Calabrese or anyone else, there is no evidence of it in these pages. I have to assume that's what his offshore account was for. It's time to find out for sure.

After I set coffee to brew, I dig out Justin Moran's business card and dial his number.

"This is Nell Flynn," I say when he answers. "Martin Flynn's daughter. His attorney, Howard Kidd, gave me your contact information."

"Is he all right?"

"He's dead."

"My condolences, Ms. Flynn. How can I help you?"

"You tell me. I've never held offshore assets before. Can you provide me with a statement of some sort? Or tell me how to close the account?"

"I'm afraid you'll have to come down here in person if you want to withdraw assets."

"To the Cayman Islands?"

"Yes. We take security quite seriously, Ms. Flynn. Security and discretion."

"And I appreciate that. But you can't expect me to fly down there only to find there's fifteen dollars in the account. It's not worth my time."

Moran pauses, considering this logic. "I understand," he says. "Let's do this. I'm going to ask you a series of questions, verifying that you are who you say you are. Social Security number, that sort of thing. And then I'll be happy to answer your questions about the account. Will that suffice?"

"Works for me."

"All right. Here we go." Moran asks me a series of mundane but personal questions, all of which I answer. I must have passed his test, because he stops and says, "Fine. That's good. What can I tell you about the account?"

"How much is in it?"

"Currently a hundred forty thousand dollars."

"Wow. Okay. I suppose that's worth the flight."

"Indeed. Ten thousand is transferred into it at the start of each month, so if you wait a few days, that will go up to one fifty."

"Transferred from where? My father's bank account?"

"No. From a corporation, GC Limited. The account was opened fourteen months ago and has received ten thousand dollars each month since."

"GC, you said?"

"Yes."

"I ought to contact the corporation. If my father was working for them, they should know he's passed."

"I'm not sure I can give you that information."

"Mr. Moran, I don't want to get technical on you here. But my father's dead. I'm the beneficiary of this account. So as I see it, you're my banker now."

"I understand," he says crisply. "Still, the bank has certain protocols."

"I'm also an FBI agent, Mr. Moran. Perhaps my father mentioned that. The Bureau has protocols, too. One of them is making sure none of its agents are harboring cash in offshore accounts. So we can do this the easy way, or we can do this the hard way. The hard way is going to involve my boss, the head of the Bureau, the IRS, and a whole bunch of subpoenas. Alternatively, you could provide me with a statement for my account, with the contact information for the corporation that was transferring money into it each month, and then we can close the account together and no one has to be the wiser. It's up to you. Personally, I'd opt for the easy way. It's going to be a lot more pleasant for both of us."

Moran clears his throat. "Yes, your father mentioned your line of work. Thank you for refreshing my memory. How would you like me to send you the statements?"

"Email would be preferable. I'll give you my contact information. Rest assured, I'll keep it in the closest confidence."

"I'll email it to you within the hour. Once you've reviewed it, call me and we can proceed with closing the account."

I hang up and flick on the television. Luz said she was going to reach out to Calabrese today, but it's still early. She's probably still asleep. So is he. I'll have to be patient. Patience is not my forte.

The TV does little to distract me. Alfonso Morales's confession is the big story on the local news; I have to wait only a minute before an anchor mentions it. The screen shows Morales exiting an SCPD cruiser in cuffs. Several officers surround him. Morales bends at the waist, ignoring the shouts of reporters and the flash of cameras. Someone from inside the police department must have called the media. It's more of a circus than your average perp walk.

"We bring you live to the police headquarters in Yaphank." The cameras are trained on the steps of the precinct; Glenn Dorsey stands at a podium, his officers lined up behind him like bodyguards. Seeing their faces makes me wince. These are my dad's colleagues, his friends, men I've known my whole life. Men I once considered family.

"Today was a testament to the Suffolk County Police Department," Glenn begins. "Our team worked quickly and effectively and were able to apprehend Mr. Morales within a twenty-four-hour period. Mr. Morales has confessed to the killings of both Ria Sandoval, the young woman whose body was found last summer in the Pine Barrens, and Adriana Marques, found two days ago at

Shinnecock County Park. Today is a sad day for our community as we mourn the loss of two young lives. But it is
also a day where we can honor the work of the officers
here and take comfort in their competency. I have time
for just a few questions."

Dorsey scans the crowd of reporters, pointing to a
man at the front.

"Is Mr. Morales a U.S. citizen?"

"He is not."

"What about the victims? Were they here legally?"

"Adriana Marques was a U.S. citizen. Ria Sandoval
was not."

"Is it true that the Suffolk County Police Department
maintains a ninety-four percent confession rate?" Ann-
Marie Marshall asks from the back of the crowd. When I
hear her voice, I freeze.

Dorsey frowns. "I don't know how accurate that sta-
tistic is. But we do have a solid confession rate, and it's
something I'm proud of."

"It's significantly higher than the national average,
and far exceeds that in comparable counties like Nassau
and Westchester."

"If that's true, it's a credit to our detectives. Next
question." Dorsey jabs a finger at the nearest reporter.

"Or it's an indication that your detectives use im-
proper tactics to obtain these confessions," Marshall
continues, her voice loud enough to hush the crowd.
"Just last year, there was a case in which homicide detectives from Suffolk County took a written statement in

English from Hector Dominguez, a man who speaks only Spanish and was not offered counsel or even a translator—"

"You are grossly misrepresenting the facts of the Dominguez case," Dorsey cuts her off. "Your newspaper's coverage of that story was inaccurate and nearly resulted in a lawsuit. It has no bearing on Mr. Morales's confession, which he gave completely and willingly, and which I personally oversaw. Mr. Morales had a guilty conscience and he wanted to confess. End of story. Now, if you don't mind—"

"What about Sean Gilroy's confession back in '97?" Ann-Marie Marshall shouts. "You oversaw that confession, too, didn't you? And in both cases, there was forensic evidence that suggested the suspect could *not* possibly have committed the crime of which he was accused, and in both cases that evidence was intentionally overlooked by your department."

"No more questions." Dorsey steps away from the microphone so abruptly that he knocks it over. An electric squeal fills the air. The camera follows Dorsey as he walks away, his shoulders pinned around his ears. When he's gone, it pans the crowd of reporters, who turn to one another, chattering excitedly about the heated exchange.

I shut off the television.

I open my laptop. I check my inbox; there's already an email from Justin Moran. I click open the attachment and hit print. In the office, I hear the printer whir to life. As I wait for it to finish, I search Sean Gilroy's name. After scanning three articles that Ann-Marie Marshall wrote about Gilroy's confession, I see what I'm looking for. At the end of the last article, Marshall quotes Glenn Dorsey as saying, "That boy had a guilty conscience. Some folks just want to confess, you know?"

I pick up the phone and dial *Newsday*'s main number.

"My name is Nell Flynn," I tell the operator. "I need to speak to Ann-Marie Marshall as soon as possible."

AN HOUR LATER, we meet at a coffee shop on Main Street in Riverhead. The place is small and plain, with a dusty front window that looks out on a parking lot and a sign on the door that reads "CLOSED." I pause and peer in through the glass. I catch the eye of a woman wiping down the counter. When she sees me she stops what she's doing. She beckons me inside.

I push the door open; the hinges whine in protest. The booths are tall and covered in a waxy, mustard-yellow fabric. The television over the counter is set silently to the local news. The place is quiet; I check my watch to make sure I have the right time. I'm still not sure this is even the right place. The woman behind the counter points toward the last booth.

"Take a seat, hon."

I nod in thanks. I'm surprised to find Ann-Marie Marshall already nestled in the corner. She smiles up at me, her red lips parting over perfect white teeth.

"Did I startle you?"

"No," I say, though she did. "Nice place to meet. All very cloak-and-dagger."

She shrugs. "I have my spots. In my line of work, it's sometimes complicated to find a good place to chat."

"I know the feeling." I slide into the booth opposite her. I eye her cup of steaming black coffee. The place is cold, and I cross my arms against my chest, wishing I'd brought more clothes to Suffolk County. I thought I'd be here for just a few days. But this is my second week, and my wardrobe of one pair of jeans and my father's old sweatshirts feels thin. The waitress comes over, a pencil tucked behind her ear.

"Can I get you something, hon?"

"Coffee would be great."

"How do you take it?"

"Black is fine. And hot, please."

"Coming up." She disappears and returns almost instantly with a mug and the pot. She tops off Ann-Marie's cup before whisking away again.

"I'm glad you called," Ann-Marie says once we're alone. She dumps a packet of sugar into her mug and stirs. "You know, I've thought about reaching out to you in the past. But I wasn't sure you'd want to hear from me."

"I wouldn't have. Frankly, I've always hated your guts."

She smiles, unfazed. "Well, I'm glad I didn't, then. Why did you call me?"

"I saw you at the news conference with Glenn Dorsey. You mentioned Sean Gilroy. From my mother's case."

Her face hardens. "If you're here to tell me to shut up about that case, you could have done that over the phone. And I would've told you the same thing I tell the SCPD. Absolutely not."

"That's not what I want. To the contrary, actually."

That catches her by surprise. "You want to know about the Gilroy case?"

"You said there was forensic evidence that contradicted Gilroy's statement."

"There was. The coroner's report stated that your mother's assailant was left-handed. Gilroy is ambidextrous. He writes with his left but plays sports with his right. So it stands to reason that he would have used his right hand if he was to stab anyone."

"That's conjecture."

"It is. But the forensic pathologist agreed with me. Conveniently, his entire report was lost shortly after the trial. And then he retired to Florida. Or at least, that's what I was told. Anyway, he became unreachable. That seems to happen to a lot of people in Suffolk County. They just disappear." She spreads her fingers wide as if to say *poof*.

"Gilroy's fingerprints were on the murder weapon," I point out. "Were the prints from his right hand or his left?"

"His left. Look, I don't doubt he picked up the knife with his left hand. He said he did. But it's possible he did so after he'd found the body. You know he recanted once, right? He said he saw her through the window and that she was already dead, and he broke into the house in order to help her."

"And you believe that."

"I don't know what to believe. I still don't know who killed your mother. But I don't believe Gilroy's confession. It was filled with small inconsistencies. The timeline didn't quite match up. He couldn't explain how he got ahold of the knife, and he said he stabbed her once by accident, when in fact she'd been stabbed multiple times. I think he was pressured into confessing, and then any evidence that contradicted it disappeared. Maybe Gilroy was the killer. But that case was never as neat and clean as Glenn Dorsey wanted people to think it was."

"But why? What possible motive would Glenn Dorsey have for framing Sean Gilroy?"

Marshall sighs. "I can think of a few. I'm sure you can, too."

"You think my father killed her."

"You'd know better than I would about that. You were his alibi after all."

I shift against the hard seat and wonder if coming here was a mistake. "I wouldn't have lied about something like that."

"He was your father. You were young. Maybe you didn't even know he was gone."

"We were camping in a two-person tent, thirty miles from our house. I would have noticed if he had left. And he wouldn't have abandoned me in the middle of the woods at night."

"Fair enough." Ann-Marie raises her palms. "Look, Nell. Can I call you Nell? I'm not saying Gilroy *didn't* kill your mother. He very well may have. But he is still entitled to due process. I think he was intimidated into giving that testimony. I don't believe he was properly Mirandized. I think there was substantial evidence tampering to make the whole thing go away as quickly as possible, and Gilroy didn't have—doesn't have—the resources and the mental wherewithal to defend himself. Dorsey decided he was the guy and he made sure he went down for it, no matter what. That's my point. That's always been my point."

"So you think the SCPD is corrupt."

"Yes, I do. Gilroy is not an isolated incident. This has been a chronic, systemic problem in Suffolk County for decades. I've talked to men who've been hit with phone books and had their testicles squeezed during interrogations. Because those things don't leave bruises, see? I've talked to officers off the record in Nassau County who say it's an open secret that the cops in Suffolk County do whatever they want, that they're total cowboys, that they skim off the top whenever there's a drug bust, that they accept bribes from gang leaders and drug dealers so that they can keep doing what they do, that they frame people all the time. Everyone says this has only gotten worse since Glenn Dorsey became the chief of detectives."

"So why hasn't the department been investigated? If it's such an open secret."

Ann-Marie gives me a look like I'm stupid. "They *have* been investigated. At least twice that I know about. Once under Governor Baldacci, back in the 1990s, and the commission found widespread misconduct in both homicide and narcotics investigations. That's a direct quote. You can look it up. Two detectives named in that report were ultimately sent to prison. Detective McCrary for taking kickbacks and Moynahan for assaulting a suspect during an interrogation. Maybe you were too young to remember them?"

I open my mouth but nothing comes out. I do remember them both, but only a little. I remember that Maureen McCrary used to come over a lot after my mother died. She'd bring casseroles and wear blue eye makeup and skirts that were just a little too short. She'd flirt with Dad and ignore me as best as she was able. One night after she brought over some baked ziti and a bottle of wine, I asked her where her husband was. Dad sent me to my room. Later, he told me that the McCrarys were getting a divorce, that Mr. McCrary had moved away, and that I shouldn't be so rude to guests. Then he said he found Maureen every bit as annoying as I did and was grateful that I'd said what I'd said because now she'd never come back. That was the last time Maureen came by. We'd see her now and then around the holidays at St. Agnes or at the annual SCPD fund-raiser. She'd wave and keep her distance. Eventually, she married a police officer in Westchester. I never saw her again.

"When was the second investigation?"

"Two years ago. Governor Franklin called for an investigation into the SCPD after the Hector Dominguez debacle."

"What happened there?"

She shrugs. "Got me. Either it's still going on or Dorsey found a way to make it go quietly into the night. There was a rumor that the DEA had been pulled in to monitor the SCPD. A source told me they had someone inside SCPD, monitoring the Narcotics Division. But so far, nothing's come of it."

"So you think it's happening again with Alfonso Morales. A forced confession, a slipshod investigation."

"Absolutely. And you do, too. Otherwise you wouldn't be sitting here talking to me."

"But why now? If they're so quick to frame people, why didn't they arrest Morales last summer?"

"I don't know. Listen, I have friends inside the department. They said your dad and Dorsey fought about the Pine Barrens case and the way it was handled. Dorsey wanted to arrest Morales, and your father said there wasn't enough evidence. They barely spoke after that. Caused a lot of tension over there at headquarters. But now your father's gone, so Dorsey's going to handle this the way he usually does."

I lean back against the booth. The laminated fabric sticks to my skin. I stare out the window at my father's pickup. In the bright afternoon light, it sparkles. A bright candy-apple color, more red than maroon.

I sit up, struck by a sudden thought. "So you think my father actually wanted to solve Pine Barrens?"

"That's what I heard."

"He didn't want to sweep it under the rug, the way Dorsey is now."

"Right." Ann-Marie gives me a quizzical look.

"And you said there's an inside man? A source in the SCPD?"

"That's what I've heard. I've never been able to verify it."

"I have to go," I say, and pull a few dollars out of my purse. "I'm sorry. I just—something just occurred to me. I'll be in touch."

She grabs my sleeve, stopping me. "Listen, talk to Milkowski, would you?" she says quickly.

"The pathologist? Why?"

"Just talk to her. She believes Morales wasn't the killer. The killer was left-handed, but whoever cut up the body was right-handed. So she thinks someone shot Adriana and maybe Morales disposed of the body. She has solid evidence to back that theory up. She talked to me off the record. She's scared of Glenn Dorsey. She needs help, Nell. If she comes forward, she's going to need protection. Maybe you can give that to her."

"Are you writing a story about this?"

"Something like that. Hoping not to get myself killed in the process." She turned and signaled for the check. "What are you doing, exactly? Running your own private investigation? If you don't mind my asking."

"Something like that. Let's stay in touch." I drop my card on the table and sprint out the door, the hinges wailing in my wake.

19.

Elena Marques's house is just a short drive down Pulaski Street. I gun the engine and drive as fast as I can, pulling up right in front of the house, just as I had the day before. I hustle up the steps and ring the bell. As I wait for her to answer, I notice a sedan pull up and park across the street. The car's engine switches off, but the driver doesn't get out. He pulls out a paper and pretends to read it. I know he is watching me instead.

The door opens. Elena looks even frailer than when we last spoke. She gives me a wan smile.

"Agent Flynn. Come in." She waves me inside. I glance over my shoulder when she turns away, just in time to see the man in the car pointing a camera lens in our direction. I pull the door closed behind us.

"Are you all right?" she asks me. I realize I'm sweating a little. I wipe my brow with my wrist.

"I'm okay. Thank you." My voice comes out sharper than I intended. "How are you? That's more important."

She shrugs. "I heard on the news that Alfonso Morales was arrested."

"He was, yes."

"Is it true he confessed to killing Adriana? And that other girl, the one from last summer?"

"That's what I've heard. I'm not sure."

"You weren't there?"

"I'm not a police officer, Elena. I was just assisting with the investigation."

"And now it's over." She stares at me evenly, like she's waiting for me to disappoint her. "That's it."

"It's not over for me. Not by a long shot. Can we talk?"

"About what?"

"I think your sister was part of something. Something big. I think some very powerful people took advantage of her. I want to make sure every person who hurt your sister is brought to justice. Not just her killer, but people who may have exploited her before her death. But I'm going to need your help to do it."

Elena is quiet for a minute. She turns and takes a seat on the couch. "Why are you doing this?"

"Why am I doing what?"

"This. Talking to me. It's not your case. You're not a cop. So why do you care so much about Adriana?"

I sit down on the couch beside her. "Everyone should care. Your sister was a human being. She deserved to be treated like one."

Elena slides her hand across the couch. She puts her

hand atop mine and squeezes. When I look up, I see that her eyes are filled with tears. "Thank you," she whispers. "For saying that."

"Look, I need to be honest with you. My father was a Suffolk County Police Officer. His name was Martin Flynn. He came here after Adriana disappeared. He took her phone. Was it a silver flip phone? A burner?"

Elena pulls back her hand. She sits up straight, her eyes wide in fear. "Yes. It was. Flynn . . . that was your father?"

I nod. "But I think maybe he was trying to protect Adriana."

"Protect her from who?"

"Your sister was part of a network of young girls, a prostitution ring, run by Giovanni Calabrese. The man you saw in the white Escalade. Calabrese paid off members of the Suffolk County Police Department to look the other way. There's an investigation into the department right now. Apparently, the Feds have a mole inside the department. I think my father was that mole. And I believe your sister and Ria Sandoval were helping my father with that investigation."

"The police department had her killed?" she says, sounding incredulous.

"It's possible. Or maybe Calabrese did. Or James Meachem. He's a frequent client of Calabrese. And Adriana's body was found near his house."

"James Meachem. The man with the house on Meadow Lane." Elena pales. "Oh, God. This is all my fault."

"It's not your fault, Elena. You can't think that."

"No, it is. It is. You don't understand. I used to work for James Meachem. I brought Adriana once. To work with me. That must be how this started."

"Okay." I take a deep breath, trying to maintain my composure. "Go back. How did you meet James Meachem?"

"For years, I cleaned houses for summer people," Elena starts slowly. "I was part of a team. We'd just go wherever we got called. The summer was our busiest time. Between Memorial Day and Labor Day, we made thirty dollars an hour. I worked six days a week, sometimes seven. Sometimes we'd be in one house all day. Twelve, fourteen hours. The houses were so big. Eight, ten bedrooms. So much laundry. Beach towels and sheets and linens. And all the silver, *Dios mío*. Do you know what it's like to clean silver for eighty-person dinner parties? And crystal glasses so fine I thought they'd crack in my hands. I will never understand why rich people can't buy silver and glassware that goes in a dishwasher! It's almost like they like to see us on our hands and knees, scrubbing their floors."

Her eyes glisten with tears, like she's remembering something painful, something she'd tried hard to forget. I nod, urging her to continue.

"Anyway, it was hard work, but it paid so well, much better than cleaning at the hospital, honestly. At night I'd come home and everything would ache. My back, my legs, my hands. But if Gladys—she was the one who organized our crew—called me, I always said I was free to work.

"Gladys got a call about a house on Meadow Lane that needed cleaning. One of her regular girls couldn't do it, and she asked me if I knew anyone who could help. I told Adriana that she could make some extra cash. She was just fifteen, on summer break from school. She was happy for the money. The house was incredible. All glass, overlooking the ocean. The owner wasn't there; he was supposed to arrive the next day. There was a French woman. Manon, her name was. I thought she was the house manager, but I wasn't sure. She told us what to do. She was very stern with us. She wanted everything pristine and perfect. She screamed at one of the girls because she didn't like the way she made the bed. And the rugs were all white, so she made us work barefoot.

"The whole time people were coming in and out, delivering white orchids and champagne by the case. It looked like they were having a big party. Gladys sent me and Adriana upstairs. We were supposed to steam and press all of these clothes. Fancy dresses and nightgowns and lingerie. The French lady came in and watched us do it, and she started arranging the clothes onto racks, like what you see in a department store. It was all new. Sent in bags from Bergdorf Goodman and Barneys. I thought maybe they were gifts for the owner's wife or girlfriend.

"The lady, she stared at Adriana while we worked. I got nervous, I thought maybe Adriana looked too young and that worried her. But then she asked Adriana if she could try on one of the dresses. She held up this beautiful dress—it had one shoulder and was made of silk—and

Adriana took it and started walking toward the bathroom. The lady stopped her and said she didn't need to be shy, she could change here in front of us.

"So Adriana took her clothes off. I think she was embarrassed because she was wearing an old bra and panties that didn't match. She took those off, too. Then she slipped on this dress and the lady smiled. Adriana did, too. The woman told her she looked like Aphrodite, the Greek goddess of beauty. She asked Adriana if she ever thought about modeling. Adriana said no. The lady walked over to her. She stood behind her and they both looked into a mirror. She pulled Adriana's hair back and twisted it into a bun. She said, 'See how elegant you are? You look like Helen of Troy. You look like Leda.' And that's what she called her after that. She called her Leda."

I grimace. "Leda was raped. It's a Greek myth. Zeus took the form of a swan and raped her."

Elena says nothing. She bites her lip; her nostrils flare.

"Did you ever see her again? This woman?"

"She handed Adriana a card and said to call her if she ever changed her mind about modeling. She said she worked in entertainment and was always looking for pretty new faces. Once we left the house, I told Adriana to stay away from her."

"And you don't remember her last name?"

"I don't. I'm sorry. I haven't thought about her in years."

"Did you ever meet Mr. Meachem?"

"No. We cleaned that house a few times. Before Mr. Meachem would arrive and after he was already gone.

But I never saw him. And the French woman, she never spoke to me or to Adriana again."

"You don't think Adriana called her?"

"I didn't think so. But now I'm not so sure. Oh, God. That house. It was right next to the park, wasn't it? Where her body was found."

"Yes."

"Do you think he killed her? James Meachem?"

"I don't know. But he hires young escorts for his parties. He's a predator, and I want to make sure he never hurts another girl again."

Elena nods, silent. A tear slides down her cheek and drops onto the carpet.

I reach into my bag and pull out the photograph of Dad and Glenn Dorsey. I hand it to her, tapping my finger on my father's image. "Elena, is this the police officer who came to your house after you reported Adriana missing?"

She studies it carefully. "Yes. That's him."

"Could you look out the window? There's a car parked in front."

She stands up and walks to the window. She peers outside and her eyes widen in fear.

"Is that—?"

"It's my father's pickup. The man in the photograph."

"That's the red truck. The one I saw outside the house before Adriana died."

"You're sure. Take another look. It's important."

Elena turns back to the window. Her hand presses against the glass. "Yes, that's it. It was parked right where it is now. I'm sure. It was like he was watching us."

"I just have one last question." I fish the Polaroid photograph out of my purse and hand it to her. "This is Adriana, isn't it?"

"Yes." She nods. She touches her finger to her sister's image. "That's her. Where did you get this?"

"My father had it. Do you know who the other girl in the picture is?"

Elena frowns, considering. "Her name's Maria," she says after a few seconds. "Maria Cruz. They went to St. Mary's together for First Communion. She was a nice girl."

"I'm trying to find her. You don't know where she is, do you?"

"No. I'm sorry. I haven't seen her in a long time. I hope she's all right."

"I hope she is, too."

20.

Outside, I listen to a message from Luz.

I spoke to Gio, she says. *He told me to come by today or tomorrow with my friend. He said he's always looking for fresh blood. Let me know what you want to do.*

I dial Sarah Patel's number.

"Luz can bring me to Calabrese's today," I tell her. The sedan is still outside, waiting for me. The driver hides behind his newspaper, the front page rustling a little as he peers over the top of it. I make a mental note of the license plate: HB-778.

"Nell, it can't be you. It's too close for comfort. What if Calabrese recognizes you?"

"How would he recognize me?"

"He knows your father. And what if he wants you to work a party? You can't go in there. It will be swarming with cops."

She has a point.

"So what do we do?"

"Can Luz go in herself? We could wire her up and send her in."

"That's too risky. She's just a kid."

"I can't get an agent up there today. It's too tight."

"Why don't I go with her? Just to meet him. She can always tell him later that I changed my mind."

"I don't think it's a good idea."

I sigh. "Okay. I'll think about it. But we have to move fast."

"Just be smart, okay? Don't take unnecessary risks here."

"I never do," I tell her, even though it's far from true.

I hang up the phone and cross the street in a few long strides. I stare straight ahead, my shoulder aching but held back; I'm careful to move quickly but not too quickly. I won't let him see me sweat. Before I left, I told Elena to lock her door and call me if she felt uncomfortable. As I lock the truck, I wish I had someone to call myself.

I'm pulling away from the curb when my phone rings. It's Lee. I clench my jaw, debating whether or not to answer. I still haven't worked out how I feel about him. On one hand, I don't think he would have dragged me into this investigation if he knew it would lead back to the department. On the other hand, Dorsey's his boss. It's possible that Lee has been watching over me all this time, just like the guy in the sedan.

Curiosity gets the better of me, as it usually does.

"What's up, Lee?" I turn the phone on speaker and pull out onto Pulaski Street. It only takes a second for the sedan to do the same. I speed through a yellow light, testing him. He guns his engine so as not to lose me, causing an oncoming driver to lean on his horn.

"Where are you, Nell?"

"Riverhead. Why?"

"Morales confessed to both murders."

"I heard. Shouldn't you be out celebrating?"

"Dorsey's organizing something tonight. Hank's place, five o'clock. He wants you to be there."

"Great. Can't wait for that."

"We really need to talk."

"I'll be there tonight."

"Can you meet before that?"

"I'm a bit tied up right now, to be honest." I glance back in my rearview mirror. The sedan's still there, despite my foot pressing down on the accelerator like lead. I'm doing nearly eighty in a forty-five zone, and it's possible I have a cop on my tail. I probably shouldn't have picked up the phone.

"I ran a check on the clothes. From Adriana's closet."

"Oh yeah?"

"A woman named Manon Boucher purchased them. She works for James Meachem."

"Mm-hmm."

I can't focus on what Lee is saying with this asshole on my rear. I consider my options. It could be anyone. One of Dorsey's guys, keeping tabs on me. It could also be Giovanni Calabrese or someone who works for him. Maybe he checks out his girls before he sends them out to work. It's possible it's one of Dmitry Novak's henchmen, here to finish what we started a month ago, but I doubt it. Novak's a trained killer. If he wanted me dead, I'd be dead. I wouldn't see him coming, either.

"Also, I tracked down some info on the woman you mentioned. Maria Cruz."

"Oh yeah? Do you know where she is?"

"I think she's in Miami. Let's talk about it in person."

"Fine. I'll see you at Hank's tonight."

"Okay. Are you all right? You sound tense."

As he says it, I swerve from the middle lane onto the exit for Hampton Bays. I skate in front of an SUV, its fender barely missing the broadside of my truck. Horns go off all around me, but I don't care. I can't care. If the sedan gets me alone on an empty stretch of road, there's no telling what will happen. As I turn onto the roundabout, I see the sedan fly past. The driver's head swivels around. I smile and give him a wave. He'll be back, I'm sure. But for the time being, it feels good to be alone.

"Yeah, everything's okay," I say, exhaling slowly. "It's just been a long day."

"For you and me both."

"Listen, I need another favor."

"What can I do?"

"A car's been following me around all day. Maybe it's nothing, but I want to be sure. Could you run the plate for me? It's a New York plate, HB-778."

"Yeah, I'll do it now. See you tonight."

WHEN I PULL into the lot outside of Ty Haines's garage, I cut the engine and sit still, listening to the rush of traffic on the Sunrise Highway. My heart is pounding. It takes me a minute to unwrap my fingers from the steering wheel. I've lost my tail, at least for now. I have to assume he'll find me again soon. Next time, he might get aggressive.

Ty Haines's place is one of a handful of auto-body shops in town, but it was the only place Dad trusted to take care of his bikes. Ty, like my dad, was a Marine Corps vet and a collector of classic motorcycles. He approached them with the same meticulous touch that my father did; a tenderness that I can only describe as love. When my father was having trouble finding a new part or fixing something on his own, he'd take the bike over to Ty's. Some Saturdays, I'd come along. I'd watch them tinker together in near silence, amusing myself with whatever I found around the shop.

I find Ty in the back, lying beneath the carriage of a vintage Aston Martin. I wait until he slides himself out so as not to startle him. When he sees me, his face lights up.

"Look at you," he says, pushing himself up to stand. He opens his arms and wraps me up, holding me for an extra second or two. "It's real good to see you. Man, the last time was, what, ten years ago?"

"Something like that. It's good to see you, too. Thanks for doing this."

"You kidding? Anything for you."

"This a bad time?"

"No. I was going to call you today. Follow me. I want to show you something."

I follow Ty past a row of cars to the rear door of the

garage. There's a small yard out back, with tarps set up to cover spare parts from the rain. At the edge of the property, there's a shed with a padlocked door. Ty pops the lock and ushers me inside. A shaft of light filters through the screened-in window, glinting off the silver body of my father's bike. It lies on its side on a drop cloth, like a patient undergoing surgery.

"I want to talk straight to you, Nell."

"I'd appreciate it."

"I'm no crime lab expert, but looks to me like someone cut your dad's brake line."

"You're sure?"

Ty grimaces. I can read the answer in his face. "It's a clean cut. Look, I can show you." He squats down, beckons me to do the same. "See this here?"

"Yep."

"Brakes usually fail when there's rust from poor maintenance. Now, you and I both know your dad. He kept his bikes in pristine condition. And there's no sign of rust in the fluid. Everything is in perfect working order, except the line is severed clean across."

I stare at the brake. It looks like a bone that's snapped in half. Ty doesn't need to explain it to me: I can see it myself. The cut was intentional. The intent was murder.

"Any idea who would do a thing like this?" he asks.

"I have a few ideas." I stand up. "Listen, Ty, can you keep this between us? Don't let anyone know you have this bike in your shop. Okay?"

"Of course. Between us. That's why I have it out back here."

"Do you mind keeping it for a day or two?"

"Nope. No one comes back here but me." He crosses his arms and stares down at me, his brow furrowed. "You gonna be okay? Maybe you should call one of your dad's buddies from the force."

"No. I'll be fine. This is something I need to handle on my own."

"Listen. Whoever did this to your dad's bike meant business, so be careful. Watch your back. I don't want to see you getting hurt."

"That makes two of us."

As I walk away from Ty's garage, I dial Luz's number. There's no time to lose.

"Call Giovanni," I tell her. "Tell him we'll come by tomorrow."

"Okay," she says. I can hear the fear in her voice. "And then what?"

"You just have to introduce me, that's it. I'll take care of everything else. By the time I'm meeting with him, I'll make sure you and your brother are on your way into protective custody."

"Be careful. Gio's got a temper. He's not someone you want to piss off."

I cock the phone between my ear and shoulder to check my weapon. "I get it. But listen, Luz: neither am I."

21.

The parking lot outside of Hank's is mostly empty. I pull in next to Dorsey's Jeep and wait, hoping that Lee will materialize. It's a few minutes past. It's possible he's already inside. I stash my weapon in the glove compartment. I check my phone one last time and step out of the car. My breath crystalizes in the cold night air. I turn up my collar, shove my hands in my pockets. In the distance, I hear a motorboat out on the bay and the whir of traffic crossing over the Ponquogue Bridge.

The lights are on inside. There isn't any music playing, at least not yet, and if a crowd has gathered, it's a small one. I push the door open and scan the room. It's empty but for the back booth, where two men sit in close conversation.

Their heads swivel as I enter. Dorsey and DaSilva. They stand to greet me. I glance sideways at the bar, hoping to see Hank, at least. He's not there. No one is. The whole joint is empty except for me and the two men.

"Hey, Nell, glad you could join us," Dorsey says. His voice is congenial. Friendly, even. Still, there's something off about him, about this whole scene. As he strides toward me with a thin-lipped grin, my stomach tightens in fear.

"Can I get you a drink? Bar's open."

"Am I early? Or late?"

"Neither. You're right on time."

"Where's Hank?"

"He stepped out. We asked him to give us the place for the night. I'm sure some other guys will be along shortly."

I consider the distance to my truck and then from the parking lot to the road. I won't get far. The parking lot is empty and surrounded by boats on dry docks. If Dorsey wants to shoot me right here, right now, he can. Most likely, no one will hear it.

DaSilva stands at the back of the bar, his thick arms crossed against his chest. With angry, blunt features and a reddish face, DaSilva always looks like the kind of guy that's out for a fight. Of Dad's friends, he was the only one who lingered in the Third Precinct. Maybe he liked the violence. Maybe he hated the residents. Even as a child, I was aware that my mother didn't like him or maybe, more accurately, that they didn't like each other. I think about the way Luz's face soured when she said his name.

"Take a seat," DaSilva says, more of a command than an offer. "Let's have a chat."

I do as I'm told. I didn't want to excite anyone by showing up armed, but now I realize that might have been a foolish decision. Then again, I'm outnumbered. Even if I had a weapon, I'm not sure it would do me any good. I wonder if there's a chance that Lee is going to show up. He could be running late. Or maybe he sold me out. Heat rises to my cheeks as I consider that possibility. I've always sensed there is something amiss about Lee, about the quick way he drew me in and tried to befriend me. It's my fault. I should've known better. Right now, I shouldn't trust anyone at all.

"What can I get you?" Dorsey says from behind the bar.

"I'm fine."

"Oh, come on, Nell. Have a drink with us at least. We're celebrating."

"Okay. I'll have a Macallan neat."

"Just like your old man."

"I heard he was on the wagon, actually."

Dorsey chuckles. "Who told you that?"

"Hank. In fact, he said Dad was sober the night he died." I look at DaSilva. "He was supposed to meet you that night, right? But you didn't show?"

"No. I don't think so. Must've been a mix-up." DaSilva frowns. A vein pulses at his left temple. He's not a particularly convincing actor.

"Well, it got me thinking about his accident."

"Thinking what, exactly?"

"Well, if he wasn't drunk, maybe it wasn't an accident after all."

"What does that mean?"

"It means maybe someone cut his brakes."

"Who would do that?"

"All cops have enemies."

DaSilva swallows. "That's true. But it was a foggy night. And it was late. And the curve where he crashed was a tricky one. They oughta put a sign up. It can sneak up on you if you're not paying attention."

"Yeah. A sign."

Dorsey sets the drink down in front of me. He slides into the booth next to DaSilva, breaking the tension between us.

"Cheers," I say, raising my glass. I look Dorsey in the eye as he raises his drink and touches the rim to mine. "To Dad."

"To Marty."

"Your dad worked that Pine Barrens case for a year. He'd be proud of you."

"For what?"

"For helping out with the Morales arrest. You finished what he started."

"Did I? He didn't think Morales did it."

Dorsey shakes his head. "That's not true. He just couldn't prove it."

"What were you doing at Elena Marques's house today?" DaSilva asks, impatient. He's tipped his hand, but he doesn't care. That alarms me. I sit up straight, unnerved.

"Elena told me a cop had come to her house the day she filed the missing persons report. This cop had the same last name as me. Flynn. Now, why do you suppose my father did that? Go pay a visit to a missing girl's family?"

DaSilva glances at Dorsey. They both shift in their seats, unsettled by this information.

"She'd only been missing a day or two; there was no reason to suppose she was dead. Unless, of course, he knew she was dead. So I started to worry that maybe he was the one who killed her."

"That's way out of line," Dorsey snaps. He holds up a finger, a warning.

"It occurred to me, as I drove around in Dad's red pickup, that maybe the truck Elena said she saw outside the house wasn't Morales's truck. Maybe it was Dad's. And maybe the truck that turned up in the parking lot where Ria Sandoval went missing was Dad's, too. I went over there to show her the truck. See if she recognized it."

Dorsey is seething. His face has frozen in a mask of rage. His hands are fists, white-knuckled and resting on the table. I push back against the wooden booth, aware that he wants to hit me. If he does, I'm done for. I can't take him and DaSilva. Still, I can't stop myself. I've thrown them off guard, and right now, that's the only thing I have going for me.

"Elena mentioned that Dad took Adriana's phone with him, that night he was at their house. That phone isn't in evidence. I checked. Why would he take her phone? Unless he was covering something up. So I started doing a little digging. Turns out Dad was getting kickbacks from Giovanni Calabrese. The same guy who was pimping out

Ria and Adriana. Ten thousand a month, straight into an offshore account. Do you see where I'm going with this?"

"You don't know what you're talking about," Dorsey says.

"See, the bank account in the Caymans is mine now. And to be honest, I'm happy to have the money. But I just want to know what it was for. If Dad killed those girls, then it's not right for me to keep that account. I do have some standards, you know?"

"Morales killed those girls. End of story."

"Don't you want to know what Elena said about the truck?"

"No!" Dorsey shouts. His fist bangs hard on the table. Even DaSilva flinches. "I don't give a fuck what Elena Marques thinks she saw. Your father did not kill Adriana Marques. And he didn't kill Ria Sandoval, either. Why would he? That's crazy."

"Well, that was my question. For the record, it *was* his truck she saw outside her house. He was watching Adriana right before he died. And of course, Dad was a lefty. And an expert marksman. From where I'm sitting, he's the most obvious suspect you have."

"What was his motive? Those girls made him money!" The words tumble angrily out of his mouth before he can stop them. Our eyes meet. He's fucked up and he knows it.

Holy fuck. Dorsey just admitted that my father was involved. *I need to record this.* I'm too frightened to reach for my phone. One wrong move and it's over.

"What's Morales's motive?" I say, trying to keep my cool.

"Morales is a pig with a violent temper."

"Come on. We both know Dad had a hell of a temper himself. And he had a lot to lose. Maybe those girls decided to come clean about Calabrese's business. That would cause a lot of trouble. Or maybe they just reminded him of my mother? Let's just be honest and admit that neither of us was ever really sure what happened there, either."

Dorsey hops to his feet and leans over the table, glowering down at me. "Enough," he hisses. "You're out of your fucking mind. Martin Flynn was a good man and a good cop. One of the best."

"Aren't you tired of covering for him? Seriously. You framed Sean Gilroy twenty-one years ago. And now Morales? All for what? What's the point, now that Dad's dead?"

"You should be fucking thanking me for what I've done for your father."

My lips part. My breath catches. "What did you do?" I whisper. "That's all I want to know. Did you cover for him? Did you set Gilroy and Morales up because you were protecting him? I'll never tell a goddamn soul, I swear. But I need to know who my father was. What happened to my mother that night? Don't I deserve to know?"

I begin to cry. I put my face in my hands, my shoulders shaking. It's not an act. The guys can tell. I can feel the tension deflate, like air rushing out of a balloon.

Dorsey relents. "Vince, why don't you give me and Nell a minute, okay?"

Vince hesitates.

"Vince."

"You sure, Chief?"

"I'm sure. Wait for me outside, okay?"

Vince flips a toothpick up from his pocket and into his teeth. "Sure thing, boss." Dorsey stands up and lets Vince out. I feel his eyes on me, but I don't look up. I wipe my eyes with the sleeve of my sweatshirt and shove my hands deep into my pockets. One hand closes around my phone. *Now. I have to do this now.*

I wait until the door bangs shut. "Do you think I could have another drink?"

"'Course." Dorsey walks over to the bar. "Macallan?"

"Just some water. Thanks. I really appreciate it." I pull out my phone, pretend to be checking it. Instead, I turn on the audio record button and slip it back into my pocket.

Dorsey returns and sits across from me. He pushes the water across the table. "Look at me, Nell."

I look up. Dorsey's eyes soften at the corners. He smiles then. "You remind me so much of Marty."

"People keep telling me that. It's probably not a good thing."

He chuckles. "It is. He was stubborn as hell. But he was a good guy. Cared a lot about truth and justice and all that."

"Did he kill her? Did he kill my mom?"

He lets out a long sigh. He folds his hands on the table and closes his eyes for a minute. "I don't know, Nell. And that's the God's honest truth. The only person who really knows what happened that night is you."

"I was seven years old."

"I know that. No one would blame you if you lied to protect him. Or maybe you didn't know what happened. You were young. It was late. You were confused. That's understandable, too."

"I really don't know. I can't remember. Believe me, I've tried." I've never told anyone that, not in so many words. Tears rush down my face, sliding onto the table in fat, hot drops. "I don't think he left our tent. But you know how, if you tell yourself a lie enough times, you start to believe it to be true?"

Dorsey reaches across the table and extends his hand, palm up. I look at it, and then back at him. I put my hand in his. He squeezes it, and a shiver runs through my body.

"Yeah," he says. "I do."

"That's how I feel about that weekend."

"It's okay, sweetheart. I know. When we talked to you at the station, I could tell you weren't sure what happened. And so I worried. I worried that maybe Marty did something stupid. You know she was leaving him, don't you?"

"No," I say, stunned. "I didn't."

"I'm sorry. Shit. I shouldn't have said—"

"Just tell me the truth. That's all I want. Just closure."

Dorsey nods. He chews his lip for a few long seconds and stares off into the mid-distance. "Your mother met someone," he says finally. "Another cop. She'd just told Marty. They weren't happy, Nell. Hadn't been for years. They weren't right for each other. She was all passion, and he was . . . well, you know who he was. He wasn't the best husband, to tell you the truth. He didn't cheat on her, nothing like that. But he put work first, every time. He would miss important things like her birthday. Your birthday."

"I remember," I say, my voice small.

"But he didn't see it coming, I guess. He just had his head in the sand. Marisol told him she wanted out and Marty went ballistic. Charged into the office screaming that we'd all betrayed him, that we all must have known. I think he felt blindsided. He took it out on everyone in striking distance. He punched a hole in the wall right next to my desk. We were all pretty worried about him after that. He took off for a couple of days and I wasn't sure if he was coming back. Do you remember that?"

I shake my head. I don't. And yet, something deep in the recesses of my memory stirs. A door slamming. The sound of my parents arguing downstairs. My father's motorcycle engine firing up, and then whirring off down the street until the house fell silent and all I could hear was my mother whispering to someone on the phone and the buzz of cicadas out on the lawn.

"He came back, of course. A few days later. He told me he was taking you camping that weekend. He was going to give Marisol some space, to think things over. I actually thought that was a good idea. Everyone needed to cool down. But then . . . well, you know. She was murdered that weekend. And so of course, I thought about it. Could he have done that? Did he have it in him? It scared me, but the answer was yes. I thought he was capable of that kind of rage."

"Did you ask him?"

"Of course. I said, 'Marty, I'm only going to ask you once.' And he looked me straight in the eye and swore to me that he didn't do it. I wanted to believe him. More than anything. He was my best friend. And Marisol—your mom—she was . . ." His eyes glaze over with tears.

Suddenly, I understand.

"Did you love her?" I whisper.

"Very much."

"Did she love you?"

"I think so. Yes. I think she did."

"And so you felt responsible."

"Of course I did. Your dad never knew that it was me she'd fallen for. She didn't have the heart to tell him. And neither did I. So it was my fault. It was all my fault. If we hadn't—if I just hadn't . . ." He shakes his head, unable to finish the sentence.

I believe him. "There's no point in thinking that way now," I say, my voice softening.

"I'll tell you something, Nell. I looked into his eyes and asked him if he killed Marisol, and a part of me thought, *I will kill him if he so much as laid a finger on her.* I loved that woman. I was heartbroken myself. But he said no. And I believed him. I still believe him."

"And Gilroy?"

"A neighbor—the woman across the street, the one who called 911—remembered seeing Gilroy leaving your house. We went straight there. The kid was covered in her blood. He was wearing your father's clothes. He couldn't explain how he ended up in the house, or why his fingerprints were on the knife. Did I lean on him in the interrogation room? Yeah, I did. But only because I knew he did it and I wanted it to be over. For Marty's sake. For your sake. It just needed to be over. You see that, right?"

Dorsey looks tired. He pinches the skin between his eyes, massaging the place where his brows come together. "I did what I thought was right," he says, more to himself than to me. "And I stand by that decision."

"And what about Morales? Did he kill those girls?"

"Your dad didn't, that's for sure. Look, the business with Calabrese. Your dad needed that money. He'd gotten himself into some trouble, financially speaking. He had debts to pay. He asked me for help and I gave it to him. He wouldn't kill those girls. All that would do was stir up trouble."

"Did you lean on Morales, Glenn?"

"I lean on people who deserve to be leaned on."

"Are you sure Morales killed them? You don't sound sure."

"He had something to do with it. I'm sure of that. Maybe he didn't shoot them, but he sure as hell chopped them up."

"Who do you think shot them? It can't be Morales. He's not tall enough. He's not a lefty. You must have an idea."

"I don't know. Maybe it was Calabrese. Look, we heard rumors that there was an investigation into the department. Everyone was getting a little nervous. Calabrese runs a tight ship. I don't know what Marty was doing hanging around Adriana's house after she went missing, but I never once thought he killed her. And I'll be damned if I let anyone—especially you—drag his name through the mud."

I raise my hands. "I don't want to drag anyone's name through the mud. Especially not Dad's. I just needed to know what happened to my mother. And now I do. So thank you for your honesty."

"This is Lee's fault. He shouldn't have pulled you into this."

"Is Lee involved with Calabrese?"

Dorsey snorts. "No way. That kid's a Boy Scout. Look, Calabrese would be doing what he was doing with or without us. You gotta understand that. So what if he slipped us a few dollars to look the other way? What's the harm? Your dad was getting his life in order. Eventually, he was planning to tuck some money away for you."

I inhale sharply. He's just confirmed everything on tape. "I get it," I say slowly, trying not to react. "Look, I'm not complaining."

"We work our fucking asses off. And we get paid like dogs."

"You deserve better."

"Damn straight. You think it's easy to manage a department? I have guys quitting all the time because they can't live off what we get paid. How can you ask some kid to put his life on the line every day if he can hardly afford the mortgage on his house? Suffolk County is so damn expensive. Working folks can't afford to live here anymore. These rich people, they want us to cater to them. But where are we supposed to live? Where can our kids go to school? The way I see it, this is what we're owed. I'm just trying to even the playing field a little for my guys."

I think about Luz's house in Brentwood. About Elena living across from the cemetery in Riverhead. About Adriana and Ria, selling their bodies so their families can eat. In that moment, rage wells up inside me. I want to grab Dorsey's neck and snap it. I want to hurt him the way he hurt those girls. He deserves it.

"The world is not fair," I say carefully.

"No. It's not. I have to make sure my best guys are taken care of. And then they stay. And everyone's happy." Dorsey shakes his head, like he can't stand the inequity of it. "Anyway, it's over. We buried your dad. Let the man rest in peace." He rises to his feet. "I should be getting home. I think you should do the same."

I stand, my legs trembling beneath me. Dorsey reaches out, puts his hand on my elbow. It takes all my strength not to pull away.

"Be safe, Nell. I wouldn't want anything to happen to you. I've lost enough people I care about."

"I think it's time I head back to DC."

Dorsey nods. "That makes sense. It's for the best. I love you, sweetheart. Don't forget that."

DASILVA IS GONE. The parking lot is empty. When I start up my truck, the engine sputters. I panic and cut the ignition. For a minute, I sit still, paralyzed. I focus on my breath, trying to slow it to a normal rate. My head is spinning. The realization that Glenn Dorsey loved my mother—and that she might have loved him back—shakes me to my core. And yet, it makes a certain amount of sense. Dorsey was always around. Even when Dad wasn't home, I would find him unloading grocery bags for Mom or fixing the boiler for her. After she died, he watched over me with the protectiveness of a second father. I used to think his attachment to me—to us—was born out of his love for Dad. Now I realize I was wrong. He loved my mother more.

How could Dad not have known? Did he ever suspect that Dorsey had feelings for my mother? Had he ever glanced across the room at a party and seen them sharing a laugh together and wondered? Had he seen my mother flex onto her tiptoes and kiss Dorsey on the cheek, her lips lingering just a half second too long against his skin?

It's hard for me to believe that Dad wouldn't have sensed what was happening between them. Dad was incredibly perceptive. He could sit in a blind for hours just waiting and watching the trees before he executed a deer with one single, perfect shot. His intuition made him a skilled hunter and a first-rate detective. So how could it have failed him so miserably at home? But then, if he had known about them, how could he have worked side by side with Dorsey for so many years without wanting to murder him? Dad, like Dorsey, was tough, cutthroat, and prone to rage. Wouldn't the tension between them have eventually boiled over into violence?

Maybe it did. Maybe Dorsey cut Dad's brakes himself. I picture my father getting on his bike for that last ride.

Did he have time to realize what had happened? Had he felt it coming?

I take a breath and turn the key again. This time the engine starts up without a hitch. Still, fear rises in my throat. *Breathe, breathe*, I tell myself, fighting the urge to panic.

As I cross the Ponquogue Bridge, I call Lee. I can't help feeling like he left me there on purpose. The thought enrages me. As angry as I am with Lee, I'm even more so with myself for trusting him. Maybe he wasn't involved in Giovanni Calabrese's enterprise. But there's something Lee isn't telling me about himself. Given that I almost died tonight as a result of his damn investigation, I feel like he owes me some answers.

"Nell?"

"Where were you?" I snap when he answers.

"I went to see Milkowski. She wasn't at the lab, so I went to her house and—"

"It was just me, Dorsey, and DaSilva. Not exactly the celebration I was picturing. You left me there. I swear to God, Lee, I thought they were going to kill me."

"I'm sorry. I—"

"Dorsey admitted to everything. His involvement with Calabrese. How he forced a confession out of Morales. The ends justify the means in his world."

"Nell."

"I recorded it all. I want you to have it in case anything happens to me, okay? I know you probably think I'm being paranoid, but I have a bad feeling. The brakes on my dad's bike were cut. His death was no accident."

"Nell, you have to shut up. Please. Listen to me. Jamie Milkowski is dead."

"What?" I slam on the brakes, and the tires squeal angrily on the road. I pull the car over to the side and put it into park. "When?"

"A few hours ago. A hit-and-run, not too far from her office."

"Holy fuck. They killed her, too, didn't they?"

"I think so. She and Dorsey had a shouting match this morning. She said there was no way Morales was the shooter and Dorsey was just sweeping her report under the rug. I heard her tell him she was going to the press."

"Oh my God. She did. She spoke to a journalist earlier today."

"Who?"

"Ann-Marie Marshall. You have to find her. Make sure she's okay."

"Nell, where are you? I'm worried. Let me come get you."

"I just turned onto Dune Road. I'll be home in a few minutes."

"I'll meet you there."

"I'm fine, Lee."

"No. You're not fine. We have to get you out of Suffolk County. Tonight. Everyone who touches this investigation ends up dead."

22.

At home, I lock every door and window. I check my Smith & Wesson. I place a second loaded handgun in my nightstand, just in case. When I hear the rumble of car wheels on the drive, I peer out through a slit between the curtains. My pulse slows a little when I see that it's Lee. His face is drawn. Deep circles are printed beneath his eyes. He's wearing an SCPD sweatshirt with a coffee stain down the front. He holds two large foam cups in his hands. I'm not sure he's slept or showered since I saw him last.

"You look like shit," I tell him when I open the door.

"You don't look so great yourself."

"It's been a long few days. Thanks so much for pulling me into this mess."

"Sorry. Misery loves company." He hands me a coffee. "I figured you could use one, too."

"I was going to offer you a scotch, but this is probably a better idea."

"Let's keep our wits about us for the time being, shall we?"

"Come in. Let's sit outside." I lead Lee to the deck. I have no reason to think the house is bugged, but that's how my suspicious mind works. Anyway, the rain has cleared. The chairs are still damp, but that's fine. The fresh, cold air fills my lungs. Overhead, chevrons of geese move across the fading blue-gray sky. I switch on the porch lights. I scan the sawgrass for egrets but see none. It occurs to me that we're about to slip into October: height of hurricane season. The beginning of the migration.

"So first things first. I traced the plate number," Lee says. "You want to tell me what Vince DaSilva's doing tailing you around town?"

"Maybe you should ask him."

"That's probably not the best idea. I'm kind of persona non grata around the office right now."

"You? The hometown hero?"

"Dorsey's got strong opinions about this case. If you hadn't noticed."

"And you disagree with his opinions?"

Lee swills his coffee before answering. "Your dad didn't believe that Morales was the guy. Personally, I think Morales was involved. But he's just the muscle. Someone paid him to dispose of those bodies."

"But he confessed. So case closed. At least, that's what Dorsey said to me earlier today."

Lee sighs. "It's not that simple."

"So case not closed?"

"No. Not for me. Look, if I tell you something, can you promise it will stay between us?"

We lock eyes. "I've got no one to tell."

"I don't know what happened in that interrogation room. It was just Dorsey and Morales. Video feed was switched off."

"Intentionally?"

"Yes. Dorsey switched it off himself. He looked me in the eye when he did it. Like he was daring me to say something."

"Did you?"

"Of course not. He's the fucking chief of D's. What am I supposed to say: 'Hey, Chief, that's not proper protocol'?"

"Did Morales have counsel?"

"No. Either he never asked, or if he did, Dorsey ignored him. All I know is, they were in there for less than an hour. And when they walked out, Dorsey had a signed confession from Morales stating that he killed both girls."

"Jesus. You think he roughed him up?"

"Worse. I think he paid him off."

I sit up, alert. "You think Morales is taking the fall on purpose?"

"Less than an hour, Nell. It takes me more than that to just write up a fucking confession. This was typed up, signed, sealed, and delivered. I think the whole thing was prearranged."

"Why the whole showdown at the farm, then? Morales was armed. Someone could've gotten hurt."

"Theatrics. Some woman happened to be there to videotape it? Come on, Nell. Think about it." He crosses his arms, shoots me a look.

I slump back in my chair. "Oh my God. I almost shot him, you know. I could have killed Morales."

"If you had, even better. Problem solved."

"But why? Why would Morales agree to take the rap for two murders? He'll either get deported or he'll spend the rest of his life rotting in jail."

"I don't know. Either someone paid him a ton of money, or else he made sure his family gets citizenship. Those are the only two things I could think of."

"Come on. Dorsey's powerful, but not that powerful. And he's not rich, either."

"He's not. But the people he's covering for are." Lee gives me a look. "I know you know about Giovanni Calabrese and his arrangement with certain members of the department. Calabrese has got sway. And his clients are incredibly rich, very powerful, and definitely motivated to make sure the whole operation doesn't get exposed."

I raise my eyebrows. "I didn't realize you knew that cops were on Calabrese's payroll."

"I've known for a while."

"Why didn't you tell me?"

"I had to decide whether or not I trusted you first."

"You kept pointing the finger at Morales. Why?"

"Because I think he did it. Or at least, I think he helped. But I've also been playing along with what Dorsey wanted me to do and say. It's the only way I could stay inside the department. And that's always been my goal. To investigate the department."

"Wait. Are you telling me that you've been running an investigation into the SCPD this whole time?"

Lee gives me a small smile. He nods. "I'm one of you," he says. "For better or for worse."

"One of who?"

Lee chuckles. "I'm a Fed. Have been for two years now. I'm DEA. I'm part of a joint task force that the Bureau had started to investigate the narcotics operation Dorsey and his guys have been running. I'm their man in Havana, so to speak. Their man in Yaphank."

"Come on!" I let out a sharp laugh. Lee looks wounded. "I'm sorry. I'm not laughing at you. I just—I seriously can't believe it."

"Believe what? That I'm a federal agent and not some local cop?" Lee frowns.

"No, I don't mean it like that. I just—look, I'm BAU. It's my fucking job to profile people. I always thought you seemed like a bit of a misfit in homicide. Too, I don't know, nerdy? Intellectual?"

"Thanks so much."

"But I never in a million years would have figured you for the mole."

"I prefer the term *undercover*."

"You know what I mean. Why didn't you tell me right away?"

"Because Dorsey's your fucking godfather! Think about it, Nell. I was hoping you'd be on my team here, but I couldn't be sure. It never occurred to me things would escalate this quickly. And you kind of threw me for a loop when you started suspecting your own dad. That wasn't a possibility I'd even considered."

"So what *was* Dad's role in Calabrese's organization? Be honest."

Lee shakes his head. "That was the best break I've had. Total coincidence. I knew what was going on with Dorsey and DaSilva. Narcotics, prostitution, they had their hands in everything. Your dad wanted none of it, and Dorsey respected that. They basically left each other alone.

"Last summer, your dad connected with Maria Cruz. She was one of Calabrese's girls. She's young, maybe nineteen years old. I never understood what their relationship was. I didn't want to ask, and he never brought her up. I only knew about her because I saw them together once and I got curious. Your father seemed pretty devoted to her. He wanted to get her out of that life. He rented her that apartment, got her to enroll in community college. And then he really went on the warpath."

"Meaning what?"

"It was pretty ingenious, really. At first, I thought he was having some kind of a breakdown. He started going out a lot, making a big show of hanging with the boys. Always up to party. And he got into gambling. Big-time."

"That does sound like a breakdown."

"It wasn't. It was all a show. I started watching him pretty closely. He wasn't drinking at all. He'd order one drink, swirl it around, and then switch to soda. He gambled, but never a lot, and never in a way where he was out of control. He did all that so that he could get in with Dorsey and that crew. Eventually, he told Dorsey he'd racked up a bunch of gambling debts. He was desperate for money. And so Dorsey brought him into the fold."

"Did Dad tell you this?"

"No. I was just this annoying newbie who managed to get myself assigned to him. But I was watching him. And I figured out what he was doing."

"What was he doing?"

"He was building a case. My guess is he was recording conversations, taking photos, collecting evidence. And he was watching over the girls. Making sure nothing happened to them. He got a few of them to talk. One of them was Ria. When she was murdered, he totally flipped out. I guess he felt responsible. He became obsessed with solving her murder."

"Oh my God." I slap my hand to my forehead. "Everything makes sense now. That's why he was following Adriana."

"Right. He knew Morales wasn't behind it. He figured Morales might have disposed of the body, but he was just helping the real killer out. He thought it was Dorsey, or Calabrese, or one of the clients. But he couldn't prove it. So he kept at it. And then Adriana went missing, and two weeks later, he was dead."

"That's why you wanted to get into his office."

"I still do."

"There's nothing there. He must have cleaned it out before he died."

"Still might be worth letting me have a look."

I stand up. "Fine. But I'm going to open the scotch, if that's all right with you."

"Whatever it takes."

"Hey." I grab him by the arm, stopping him in his tracks. "Is your mom really sick? I thought you moved back here to be near her."

Lee flushes. "She is. That's true. But to be honest with you, it's a damn good cover. I was hired by DEA straight out of law school. One of my professors recruited me. Then this came up and we all saw it as a good way to get someone inside the department. Dorsey's one of the biggest distributors of narcotics and opioids in New York State. Eighty percent of the shit that's out there on the market is there because he either got paid off by someone or because he's selling it himself. He's a bad guy, Nell. And his team is no better than a cartel."

I nod slowly. "And what about me? Did you just want to get into Dad's office?"

"As opposed to what? Getting into your pants?"

"No!" I snap, before realizing he's joking. "Fuck you."

"No, listen. I was hoping you'd be a partner. I've been here for two fucking years, Flynn. It's been pretty dismal. Dorsey and his cohort are a tight-knit bunch. I thought I'd be able to charm my way in, but it wasn't so easy."

I can't help it, I laugh. "Because you're so suave?"

"Well, yeah. And I'm local. I thought they'd see me as one of their own."

"But they didn't."

"It takes a while to gain Dorsey's trust. I started realizing that my best shot was to befriend someone he was close to. I thought I had an in when I got paired up with your dad. But then he went and died on me. So yeah, I was pretty lonely until you showed up."

"They killed him, Lee. I know it. Who else would cut his brakes?"

"Well, to be fair, your dad was kind of an asshole. I imagine he accumulated more than a few enemies over time."

"Please be serious."

Lee stands up. "My money's on either Dorsey or Calabrese. Come on. Show me the office. We're going to nail their asses to the wall."

23.

I told you. There's nothing in here."

Lee walks another loop around Dad's office. We've been in here for the better part of an hour and found nothing of use.

"What about his apartment in Riverhead?" Lee asks, for the second time.

"We can look again. But I didn't find anything. Anyway, I don't think he would have stored evidence there. It would've put Maria at risk."

Lee shakes his head, frustrated. "I fucked up. I should've been straight with him. We could have worked together."

"Don't do that. Don't blame yourself."

"I tried a couple of times. To tip my hand a little. Show him that we were on the same side. But he just wasn't having it."

"Dad didn't play all that well with others."

Lee sighs. "I know. But I could've just come clean with him."

"That would have been a huge risk. If he told Dorsey, you'd have blown two years of undercover work and maybe gotten yourself killed in the process."

"I know."

We're both quiet for a minute.

"We have Dad's bank statement from Cayman International. That's enough to subpoena Calabrese's financial records. And I have a meeting set with him tomorrow. Luz Molina is going to bring me there."

"That's way too risky. For you and for Luz."

I swallow hard. I know he's right, but I'm desperate. "I have Dorsey basically spilling his guts to me, not just about the forced confessions, but about taking money from Calabrese. That alone is enough to arrest them both."

"But is it enough for a jury?"

"Maybe. I don't know. Maybe not."

"What about Luz? If she can testify . . ."

"She's not going to stand up as a witness. She's a kid. And she's undocumented. A defense attorney will tear her apart on the stand."

"Dorsey is such a prick." Lee scowls. "Imagine preying on a girl like that."

"We need to get her out of here before we start arresting anyone. I promised her I'd get her into protective custody."

"And we will. Look, we have a narrow window here. Maybe twenty-four hours, and that's it. Right about now, Dorsey is probably seriously regretting his little heart-to-heart with you."

"I know. I've thought that."

"Let's call Sarah Patel. And Lightman. We'll get a team mobilized. Tomorrow we go in and seize everything at SCPD and GC Limo."

"We still don't know who killed those girls."

"We could lean on Morales. Or"—Lee snaps his fingers—"we trace his bank accounts. See who paid him off."

"We're leaving a lot to chance. I don't like it. We only have one shot to raid the offices. We better be damn sure we have enough evidence against these guys before we do."

Lee walks over to the map. He leans in, studying it. "Was this always here?"

I step next to him, our shoulders touching. "No. I mean, it wasn't here when I was a kid. Why?"

Lee reaches up and rips it off the wall.

"What the f—" I stop midsentence.

Behind the map, carved out from the wall, is a safe.

"Any chance you know the combination?" Lee says, his voice a near whisper.

"I have a guess," I say. I move forward and press in my mother's birthday, the same combination of numbers that opened his file cabinet. There is a second of silence, followed by a whirring sound. I reach for the handle and pull the safe open.

"Holy shit," we both say at the same time.

Stacked inside the safe are a laptop, a notebook, files, photographs, and a recording device.

"Let's call Sarah now," Lee says. "We need to get a team on this. Tonight."

24.

"I have to hand it to you, Flynn. You somehow managed to stumble into one of the largest raids in Bureau history despite being out on administrative leave."

Lightman is on speakerphone from midair. He and a team of agents from BAU are en route from DC, aboard a private jet that is scheduled to touch down within the hour. We've been up all night, sorting through the photographs, audiotapes, and other evidence my father had accumulated against Dorsey, DaSilva, Anastas, and various other members of the SCPD, as well as Giovanni Calabrese and a handful of associates who kept his prostitution business up and running. There are flash drives filled with pictures of Meachem's parties, which will end the careers and marriages of men around the globe. Sarah is combing through evidence down in Miami, too. We have stacks of financial documents to examine. Even with a team assembled, this may take days, even weeks. But for now, it's enough to arrest half of the detectives in Suffolk County and lock Giovanni Calabrese behind bars for good. I've also negotiated a protective custody arrangement for Luz and her brother, Miguel. After Lee and I oversee the raids this morning, I will take her statement and then get them on a private plane at Gabreski Airport in Westhampton. I will, in all likelihood, never see her again. The thought is a bittersweet one. In the short time I've known her, I've come to care about her. I want to care *for* her. No one else ever has.

"I told you I'm not going to lie on a couch and talk about my childhood," I say to Lightman. He chuckles. He's still mad at me, I can tell. But for now, he's going to let it slide. This case is too big for him to carp at me about protocols.

"Don't think you get to bypass Maloney," he says. "Your leave is still in effect."

"Come on," Lee interjects. "I don't mean to be disrespectful, but Nell's managed to pull together a case against one of the most corrupt police forces in history. She's done in a week what I couldn't do in two years."

"Son, that says more about you than it does about her," Lightman says.

Lee turns crimson. I can't help it: I burst out laughing.

"Oh, shut up," Lee mutters, but he's grinning, too.

"How long do we have to wait?" I ask. I stand up and walk over to the window. It's morning, technically, but it's still dark outside. I haven't slept or eaten, but I feel shot through with nervous energy. "We've started our descent. We'll be on the ground soon. By eight a.m., we will be at both locations."

I want to move now. Every car that passes on Dune Road sends a charge down my spine; every sound from the marsh outside sends my hand straight to my firearm. We have three hours to go: an eternity. Still, I know we're lucky to have such a large team mobilizing so quickly. And for the moment, anyway, Lightman is treating me like I'm back on the team. If everything goes smoothly today, he'll have no choice but to reinstate me. Hell, he should probably give me a fucking promotion.

Sarah dials in. "You guys hanging in there?" she asks. I can hear the fatigue in her voice.

"Hell, yeah." Lee rubs his hands together. "I've been waiting for this for two years."

"You just needed Nell to come in and get the job done."

Lee laughs. "Sam, if you don't need her at the BAU, we sure could use an extra set of hands over at DEA."

"Or down here," Sarah adds. "Human Trafficking Task Force could be your calling, Nell."

"After today, I think I'm going to put in for vacation."

"Okay. We're starting our descent into Gabreski," Lightman announces. "I gotta turn this off. One of you want to drive over here and get us up to speed?"

"I'll go," Lee says. He turns to me. His hand finds its way to my arm. He gives me a soft smile and his fingers tighten around me. I feel my heart contract just a little bit. "You going to be all right?"

"I'll be fine. You go. Call me when we're ready to roll."

"Hey, Nell?"

"Yeah?"

"I'm sorry I ever called you *kid*."

"It's okay."

"No, it's not. I'll come up with something better. Deal?"

"Deal."

He winks. I turn away, unwilling to let him see me blush.

LEE WALKS OUT of the office. A few seconds later, the front door opens and shuts. The house falls silent. I've just started to move again when a deafening boom knocks me flat on my back.

The window of the office shatters. A rush of cold air fills the room, along with the acrid smell of smoke. A piece of paper floats by.

It takes me a few seconds to stand up. My head is whirring with sound and light. My knees give as I do, nearly folding beneath me. I look down at my hands. A shard of glass has embedded itself in my palm. Wincing, I pull it out and wipe the blood down the front of my pants.

I withdraw my weapon and move to the window. I'm having trouble seeing clearly out of my right eye. I reach up and realize it's swollen shut. When I see the smoking black mass in the driveway, I let out a scream. There is a crater in front of my house. Inside it is Lee's car. It's been reduced to a mass of smoldering metal.

Lee, I know, is gone.

25.

In and out.
    In and out.
In and out.

I remind myself to keep breathing as I slip out the back door of my house. My feet sink into the wet sawgrass. I'm wearing a backpack stuffed with as much evidence as I can carry: photographs, audiotapes, financial records. I'm packing two weapons: one at my hip, one at my ankle. I need to get away from the house as fast as I can. I have to assume that Dad's truck, parked across from Lee's, is fitted with the same car bomb that turned my driveway into a moonscape. Whoever rigged it will, no doubt, be back to check their handiwork. They may be watching me already. If they know I'm alive, I am dead woman running. If they don't, I have a narrow window to escape before they return.

It takes me less than five minutes to cross the half acre

of preserved land that borders my house. It's the longest, hardest run of my life. There is no cover in the marsh. Just thick, unwieldy underbrush to push through and pockets of muddied water. My backpack slaps hard against my spine as I move. I feel my left shoe come untied and I have to flex my foot hard to keep it from falling off altogether. I'm breathing so hard my lungs feel like they're on fire. The smell of ash hangs heavy in the air.

I'm halfway across the marsh when a car backfires on Dune Road. I throw myself down into the muck. For a few seconds, I lie still. An egret lifts up into the air, unfolding its wings overhead. Daylight is breaking: a bad sign. I can see a column of smoke rising from in front of my house. The air smells like burnt metal and rubber. Someone will see it; someone will call the police. Soon, cop cars and ambulances will descend on this corner of Dune Road. They may already be on their way.

I get up, keep going. When I reach the other side of the preserve, I take a deep, grateful gulp of air. Then I force my way through the neighbor's hedgerow; I emerge behind the garage. It doesn't appear as though anyone is home. The windows are dark; there are no cars in the drive. I grab the garage door and manually hoist it up. No alarm sounds. Inside, there is an old station wagon, the keys tossed casually on the driver's seat.

I let out a shaky exhale. Thank God for small miracles. My odds of survival just went up.

I slide into the driver's seat and put the keys in the ignition. As I adjust the rearview mirror, I catch sight of myself. My right eye is purple and swollen, like a boxer's after a fight. A cut at my hairline wells with dark blood. I hadn't even noticed it. I reach up and touch it, and wince when my fingers feel a sliver of glass pressed beneath the skin. My fingers probe my scalp. There's clotted blood there, too. I have a dull ring in my ears and I'm starting to feel woozy. Light streaks in front of me. I close my eyes for a second, willing myself not to lose consciousness.

My eyes pop open. I have to go. Light glints off the glass embedded near my hairline. I extract it with my nails, groaning aloud as I do. I blot the blood away with my sleeve; the blood is coming hard and fast now, and I have to stop it. I slip off my T-shirt and tear one sleeve off at the seam. I wrap the fabric as tightly as I can around my head, my eyes welling from tears as I do. Bursts of light pop in front of my eyes; the pain is blinding. I put the car in drive. I don't have time to worry about a few cuts and bruises. Lee is dead. If I don't move, I will be soon, too.

Before I pull onto the street, I take the SCPD baseball cap that Lee lent me at the crime scene and slap it on over my makeshift tourniquet. My head screams with pain, but I need to cover myself. It's hardly a disguise, but at least my face is partially obscured. I'm also driving someone else's car. I'll have to write the neighbors a nice thank-you note when this is all over. *Thank you for letting me steal your car. Please enjoy this bottle of scotch.*

I'm almost to the Westhampton Bridge when I hear sirens. My pulse escalates. I have to fight myself not to press down hard on the accelerator. The speed limit here is an excruciatingly slow thirty-five miles an hour. I flip on the blinker and make my way onto the bridge, just as an ambulance squeals by me, heading east on Dune Road.

My phone is vibrating on the passenger seat. I lean over and turn it onto speaker.

"Nell!" Sarah shouts into the phone. "Where the fuck is Lee? Everyone is on the ground waiting for him. We're ready to go. I've been calling him and he's not picking up."

"He's dead." My words come out heavy and slow. As I drive through town, my vision starts to blur. I blink back what I think are tears; I realize quickly that it's blood. I drive straight through a red light, only half realizing what I'm doing. I should pull over. But then I hear sirens again—maybe a block or two away—and I sit straight up and drive.

In and out. Keep breathing.

"He's *what*? What happened?"

"Car bomb. In my driveway."

"Where are you? Are you hurt?"

"I'm in Westhampton Beach, less than ten minutes from the airport. But I need to go to Brentwood. I have to get Luz."

"You go straight to the airport, do you hear me? Straight there. Sam is there. He'll keep you safe. I'm going to send out the teams now. We have to move."

"Call Luz. Make sure she's safe. She's a key witness, Sarah. They'll get to her. They'll hunt her down."

"I'll take care of her. You just stay alive. You hear me, friend?" She's screaming at me, and yet I hardly hear her.

I'm slipping into an almost dreamlike state, somewhere between waking and unconsciousness.

"I'll be fine," I whisper into the phone, just as it slips through my fingers. My eyes close. The car runs off the road and hits something, hard and fast. The last thing I hear is the hard pop of the airbag deploying. Then there is nothing. Only darkness.

26.

My eyes open. The light is so bright it burns. I let out a small moan and squeeze them shut. I feel my body hurtling through space. A wave of nausea rolls up from my stomach. I turn my face to the side, preparing to vomit.

"Nell." A familiar voice. More urgently this time: "Nell! Can you hear me?"

"Sam?" I croak, peaking through one eye. I can't see anything, it's all a blur. But I can hear him. He's right beside me. I feel a wash of relief.

"Sir, you're going to have to stand back now," an unfamiliar voice dictates. "She's going into surgery."

"Nell! Can you hear me? I'm right here. You're going to be okay."

"Sam!" I try to sit up, but I can't. My head feels like it's made of lead. I force my eyes open. A doctor, wearing a mask, trots alongside me. The white walls pass in the blur. We stop; I hear doors opening. I'm on a stretcher, I realize. Overhead are the halogen lights of a hospital. I don't remember how I got here or how long it's been since I was pulled out of the stolen station wagon. The last thing I remember was the punch of the airbag and the sickening sound of crumpling metal.

"Ma'am." The doctor sounds agitated. "Please try not to move. We're bringing you in for surgery. Everything's fine. Just need to stitch you up. Okay? Try to relax."

"Sam!" I shout. "Where's Lee?"

Lightman doesn't answer. He doesn't have to. In the back of my mind, a voice reminds me: *Lee is dead. Lee's car exploded in the driveway.* The doors swing shut behind us. Someone is adjusting my IV; I feel a warm surge of fluid flooding my veins. My eyes drop closed, and I slip back into a deep, hard sleep.

27.

"There she is."

My eyes flicker open. I look right and then left. Lightman beams at me from my bedside.

I attempt a smile back. Pain radiates through my body. "Where am I?"

"You're at Southampton Hospital. You just came out of surgery. You're going to be just fine."

"What happened?"

"When the car bomb went off in your driveway, the windows shattered. You were cut up pretty badly. You ended up passing out while you were driving to the airport. You've lost a lot of blood. Thank God you were on the phone with Sarah. She knew where you were. I came and got you myself."

"Where is Lee?" I am awake now, alert. Everything comes rushing back. The sound. The smoke. Running across the sawgrass. "Is Lee—"

"He's gone, Nell." Lightman puts his hand on mine. "I'm sorry."

"You're sure?"

He nods. His eyes well up. He takes off his glasses and dabs them dry. "It could've been you, you know. We found one on your truck, too."

For a few seconds, we are both quiet.

"We got them," Lightman says, finally. "We arrested them all."

"Dorsey? Calabrese?"

"Yes. And DaSilva and Anastas. A bunch of others, too."

"What about Meachem?"

"He's out of the country. We can't—"

"Don't tell me he's going to get off for this."

"He's not. He won't. It may just take some time."

"What about the others? The clients? The men at Meachem's parties?"

"We have a lot of evidence, Nell. We're going through it now. This will all come out in due time. The important thing is that we got Dorsey and Calabrese. And they're done for. But you, you need to rest. You've been through a helluva lot."

"What about Luz? Is she safe?"

Lightman nods. "Safe. She and Miguel left from Gabreski a few hours ago. They'll go into protective custody. Luz has been amazing. She's already given us some really helpful information, about Calabrese, the organization, the involvement of the SCPD, and the clients she met at Meachem's."

He pauses. I can tell he's holding something back.

"What is it?"

He sniffs back tears. "You gave me a scare, that's all. I'm glad you're all right."

"Any idea when I can get out of here?"

"Another day or so. I'll arrange for you to come back to DC." He points his finger at me. There are tears sliding down his cheeks. "And this time, you are going to therapy."

I laugh. Then I'm in his arms. I press my face against his chest and let out a sob.

"Lee was a good guy," I whisper.

"He was."

"I need to stay in Suffolk County. Just for a little while."

He gives me a look of exasperation. "Nell—"

"There are just a few things left to do. A few days, tops. I'll be back at my desk next week."

"Nice try. You still need to do the evaluation. And I'm sure Maloney's going to be thrilled when he hears about what you've been up to."

"Oh, fuck Maloney. Tell him there's no point in having me on leave. I end up working, anyway."

"Sarah's worried about you. She wanted to come see you."

"She's got enough going on. I'll give her a call when I get out of this place."

"Where will you go? You can't stay at your dad's house."

I shrug. "It's my house now. It's time to pack it up and say goodbye."

28.

Thunk. Thunk. Thunk.

    My hammer hits a nail square on, pinning another shingle to the roof. The row is finished. Just three more to go.

I sit back on my haunches, admiring my handiwork. When I began this project a week ago, I thought I'd just cover the leaks and replace the rot. I found the work enjoyable, almost meditative. I didn't want to stop. It's hard, certainly. I do it in small bits, an hour or two at a time. When I see the new shingles, when I hold them in my hand and feel their clean, straight edges and their heft, twice as dense as the old ones, I can't help but think the whole damn roof needs replacing. I have the time. I like saving the money. And I really enjoy the view. From up here, I can see over the dunes to the ocean. On a clear day, I can see past the looming arc of the Ponquogue

Bridge all the way to the rocky point of Shinnecock County Park.

As it turns out, I'm pretty good at home repairs. Once I was released from the hospital, I got a contractor to put in new windows, but I fixed the boiler and the fridge on my own. Next, I want to tackle the deck. The stairs creak and the railing isn't sturdy. Lightman tells me I should hire someone to do the outside work, especially now that it's getting so cold. But I enjoy being outside. It's like physical therapy for my shoulder. Every day, I feel myself getting stronger.

Before I returned home, Lightman made sure that any trace of Lee's car was removed. The driveway was repaired; new gravel filled it. There is still a shallow indent where the explosion occurred. I want to leave it that way. I think about him every time I see it.

I haven't yet decided what to do with the house. Maybe I'll list it in the New Year. For now, I'm content to live in it as I fix it up. As Dr. Ginnis says, I'm taking it one day at a time. I speak to him most mornings, usually for longer than either of us expect. He tells me that he'll sign my medical evaluation form whenever I'm ready to go back. For the time being, he isn't pushing me. Neither is Lightman.

Thunk. Thunk. Thunk.

I have just started another row of shingles when I hear a car pulling into the driveway. I stand up, shield my eyes from the late afternoon light. Sarah Patel emerges from a gray sedan. She wears black jeans and motorcycle boots, just like the first time I met her.

"Sarah!" I call out. I wave when she looks up.

"You're unbelievable," she says, shaking her head. "You're supposed to be in bed! What the hell are you doing up there?"

"Just a little home repair." I laugh. "I'll be down in a sec."

We hug by the front door. After a few seconds, she pulls back, holding me at arm's length.

"Well, we obviously need to fatten you up. But all things being equal, you look pretty good."

"You, too. You didn't need to come. You must be exhausted."

She makes a face. "Oh, please. I've been meaning to visit you for weeks. But this investigation . . . well, you know. You really opened Pandora's box, my friend."

"Come sit. I want to hear all about it. First, though, I have something for you."

In the living room, I set a log on the andirons and light a fire. We settle on the couch, Sarah on one end with her boots off and her feet tucked up beneath her, me on the other with a blanket draped across my waist. The fire crackles, filling the room with light and heat.

I take off the cross from around my neck and hand it to her. "This belonged to Adriana Marques. She's wearing it in the photos my dad took of her."

She turns it over, examining it. "It's lovely," she says. I can tell she doesn't understand why I want her to have it.

"It's a recording device."

"Oh!" Her eyes widen, amazed.

"I didn't realize at first, either. But it kept bothering

me: why did Dad have it? Last night, it occurred to me: of course. She was recording all of her meetings for him. Look here." I point at a small gold ball at the back, no bigger than a pinhead. "This is it."

"Wow. Thank you. I will get this to the team as soon as possible." She tucks it into her bag. Then she hands me a folder. "I have something for you, too."

"What's this?"

"Film stills of one of Meachem's parties. From the video footage inside his Palm Beach home. Some heavy hitters in attendance."

I open it and start to flip through them. I whistle. "You're not kidding. Half of Washington is at this one."

"As I said. Pandora's box."

I stop on one photo in particular. It shows a cluster of people gathered by the edge of the pool. The men wear suit jackets, linen pants. The women—girls, really—are in cocktail dresses and high heels, their lithe bodies cast into relief by the setting sun.

I inhale sharply when I see a face I recognize. My head spins as I process this new information. Of course. The answer has been in front of me all along. Now I have to prove it.

I shut the folder.

"Any more arrests?" I ask.

"A few. The police commissioner down in Palm Beach—I think I told you about that one. A few of his underlings. Thanks to you, we went back into the Palm Beach records and found two Jane Does that were murdered in the same way as Ria and Adriana. They both fit the profile to a *T*. We were able to match one of the bodies to a missing person. Heather Valdez, a seventeen-year-old from West Palm."

"And the other?"

"Still working on it, but the records are spotty. We may not get lucky there."

"Where is Meachem?"

"No trace. We're looking."

"Bastard. Calabrese doesn't have any connection to the Florida girls, does he?"

"No. Calabrese's just local. There's a Calabrese equivalent down in Florida. A pimp named Joe Lentz. He supplied girls to Meachem. He's in custody. He's not talking yet, but we'll see."

She pauses then, pressing her lips together as if deep in thought.

"What is it?"

"There's someone I want you to talk to. Not right away. Just when you're ready."

"Sure. Who?"

"Maria Cruz. I met with her yesterday. She wants to meet you."

"Oh." I sit forward. "Of course. I can fly down there."

"No need. She's coming back to Suffolk County in the next day or so to give her deposition. She's been really helpful with the investigation."

"Shouldn't she be in protective custody?"

"We are protecting her. She's a key witness against

Dorsey and Calabrese. I want you to meet her. It's important. There are things about her I think you should know."

"Anytime. I want to. First, though, finish telling me about the case." I stand up and walk over to the sliding glass doors. I stare out at the fallow marsh. It's mostly golden now, the color of wheat. The birds are gone. In the mornings, there is frost on the sawgrass. As I stare out at the dormant marsh, something clicks.

I turn around, frowning. "Have you checked national databases? For murder victims who match the same pattern we've seen in Long Island and Florida?"

"I have two agents working on that now. Why? What are you thinking?"

"When did Heather Valdez go missing?"

"In January 2016." Sarah shakes her head. "Meachem was out of the country that whole winter. So unless he had someone do his dirty work—which, of course, is entirely possible—he's not responsible."

I shake my head. "I have another idea. I saw someone I recognize in one of the photos. I'm not sure. Call your agents. There's one location in particular I want to focus on. This may be a stretch. But if I'm right, then I can tell you who our killer is."

29.

Sarah pulls up on the sandy shoulder of Meadow Lane, across the street from James Meachem's house. I'm in the passenger seat. I haven't been able to drive since the explosion. Even getting into a car sends my heart racing. I've made do by biking across the bridge to the grocery store every few days, returning with supplies in my backpack. Otherwise, I rely on rides from friends. Hank stops by regularly. So do Ty and Cole Haines. I've found a few friends at SCPD, too: detectives who, like my dad, were disgusted by the corruption that had eaten away at their own force like a cancer.

Sarah and I hop out of the car. We meet in the middle of the deserted street. A sharp, cold wind howls across the rocks that line the bay. I shiver under my jacket. It's just a thin shell; beneath it, I'm wearing a sweatshirt and a fleece vest. It's not enough. My fingers sting from the cold. I wish I had a hat and scarf. If I stay here much longer, I'll have to buy some proper winter clothes. It's been nearly two months since I arrived.

"There it is," I say to Sarah, pointing at Meachem's property. "The house of horrors."

"Jesus. It's soulless."

"And there"—I move my finger toward the dunes at the edge of the property—"is where Adriana Marques's body was buried."

Sarah crosses her arms against her chest. "That poor girl," she says quietly. She glances around. "This place is so desolate."

"It always is this time of year. A ghost town. These are all summer homes."

"But Grace Bishop is here."

"She told me she stays here until Thanksgiving. Said I could stop by anytime."

At Grace's gate, I nod to Sarah. "I'll go in alone. Okay?"

"Are you sure?"

"Yes. I think it's better that way."

Sarah hesitates and then nods. "Okay," she says. "Shout if you need me."

I WALK UP to the gate, press the buzzer. When I announce my name, the gate swings open. I follow the long drive toward the house. It appears empty. The lights are all off even though the sun is beginning to set. When I hear a stirring in the garden, I pivot. Over the top of a hedgerow, I glimpse movement. Grace is there, digging.

She pauses and then straightens up. When she sees me, she smiles.

"Hello, there," she calls out. She's wearing only a sweater and a little scarf, tied neatly around her neck. Her hands are covered in gardening gloves; in one, she holds a spade.

"You're working late."

"Have to put my gardens to bed for the winter. No rest for the weary."

"I thought it was 'no rest for the wicked.'"

Grace raises one eyebrow. "Is it? Oh, my. I've been saying it wrong all these years. Would you like to come inside?"

"I'm all right. The fresh air is nice."

Grace clenches her jaw ever so slightly. "I was sorry to hear about your partner."

"He wasn't my partner. He was a friend."

"So sad. Did the police officers that they arrested take responsibility?"

"No. But we're building our case."

"I told you those men were corrupt. You should've listened. Of course, at the time, I didn't realize your father was one of them. In fact, it was your father who came to speak to me about Alfonso Morales, wasn't it?"

I nod. "It was, yes. He died right before Adriana's body was found."

"And so you wanted to close his case for him. How noble of you." There's a coldness in her voice that I haven't heard before. Her eyes, too, have narrowed. They're an unsettling ice blue. I want to look away, but I don't. For a few seconds, we face off, just staring at each other in silence.

"You feel that I lied to you," I prompt.

"No one likes being lied to, Ms. Flynn."

"I agree. I would argue that I didn't lie. Merely omitted the facts."

"Isn't that the same thing?"

"Not really. See, you lied to me. You said you hadn't met Mr. Meachem before. You said you didn't socialize with him."

Her body goes rigid. When she speaks, she practically spits. "I do not socialize with that man."

"You don't, that's true. But your husband does. He was over at Mr. Meachem's on a number of occasions, in fact. Not just here, but also down in Palm Beach."

"Eliot would never."

"But he did. We have photos, unfortunately."

"You're wrong."

"Such a sad story. Those girls were his downfall. One tried to extort him. Isn't that right? And then Adriana, well, that was worse. Eliot got her pregnant. So that was awfully complicated. After everything you did for him. After all you endured to secure his position in the Treasury. How could he do that to you? And he'd done it before, hadn't he? He'd paid them off before. But this time, because of the baby, it wouldn't be so easy."

"That disgusting little bitch got herself pregnant," Grace snarls. "Eliot didn't do it. He couldn't have. He can't. I told you that. I confided in you."

"And that's why it was so enraging, wasn't it? Because you realized that your husband *could* get someone pregnant. Just not you. Did he want to keep the baby, Grace? Was he planning to leave you? Adriana's sister said he used to call her late at night, promising to take care of her. She was so happy right before she died. Is that because she knew Eliot would be there for her?"

Grace lets out a bloodcurdling scream as she lunges for me. It happens so quickly, I don't react in time. She knocks me to the ground and raises the spade over her head.

I roll to the right, feeling the whir of the spade come down beside my ear. It sinks deep into the earth and sticks there. I see the opportunity and take it.

My fingers close around a rock on the ground. With all my force, I pull it up and smash it to Grace's temple. There's a hard, sickening sound as it reverberates off her skull.

"You bitch!" she screams as I hurl my body on top of her. I sit on her torso as she thrashes. She's tall—nearly six feet—so it takes every fiber of my body to restrain her. Out of the corner of my eye, I see Sarah force her way through the hedgerow. She runs toward us. I glance up, meeting her gaze. For a split second, I stop focusing on Grace. And that's when I feel it. She sinks a blade into my thigh with all her might.

I fall backward, a lightning bolt of pain coursing through my leg. Grace gets up onto all fours and then pushes herself up onto her knees. She raises the blade again, and this time, she's aiming for my heart.

A single shot rings out. Grace crumples to the ground. Sarah's footsteps grow louder. I hear her shouting into her radio, calling for backup. Soon, she is kneeling over me, pulling my torso up into her lap. Grace hasn't moved. A river of blood spills from her chest and pools in the grass around her body. She's dead; I can tell by the unnatural way her leg is bent beneath her. I turn away, my chest heaving as I breathe through the pain. The bushes behind me are each neatly wrapped in burlap.

Overhead, the sky is the color of slate. In the distance, I hear the cry of geese and the rush of the tide rolling in and out on the sand. I look up at Sarah and smile.

"You're going to be okay," she says, her voice rife with alarm. "Help's on its way."

"I know." I let my eyes close. "It's over. I'll be fine."

30.

Ann-Marie Marshall is sitting in the same booth at the same coffee shop where we met two months ago. This time, it's open. A cluster of teens hang out around one of the tables. The lunch counter is nearly full. When I slide into the banquette, I see that Ann-Marie has already ordered me a hot black coffee. I smile appreciatively.

"It's good to see you," she says. I can hear the relief in her voice. "I wasn't sure we'd get to do this again."

"Me, either."

"After Jamie Milkowski was murdered, I ran. Got straight in my car and didn't stop driving until I reached my sister's house in Vermont."

"I don't blame you. You might've been next."

She stares into her coffee. "Instead, they went after you and Lee Davis."

We're quiet for a minute. I listen to the buoyant chatter of the teenagers in the next booth. Their laughter soothes me. "Do you know if they've made any progress on the Milkowski investigation?" I ask.

"Not really," she says, her voice quiet. "There were no witnesses. I mean, everyone assumes that it was Dorsey or DaSilva. But no one can prove anything and they've stopped talking."

"DaSilva admitted to planting the car bombs. He might as well confess to running down Milkowski, too."

"He had to admit to the car bombs. They found a third one exactly like it in his garage." She cocks her head and stares at me. "What about your father's death? Have you heard anything there?"

"No. But I don't expect to."

"I'm sorry. That must be hard. Not having closure."

"I do have closure. I know what kind of a man he was, at least. I know that he died trying to protect those girls. And the men that did that to him are going to jail for a long time, regardless."

"May I suggest something? Just for you to consider."

I already know what she's about to say. She alluded to it on the phone without outright proposing it. "Sure. Go ahead."

"I'm going up to Shawangunk Correctional in a couple of weeks. To speak to Sean Gilroy. He's agreed to let me interview him again."

"Are you writing another piece about my mother's case?"

"No." She shakes her head firmly. "I'm writing about police brutality in Suffolk County. About their ninety-four percent confession rate. Sean Gilroy is part of that story."

I swirl my coffee around, considering. "Why do you want me there?"

"I don't. I just think it might be helpful for you to talk to him. He's spent the last two decades atoning for what he did. I'm not saying you should forgive him, but it might bring you peace to talk to him, to see how he's changed, and to know that he's sorry."

I turn it over in my head. The truth of it is that I think I have forgiven him, as much as anyone can forgive someone who takes the life of a loved one. I don't know if there's anything to be gained by hearing him apologize. I'm still taking things one day at a time. "I'll think about it," I say. It's the best that I can do.

"Okay." Ann-Marie nods. "Have you heard anything further about James Meachem? He still off sunbathing in some country without extradition?"

"As far as I know."

"I have to ask: what made you suspect Grace Bishop?"

I smile, take a sip of my coffee. "Is this on or off the record?"

"Whatever you want. I'd love to interview you. You know that. But I'm also happy to just talk. I can't help it, I'm curious."

"My phone rings constantly now. I had to unplug it. And my cell phone is turned off most of the day. It's been a circus. I haven't given an interview yet. I'm not sure I ever will. But if I do, it will be with you."

"I appreciate that. I imagine it's been crazy for you. You're at the center of a major political scandal."

"And it's just beginning. Eliot Bishop's arrest is the first of many. Meachem had a lot of connections. Every politician and CEO he's ever had over should be running scared."

"Do you think Eliot Bishop was an accomplice?"

I shake my head. "I don't know. It's not my case anymore. It never was, really."

"Like hell. You solved it."

"Just followed a hunch."

"So what made you suspect her?"

"Besides the fact that she's tall, left-handed, an expert marksman, and on the board of the Preservation Society?" I deadpan.

Ann-Marie chuckles. "Yes. Besides that."

"Honestly, at first I didn't. I liked her. She's very charming. And I thought she wanted to help. But once we realized that there were two bodies in Palm Beach that had been disposed of similarly, it narrowed the pool to people who frequent both areas. We started searching national databases and found another case near Grace's family ranch in Texas. That's when it clicked. Grace was so defensive of Morales and so eager to point the finger at Meachem. If Morales was really just some landscaper she'd met a couple of times, why would she be so adamant about his character?"

"So she blamed Meachem for introducing her husband to these escorts."

"Yes. I think she saw him as the devil, and he proved to be too great a temptation to her husband."

"So she planted Adriana's body near Meachem's house on purpose. And then she conveniently discovered it herself."

"Exactly. It's quite clever, actually. She destroys Meachem and also finds a scapegoat for her prior murders."

"She was a jealous woman."

"Yes. And I think Adriana's pregnancy set her over the edge. She was infertile herself, you know. So it wasn't enough for her to just kill off the girls. She wanted the whole operation shut down once and for all."

Ann-Marie's eyes widen. "That's why there were marks all over the abdomen."

"I have to believe so. In the past, she just shot the victims and then paid someone who worked for her to dispose of the bodies. But this time . . ."

"Rage got the better of her." Ann-Marie drains the remains of her coffee. "Do you think her husband would have left her for Adriana?"

"I don't know. Elena Marques thought that Adriana was seeing someone powerful or important. She overheard them talking on the phone once. The way she described it, it sounded as though he was committed to helping her at least. Either way, Grace couldn't risk it. The way she saw it, she'd given up her whole life to further her husband's political career. And he thanked her by screwing around behind her back."

"Do you know how much she paid Morales?"

"No. They're still unwinding her finances. I'm sure they will, in time."

"Are you glad she's dead?"

"No." I glance away, staring through the window onto Main Street. If I crane my neck, I can almost see my father's apartment, the one he rented for Maria Cruz. I look back at Ann-Marie. "I'm not. I would've liked her to stand trial."

"Still, it's justice."

"Perhaps." I reach into my bag and pull out my wallet. "I'm sorry. I have to run. I have an appointment."

"Please. It's on me."

"Are you sure?"

"Yes, of course." She puts her hand on mine. "I'm so glad we met, Nell."

"I am, too," I say, and I mean it.

"When are you heading home?"

"You mean to DC?"

"Yes."

"I haven't decided. I think I may stick around here for a while."

She raises her eyebrows. "Really," she says, a trace of surprise in her voice. "That's nice to hear."

"I like Suffolk County in the off-season."

"It's the reason I stay," she says, and stands up to give me a hug. "I'd love to see you again. Let's stay in touch."

"Absolutely." I hug her one more time.

31.

I cross Main Street, aware that I'm late. Just a minute or two, but still, my heart is pounding. It's hard for me to walk quickly; the best I can manage is a swift limp. At the top of the stairs, an officer is stationed in front of apartment 3. He nods when he sees me and raps on the door.

I hear the locks click. The door opens. Behind it stands a young woman. She's dressed simply in jeans and a turtleneck sweater, and her long black hair is plaited down her back. Her eyes are green, like mine. Set against her olive skin and delicate features, they are beautiful.

"Maria," I say, my voice almost a whisper. "I'm Nell."

"I know who you are," she says, moving closer, as though she wants to hug me but isn't sure if she should. I step toward her and pull her into my arms.

"I've always wanted to meet you," she says, after a minute. "I asked Marty, but he didn't want to upset you."

"You called him Marty?" I smile. Dad always hated that nickname. Only his closest friends were allowed to use it.

"Yeah." She stares at the floor, embarrassed. "I mean, he was my father and everything, but I didn't know about him until I turned eighteen. So it felt strange, calling him Dad."

"I understand. For the record, I wouldn't have been upset. It would've been nice to know I had a sister. Or a half sister, anyway. It's still nice. It's wonderful. When Sarah told me, I was honestly overwhelmed with joy."

Her face lights up. "I'm glad. I don't have any other family. So this means a lot to me."

"To me, too."

"Your dad—Marty—he was a really good man. He helped me when I needed it most."

"I'm so happy to hear that."

"When my mom got sick, I started up with Gio. We needed the money so badly. I knew Adriana from school. She was doing it, and she brought me in to meet him. And then my mom died. I had no one. I thought I was going to die, too. Some days I wanted to die. Nothing mattered anymore. And then, out of nowhere, your father came for me. I guess my mom sent him a letter from the hospital. She wanted him to watch over me. It must have come as a shock to him, finding out about me like that. But he really stepped up."

"So he didn't know about you at all?"

"No. They had a fling. That was it. It never occurred to him that my mom had gotten pregnant. She moved down to Florida not too long after. We lived there for a while. We came back to Suffolk County a few years ago, after she got sick. I guess she always felt like this was home."

"And you? How do you feel?"

Maria looks around. "This apartment is the nicest home I've ever had," she says. Then she blushes, embarrassed. "Not just, you know, because it's big and everything. It's just peaceful. No guys around with my mom, nobody bothering me. None of that. It was the only place I could ever just be quiet and forget about Gio and everything else."

"I know what you mean." I smile, put my hand on her arm. "I brought some pastries from the diner across the street."

"Thank you. I'm sorry. Please, come in. Sit."

I follow her into the apartment. I can't take my eyes off her. She's so beautiful, so young. And she feels familiar. She reminds me of someone, I realize. At first I think it's my father. She has his dark hair, his quiet nature. His narrow frame and sharp features.

But then, as she smiles up at me, her face both shy and inquisitive at the same time, I realize: she reminds me of me.

We sit at opposite ends of the sofa, one of the few pieces of furniture in the apartment. I put the box of pastries between us. The afternoon sun is beginning to soften, and it casts a long shaft of light across her face. It doesn't seem to bother her. She laughs and answers my questions without moving. I have so many, I think I could stay all night.

I don't, of course. Once it gets dark, I call a cab and return to the house on Dune Road. For the moment, Maria will stay in protective custody. She will spend her days being deposed and then, eventually, giving testimony. As for me, I'm not yet sure. I know I will be there for her whenever she is done. She's my family and I am hers. I don't know exactly what that means. Neither does she. But together, we will find out.

Epilogue

It's the last day of the year when I scatter my
mother's ashes.

I'm alone, though Maria did offer to come with me.
It's a cold, clear day. The sun is setting. I stand on a spit
of land that extends into Peconic Bay. Across it, I can see
the North Fork of Long Island. Behind me is the beach
at Meschutt County Park.

It is beautiful here, especially at this time of year. The
gentle browns and grays of the earth meld into the gray
expanse of water. My mother used to take me here all
year round to collect rocks and breathe the salt air. I have
just a few memories of her left, but some of the happiest
are at Meschutt.

Earlier this month, Glenn Dorsey took his own life.
He hanged himself in his prison cell while awaiting trial.
Vince DaSilva pleaded guilty to several crimes, ranging
from narcotics trafficking to murder. He will spend the

rest of his life in prison, as will Dorsey's other right hand, Ron Anastas, and their co-conspirator, Giovanni Calabrese.

Sarah Patel tells me, off the record, that James Meachem has signed a non-prosecution agreement with the Bureau. He has turned over his black book, as well as hundreds of hours of video footage from his homes in Southampton, Palm Beach, New York, and the British Virgin Islands, implicating scores of politicians, CEOs, and celebrities of knowingly engaging in sex with minors. According to Sarah, Meachem will be required to plead guilty to two minor charges of prostitution in Florida state court. As a result of this plea, he will serve less than a year in a low-security prison. In addition, Manon Boucher, the madame who helped recruit victims at Meachem's behest, is immune from prosecution. She is said to be spending the holidays on a yacht off the coast of Little Saint James, Meachem's private island.

Sarah has returned to Miami, where she's been internally promoted to a job she dislikes. She misses the field, and I think she will return to it soon. She's asked me to take a position on the Human Trafficking Task Force out of Miramar, and I've accepted. Maria and I both are ready to leave Suffolk County. Miami seems like a good fit. It's a fresh start in a place where Maria feels comfortable. Lightman tells me that I'll hate the people and pace of life in Miami. He says there's an office pool about how long I will last there. His money is on six months, no more. My desk, he tells me, will always be open.

I still speak to Dr. Ginnis a few times a week. He was

the one who pushed me to list the house and put down roots somewhere else. With his help, I found a charity that provides shelter, protection, and education to victims of sexual trafficking, girls like Luz and Maria. I anonymously donated the proceeds of my father's offshore account to them, as well as a portion of the proceeds from our house. The rest I've put in a trust for Maria. She doesn't know that yet, but I will tell her when the time is right.

Ginnis also suggested that I bury my mother before I leave Suffolk County for good. I'm glad he did. I thought being here with her ashes would be hard. It is. But I'm also filled with a sense of calm that I hadn't expected. After all these years, I'm finally putting her to rest. I will never know if Sean Gilroy killed my mother, but I believe he did and that is enough for me to move on. As the sun slips below the horizon line, I close my eyes and say goodbye. Then I open the urn and let her go, her ashes blowing away on the wind.

Acknowledgments

Every book takes a village. I am so grateful to the many people who helped bring *Girls Like Us* to life.

I am, as ever, indebted to my exceptional editor, Sally Kim. Sally, you are wise, kind, insightful, supportive, and patient. Without you, this book would surely not exist.

Sally brings with her the brilliant, hardworking team at G. P. Putnam's Sons. I feel remarkably lucky to work with Gabriella Mongelli, Elena Hershey, Ashley McClay, Alexis Welby, Emily Mlynek, Tom Dussel, Leigh Butler, Christine Ball, and Ivan Held, among others. I have loved getting to know you all and am overwhelmingly grateful for everything you have done to support me and this book.

I have two tireless and thoughtful advocates in Alexandra Machinist and Josie Freedman. Thank you both for believing in *Girls Like Us*, and for everyone at ICM who has worked so diligently on behalf of this project.

This book came together because of the wisdom and guidance of Taylor Rose Berry and Robert Shumacher. Thank you for sharing your stories with me. I will always be grateful to you both.

Andrea Katz, Ann-Marie Nieves, and Katie Taylor are the best cheerleaders, editors, beta readers, publicists, and friends a writer could ask for. I'm so thankful for everything you have done for me and for the book community in general. You are the best kind of people.

I will never be able to adequately express my gratitude to my family for their constant and unconditional love and support in all that I do. Emma, Owen, Mom, and Jonathan: thank you. Thank you. I love you all so very much.

Discussion Guide

1. When *Girls Like Us* opens, Nell is returning home for her father's funeral. Nell and Marty always had a complicated relationship, but how do you think the distance between them influenced Nell's perspective on the case she gets pulled into? What was the catalyst for their issues?

2. *Girls Like Us* is set in the Hamptons but shows a side of Suffolk County rarely seen in the media: the working class. How does Suffolk County in the off-season differ from your expectations of the area? In what ways are the differences in race and class between the locals and the wealthy summer visitors shown? How does Nell straddle both communities?

3. This novel has some clear parallels to recent events in the news. How does the novel incorporate current issues of sex trafficking and police corruption?

4. Loyalty—whether it be family loyalty, hometown loyalty, or loyalty to the truth—is a big theme in this novel. Who do you think Nell is loyal to? What about Marty, Lee, and the others?

5. In what ways can Nell identify with the victims in the case she's investigating? How does her connection to Luz and to the other young women impact her participation in the case?

6. Dorsey and DaSilva were father figures for Nell growing up, sometimes even more than her own father. How do you think Nell feels when she discovers their involvement in James Meachem's circle? Do you think she'll ever be able to reconcile the men she thought she knew with who they ended up being?

7. There's a late-in-the-game revelation that leads Nell to Adriana's killer. Did you suspect anything earlier on in the novel? Who did you initially think was responsible for the murders, and why?

8. Although we never find out who killed Nell's mother, Nell herself feels closure by the end of the novel. Do you have any suspicions of who it might have been? Do you agree with Nell's decision to move on from the case?

9. What do you imagine happens next for Nell in Miami? Do you think she'll settle in and build a life with her half sister, Maria? Why or why not?